FALSE ACCOUNT

FALSE ACCOUNT

Veronica Heley

Severn House Large Print
London & New York

This first large print edition published 2020
in Great Britain and the USA by
SEVERN HOUSE PUBLISHERS LTD of
Eardley House, 4 Uxbridge Street, London W8 7SY.
First world regular print edition published 2018 by
Severn House Publishers Ltd.

British Library Cataloguing in Publication Data
A CIP catalogue record for this title is available from the British Library.

ISBN-13: 9780727892515

Typeset by Palimpsest Book Production Ltd.,
Falkirk, Stirlingshire, Scotland.

One

Bea Abbot wondered why it was that some people would never follow even the simplest of instructions.

The Abbot Domestic Agency was situated in the basement of a large, cream-painted, Georgian house and reached by a short flight of steps down from the street.

The existence of these stairs was made clear both in the agency's advertisements and on the phone to clients making an appointment.

The Tredgolds, however, had decided they didn't need to behave like everyone else.

When Charlotte Tredgold and her mother arrived – an hour and a half late – they rang Bea from outside her house to say that Mrs Tredgold couldn't manage the steps down to the agency, so would Mrs Abbot please let them into her house through the front door?

Bea had the impression that Charlotte thought her mother was perfectly capable of managing the steps down to the agency rooms if she felt like it, but that today she didn't feel like it, and that was that.

Bea was not amused. Clients were seen in the agency rooms downstairs. Bea's living quarters

1

above were private and she wished them to remain so.

The question was whether she could afford to turn down a client with a mansion in Mayfair who wanted Bea to find her several new members of staff. Apparently, the Tredgolds had lost faith in the domestic agency they'd used for years and had decided to try Mrs Abbot's agency instead.

Gritting her teeth, Bea decided to see the Tredgolds and said she'd be upstairs in a minute.

Because the house was built on a slope, Bea's office at the back of the house looked out on to her private garden. She put the phone down and swivelled round in her chair to look out of the French windows. She'd been looking forward to a sandwich lunch and a coffee. The sun was shining, it was springtime and she wanted to get outside and do some tidying up.

Of course she would see these tiresome people but . . . And then she remembered that she had had an overnight guest who might still be sleeping on the settee in her sitting room upstairs.

This could be awkward.

Bea smoothed down her short, ash-blonde hair, checked that the collar of her cream silk shirt lay flat, tweaked the waist of her grey skirt into place, picked up her iPad and stepped through into the main office. Her staff were busy on their phones and their computers but Betty, her office manager, stopped work for a moment so that Bea could explain what had happened.

'They're looking for several new staff, so I decided to see them.'

Bea took the inside stairs up to the ground floor and grimaced. Was that dust on the big wooden chest in the hall? Her cleaner hadn't been that morning, had she? No. The woman had told Bea she might not make it as she had toothache and was hoping the dentist could fit her in sooner rather than later. Oh, dear. Oh, well.

Also, a man's soft leather jacket hung on the newel post at the bottom of the stairs, which led up to the bedrooms.

No cleaner and a male guest. Bea ironed out another smile.

So what! This was her house, not the agency rooms, and Mrs Tredgold would have to put up with whatever she found there.

She opened her front door and summoned up a smile. 'Do come in.'

The younger of the two women stood back to let her mother precede her into the house.

'You are Mrs Abbot? Thank you for being so understanding. I was fine until I developed back trouble. Going up steps is not so bad but going down them is painful. Don't talk to me about doctors. Keep well away from them is what I say.'

Mrs Tredgold was charm incarnate, but there was no word of apology for being late. She made her way down the hall, eyes as sharp as the diamond drops swinging from her ears, noting everything she saw, which included the dust on the chest and the man's jacket at the bottom of the stairs.

Mrs Marcia Tredgold was in her early seventies, a symphony in greyish brown with a floating scarf, but there was nothing dowdy about her. True, she flourished a stick, but her silver hair had been cut into a long bob by a master and her clothes had come from a specialist boutique. She sported diamond rings, at least two on each hand. She walked almost if not quite erect. And her shoes – Bea noted them because she liked good shoes herself – were low-heeled but superbly crafted.

Mrs Tredgold's daughter, Charlotte, slipped past Bea into the hall with an inclination of her head. She was probably in her late thirties. Mrs Tredgold was fine-boned and graceful, but Charlotte had a chunky figure with thick legs. She was also wearing an expensive brownish-grey outfit but for some reason it looked dowdy on her. Her hair was mid-brown and so was everything else about her. Her skirt was slightly the wrong length and dipped at the front, while her shoes did not look as if they fitted her properly. She had a used handkerchief tucked into the cuff of her sleeve. There were no rings on her hands.

Charlotte was the perfect picture of a down-trodden poor relation. She carried not one but two handbags, one of which hung open, stuffed with papers, used and unused tissues, crossword puzzle books, a bottle of water, a notebook and pen and some packets of pills. She was also carrying a soft brown leather purse which screamed 'designer' and which probably did not belong to her but would be her mother's.

Charlotte carried her mother's handbag for her? Amazing!

'So sorry to put you to all this trouble,' said Charlotte, fussing with the two bags.

'Never mind,' said Bea, making up her mind to be amused rather than annoyed. 'This way.' She waved Charlotte into the big reception room which ran from front to back of the house. The front windows overlooked the busy street but the French windows at the back gave on to a balcony and thence by means of a curving iron staircase led down to the garden below.

Mrs Tredgold was already there, looking down on the lanky form of a man who, half covered by a duvet, lay asleep on the settee.

Mrs Tredgold was amused. 'An overnight guest who didn't merit being given a bed?'

Bea responded to the charm. 'My ex-husband, Piers, who arrived back from America in the middle of the night and who'd forgotten the keys to his own place.'

She thought of tidying up the daily papers, half-empty coffee mug, tote bag and laptop which Piers had dropped on the floor, not to mention the rather charming gold bracelet which he'd brought back for her as a present. Oh well, this was her house, wasn't it? The Tredgolds had invited themselves in and could put up with the disarray.

Charlotte squeaked. 'Oh, dear. Does he do that often? How awkward for you.' But her eyes were avid. She might be a spinster of a certain age, but she had recognized that, even in sleep, Piers was an attractive man.

Bea's ex-husband was not handsome but he looked what he was: intelligent, humorous and successful. His clothes were expensive, his over-long mop of dark hair was beginning to grey over his ears, but his long body – without an ounce of fat – might have been that of a man of thirty.

Piers slept on. He'd been jet-lagged half out of his mind when he'd arrived at Bea's at midnight and would probably sleep through an invasion of the Body Snatchers from Mars, or wherever it was they were supposed to come from.

Charlotte dithered. 'Shall we . . . I mean? Mother? Come back another time?'

'Nonsense,' said Mrs Tredgold. She waved towards the Victorian dining table by the window overlooking the street. 'We won't disturb him. Carry on, Charlotte. You know what we need Mrs Abbot to do for us.'

Charlotte lost one of the handles of her bag, spilling some of its contents on the floor. 'Oh, but . . .'

Marcia Tredgold turned her back on her daughter. Clearly, she was not going to help picking up the things that had landed on the floor. Perhaps she found it difficult to get down to that level?

Bea assisted Charlotte to pick everything up and transferred her to the table without too many squawks and squeaks of embarrassment. Charlotte, looking as if she were about to cry, blew her nose and with some difficulty extracted a bundle of papers from her capacious handbag. Next she sought for and found a pair of pink-framed glasses and put them on.

Surprisingly, her eyes now seemed as sharp as her mother's. Her manner morphed from dither to dictator. 'So, you understand what we require?'

Bea opened her iPad. 'May I ask which agency you've used before?'

Click!

Bea swung round in her chair to see that Mrs Tredgold had opened the French windows at the back of the room and was letting a light breeze in.

Well, the old woman wasn't doing any harm, was she? And, given that she couldn't tackle the stairs down to the agency rooms, she certainly wouldn't be descending the cast-iron spiral stairs to the garden below.

Bea transferred her attention back to Charlotte who, now that she'd sorted herself out, looked a hundred times more capable than before.

'We used the Times Two agency until they supplied us with not one or two, but three incompetents. So we have decided on a change. I asked around and heard nothing but good things about your agency and—'

Click!

Bea started up from her chair. The French windows had swung to but Mrs Tredgold had disappeared!

Had she fallen down the outside stairs?

Bea started across the room, feeling for the phone in her pocket. An elderly woman falling down those stairs could very easily break her neck. An ambulance would be needed. Why hadn't the woman cried out as she fell?

Bea's heartbeat went into overdrive. What a terrible thing to happen! She could imagine the papers. The police would ask why Bea hadn't safeguarded her house.

She wrenched the doors open again and looked out.

And down.

One storey below and at the far end of the garden, Mrs Tredgold was sitting in the sun on the cast-iron garden bench, communing with Bea's large long-haired black cat, Winston. They were sizing one another up, oblivious to the rest of the world.

How had Mrs Tredgold managed to get down that winding staircase so quickly when she'd claimed to be unable to descend the stairs to the agency rooms?

What was the woman playing at?

Bea hurried down the staircase, holding on to the rail.

Mrs Tredgold looked up as Bea approached. 'Such a pretty garden. Do forgive me, my dear. I wanted to speak to you without my daughter hearing. She has stayed up top, hasn't she? She doesn't like heights, you know.'

Bea told herself to breathe deeply. To calm down.

She succeeded. Partially.

Mrs Tredgold gestured to the seat beside her. 'Will you join me?'

Bea declined. 'Why?'

'Things have been happening. Bad things. They think I don't know what's going on, but of course I do. Charlotte will tell you all about the cooks and cleaners who have come and gone. They all had glowing testimonials, but all left under a cloud. Now my daughter suggests I employ a butler. She thinks it is suitable for people in my

8

position to employ such a person. I said, "What do I want with a butler? Haven't we enough staff to keep?" She said it would keep the hoi polloi out. Me, I rather like the hoi polloi, but my daughter is always afraid I'll be conned into giving people money if I talk to someone she hasn't vetted. I must admit we've not had good luck with our staff recently but . . . a butler? Absurd!'

Bea relaxed. She retrieved a couple of padded cushions from the garden shed nearby and handed one to Mrs Tredgold. If precautions were not taken, that particular cast-iron bench printed its pattern on one's behind. Mrs Tredgold accepted the cushion with a smile and a thank-you.

Bea seated herself and prepared to be entertained. The cat, Winston, jumped on to Bea's lap but continued to assess their guest. Winston took his time to decide about people. He was telling Bea that so far he had formed a favourable opinion of their visitor but was withholding final approval.

Bea was with her cat on this one. Mrs Tredgold was something of an enigma. Was she just a delightful but semi-dotty old woman who had flashes of intelligence? Had she really engineered this tête-à-tête in the garden? And if so, how much notice should be taken of her ramblings . . . if they were indeed ramblings and not highly acute judgements on her family and household?

'You see,' said Mrs Tredgold, 'when one reaches a certain age, one begins to sort out what really matters and what doesn't. One forms certain opinions, which may or may not be the views held by one's family or indeed, of one's peer group. One is expected, being a mother and a grandmother, to adore all one's offspring, but I have never been the maternal type. I have done my best to nurture my children and my grand-child, and it is true that I have a certain fondness for certain members of my family and my staff, but I have to admit that I find others irritating if not downright annoying.'

Bea smiled, and nodded. 'Understood.'

'Yes,' said Mrs Tredgold, 'I believe you have a son and grandchildren whom you see at regular intervals but are not close to.'

Bea felt a jolt run through her. Her smile faded. Had Mrs Tredgold been researching Bea, just as Bea had been researching her? It was all true, of course. Her son was far too busy nowadays to spend much time with his mother.

'On the other hand,' said her visitor, 'you have a keen sense of duty, you have a warm relation-ship with the people you employ, you are doing a good job of rearing your ward, that clever little heiress who's been wished on you, and have managed to remain on good terms with that charming portrait painter husband of yours.'

'Ex-husband,' said Bea through her teeth.

One eyebrow twitched. 'I know about ex-husbands. I divorced my first, although he has somehow or other crept back into my life. When all is said and done, an ex-husband is useful on the occasions when you want a man to squire you around, and he knows how to summon taxis. He's also handy for changing light bulbs and batteries in the TV remote.'

She came to an abrupt halt. For a moment her

expression of determined – if not forced – geniality was missing. What seemed like panic looked out of her eyes . . . and then it was gone.

Bea was concerned. Was the woman putting on an act? By why should she? What was going on here?

Mrs Tredgold was back to being Madame Charming again. 'I observe that your ex-husband brought you back a rather beautiful bracelet from his travels.'

That threw Bea off track. She hoped she wasn't going to blush. 'So he did. When he arrived last night he begged for a cup of coffee to keep him awake while I found the spare key to his place, but he went to sleep before he could finish it.'

'You cared enough about him to put a duvet over him and let him sleep it off, but not to allow him into your bed.'

Bea ran her fingers through Winston's fur, and told herself that Mrs Tredgold didn't have second sight. She was just someone who noticed things.

She decided to change the subject. 'You want my agency to supply you with another cook and another cleaner, but not – if I read you correctly – with a butler?'

'Charlotte is the one who will talk to you about all that. Don't be fooled by her manner. She is a capable woman who is under the mistaken impression that hiding her brains makes her more attractive to the opposite sex. Humph! She ought to know better by now. You, Mrs Abbot, discarded that idea many years ago, right?'

Bea was torn between amusement and annoyance. 'Yes, I suppose I did, but—'

'I certainly never tried to hide the fact that I had brains, but nothing I have said to my daughter on the subject has penetrated her silly head. Somewhere in her teens she picked up the idea that "men never make passes at women who wear glasses". Ridiculous! She has poor sight but can't tolerate contact lenses, so goes around in a haze most of the time.' Mrs Tredgold dropped her voice to reveal a secret. 'She reads romances, you know, and writes trashy poetry.'

'Ah,' said Bea, amused. 'She hasn't realized that the real world is not like that?'

A snort. 'I learned that when I was twelve and my mother ran off with a trainer from her riding school. I do understand that Charlotte can't live without a certain amount of hope in her life, but for her to pretend that marriage gives you a pass to living Happy Ever After is sheer folly, and I sincerely hope that she never finds a man who will put a ring on her finger because she is a very bad chooser and it would only end in tears.

'However, there are compensations in her life. She lives rent-free with servants to do her bidding, not to mention the use of a secretarial person. She hosts meetings for her poetry evenings at no cost to herself. I have a housekeeper, who runs the place like clockwork, or rather, who did so until we were let down by the aforementioned cook and bottle-washer, whose absence has caused Charlotte considerable inconvenience, as one of her poetry evenings had to be cancelled at short notice. Hence this visit to your agency. She has a budget for staff. You may take down the details and provide her with whatever replacements she needs to run the rest of the house in the manner to which she has been accustomed.'

Mrs Tredgold reached out a pale, sinewy hand with a freckled back to Winston, who sniffed her fingers, and finally made up his mind about her. He stood up, stretched fore and aft, then left Bea to tread across to Mrs Tredgold and settle himself for a nap pressed against her side. Mrs Tredgold smiled to herself. 'But, Mrs Abbot, you understand that that is not why I chose to accompany her today, don't you?'

Bea felt abandoned by her cat, and considerable annoyance with Mrs Tredgold. The woman had put on a good show but every now and then there was a glimpse of calculation – or was it misery? – in her eyes. Why?

What was going on? Bea was disinclined to ask. She made a show of looking at her watch. 'Well, if that is the case, perhaps I'd better go up and speak to your daughter.' She frowned. 'I realize you came down the stairs from the sitting room all right. Will you be able to climb them again?'

'Don't be obtuse, young woman. I haven't yet told you what I want you to do.'

Bea hadn't been called a 'young woman' for many years. She blinked.

'When I'm ready, we'll go into your office through the basement, and you can help me up the stairs to the street. I will leave you with my daughter who has no doubt by now woken your ex-husband and will be trying to flirt with him. I do trust he will be polite to her. He has a certain reputation for good manners, has he not?'

13

'Yes, but—'

'Charlotte will instruct you as to finding replacements for the staff which have been found to be less than honest, or who have made lewd suggestions to my granddaughter . . . although knowing her, I would not be surprised to hear it was six of one and half a dozen of the other. I leave all that to her. No. I want you to find out who killed Mitzi and Poppy.'

Bea gaped. Who were Mitzi and Poppy? Mrs Tredgold's grandchildren? 'What happened to them? Aren't the police involved?'

'Don't be stupid. Why would the police be involved in the death of my cats? Now, give me your arm and take me back upstairs. I'm not as young as I used to be, and I need my afternoon nap before I go to the dentist this afternoon.'

Two

Wednesday lunchtime

'Cats?' Bea stood up so abruptly that Winston was startled and made himself scarce.

Mrs Tredgold got to her feet with a little help from her stick. 'Yes. My two cats.' She made sure she was balanced and set off for the house.

Bea hurried after her. 'You can't be serious! Cats? I don't believe it.'

'I don't see why not.' Mrs Tredgold was making good time down the path but paused for

14

a moment to admire the water lilies, which were just starting to bloom in the pond. 'I have lived long enough not to worry myself unduly at what human beings choose to do to one another. The papers are full of murders, rapes and conmen taking their nearest and dearest for a ride. There are people blowing themselves up here and mowing others down there. Stabbings, acid attacks, mutilations. All these are commonplace. People cheat and lie and commit crimes of all sorts and I have learned to accept that this is what human beings are like. I am aware that my own family may be no better than the rest of humanity. What I do not accept is that they should kill my cats and get away with it.'

Bea said, 'But . . .!' to thin air.

Mrs Tredgold had reached the house. She stepped through the French windows into Bea's office.

Bea hastened after her.

Mrs Tredgold plodded through the main office, inclining her head slightly as she passed each of the office girls, making straight for the door to the area stairs and the street.

Bea said, 'Don't you wish to speak to your daughter before you go? We can use the inside stairs.'

'I've had enough of her for one day.' Mrs Tredgold opened the outside door and stepped into the area from which stairs led up to the pavement. 'I'm tired and I'm ready to go home.'

She had no handbag with her, or mobile phone.

Bea said, 'Shall I call a cab for you?'

Mrs Tredgold laid hold of the railings to help

herself up the stairs. 'No need. I've made my own arrangements.'

Bea wondered what those could be. It was a puzzle, but Bea had a feeling that Mrs Tredgold knew exactly what she was doing.

The old woman climbed the steps one by one without undue haste. 'I wouldn't leave my daughter alone with your husband for too long. She will try to flirt and she has absolutely no aptitude for it.'

Bea followed closely behind Mrs Tredgold in case she were to trip and fall.

On the pavement Mrs Tredgold shook out her skirt and looked around. Bea lived in a tree-lined street, which was quiet by Kensington standards, but traffic was dense and parking next to impossible. Bea was fortunate in being able to keep her car in a property she owned in the mews at the end of the road.

So how did Mrs Tredgold propose to leave?

Simple. Mrs Tredgold pointed with her stick to a Mercedes which drew up and double-parked in front of the house. A uniformed chauffeur had timed his arrival to the second.

'That's what I like about Ahmed,' said Mrs Tredgold. 'He understands punctuality. He will come back for my daughter in an hour's time. It was good to meet you, Mrs Abbot. I wanted to see you in person and this visit has confirmed my opinion that you will be able to discover who killed my cats. I will pay a bonus if you can tell me who it was within seven days.'

The chauffeur got out of the car to open the back passenger door for Mrs Tredgold, who

16

stepped out between two parked cars with the insouciance of one who bears a charmed life, even in London traffic.

Bea said, 'I don't think that I'd be any good at—'

'Even,' said Mrs Tredgold, as she slid into her seat, 'if it proves to have been one of the family. Understood?'

The car slid away into the traffic leaving Bea standing on the kerb, not knowing whether to laugh or scream. She decided that she'd had enough of being manipulated by elderly witches and that on no account, and no matter what bribe was offered, would she consider working for the Tredgolds.

Bea went back down the area steps and into the office. It was lunchtime. Half the girls were having their break while the others continued to man the phones. Bea checked that nothing had been going on that she needed to deal with and took the inside stairs, prepared to wake Piers and tell him to go home . . . only to find him in the kitchen, being talked at by Charlotte.

Charlotte was in full seduction mode. She had taken off her glasses, undone the top button of her sludge-coloured jacket and was chatting with animation to Piers.

Piers was awake. Just. He spooned cereal into his mouth, while waiting for a cup of coffee to percolate. He hadn't shaved for a couple of days and Bea thought he looked rather like a pirate in a costume drama. As a successful portrait painter, he knew how to give the appearance of listening to others – which is what he was doing now – without actually taking in anything they said.

Yet, to someone who knew him well, he was showing signs of impatience. Perhaps Charlotte had tried him too far? After all, he must still be jet-lagged. He threw Bea a 'Save me!' look out of widened eyes and said, 'Would you excuse me?' Upon which, he seized a handful of biscuits and took his cup of coffee out of the back door and down into the garden.

Charlotte sighed, watching him make his escape. 'That poor man. He works so hard. Just back from America, he said?' She drifted to the open back door and looked down into the garden. 'Such a pretty garden, but . . . oh, my vertigo!' She stepped back, putting her hand to her heart. Sure enough, her colour had faded. She really did have vertigo.

So Mrs Tredgold had indeed taken advantage of her daughter's weakness to engineer a private word with Bea? What was going on between those two women?

Bea hungered for coffee and a sandwich for herself. She said, 'I usually break for lunch at this time of day. Your mother has been collected in her car, which she says will return for you in an hour's time, but I'm sure you'll like to be off before then. Shall I call you a cab?'

Charlotte's jaw sagged. 'But I thought . . . oh dear, didn't Mother explain? No, she probably didn't. Did she upset you? She can be very difficult and we have to make allowances. Her age, you know? Sometimes she can be quite impossible, and it's all very upsetting because they all rely on me to keep things going and everything's been so dreadful recently that it's

18

making me miserable and I wonder sometimes how I can go on.'

Part of Bea wondered in cynical fashion how much Charlotte was play-acting, while the rest of her was sympathetic. 'I'm sorry but I don't think my agency can help you this time. If you have to wait for your mother's car to return you can have a seat next door. You will excuse me if I have something to eat myself?' Bea's hospitable instincts took over. 'Perhaps you would care for a coffee or some tea while you wait?'

'I'd love it, but I'm on this new diet, you see. I mustn't eat from dawn to dusk.'

Bea was puzzled. Wasn't that the Muslim diet for Ramadan? Ramadan was not at this time of year, or was it?

Charlotte resumed her glasses and became a businesswoman again. 'So, shall we get down to business?' She trundled back to the living room.

Bea sent a despairing glance at the coffee machine and followed, half amused, and half annoyed. 'It's no use, Miss Tredgold. I really don't think I can help you.'

Charlotte seated herself at the table, which was strewn with papers spilling out of her capacious handbag, and ignored what Bea had said. 'Now, where were we? Oh yes. I was telling you that we used to get all our staff through the Times Two agency. There has been some natural wastage over the years as people relocated or retired, but the agency was always able to find a suitable replacement. I do not understand what has gone wrong with them recently. They are no longer reliable and have been totally unhelpful, not to

19

say extremely rude, when I complained. I did think of posting word of our bad experiences on Facebook and TripAdvisor and you wouldn't believe their reaction! They threatened to sue!'

Bea argued, 'They are a well-established and reputable agency. Surely—'

A sniff. 'All I can say is that I do not expect to find a thief and an abuser of children on my staff. We have had a stream of most uncomfortable incidents, any one of which might have led to the police being brought in, and – horrors! – journalists!'

'If a crime has been committed—'

'"If" Mrs Abbot? There is no question about it. A valuable watch was stolen. My young niece was importuned to display herself in unseemly fashion on social media, and . . . no,' she shook her head, 'I cannot speak of . . . No, no! And the cleaner who was responsible for my mother's flat was found with a diamond ring in her handbag which she certainly had not bought for herself. Can you believe it! Such a dereliction of trust! And so the list goes on. You may speak of a run of bad luck but it is more than bad luck. It is bad judgement. I tell myself that we have been fortunate so far. The culprits have been identified and dismissed from our employment before any great harm was done, but I can no longer trust that agency. Hence my visit to you today.'

Bea hadn't realized the problem was so grave. Her resolve not to help the Tredgolds weakened. 'You mother said you had suggested employing a butler, but she didn't seem to like the idea.'

'We could certainly do with one. Our position

in society, my poetry soirées, my brother's little dinners . . . yes, it would be appropriate, but Mother had taken against the idea. I shall have to work on her to see sense about it. For the moment, we must forget it.'

Bea managed a sympathetic nod. 'What about Mitzi and Poppy?'

Charlotte reddened. 'My mother's on about them again, is she? I might have known. I have never understood her interest in cats. I have always wanted to have a dog, but Mother has asthmatic tendencies which means she can have cats but not dogs. Or so she says. Honestly, their death is a trivial matter.'

'What did happen to them?'

Charlotte shrugged. 'They were not supposed to be allowed into Chef's kitchen, but they were cunning little creatures and would slink in if a door was opened as much as an inch. Chef detested them, of course, but my mother would never hear a bad word against him. The very night he was dismissed he took his revenge and killed them.'

Really? Mrs Tredgold had said she wanted Bea to find out who had killed them. *Did Mrs Tredgold not believe Chef responsible?*

Charlotte continued, 'Times Two have sent us a temporary replacement for Chef and someone to help him in the kitchen, but I could tell straight away that they will not do. We need people who have been thoroughly checked out as permanent replacements. Oh yes, and another cleaner, of course.'

This mention of a chef needing a job rang a

21

bell in Bea's mind. Hadn't there been something in her emails that morning? No, not in her emails, but there had been something . . . Someone asking for an interview because he'd been unfairly sacked? Could it possibly be the same man? She said, 'Why do you think your chef killed the cats?'

'He detested them, of course. And he was out for revenge. You see, he'd stolen my brother's watch, one of those which cost as much as a Mercedes. My brother was absolutely furious. The insurance people said they wouldn't pay up if we didn't have a police report on the matter. My brother was all for getting one but Mother said . . . Anyway, as soon as we let it be known that we were going to bring in the police, Chef conveniently "discovered" the watch in a tray of vegetables and restored it to its owner.'

'What proof did you have that he took the watch in the first place?'

An affronted stare. 'I can tell you, we searched the whole building high and low for it and, yes, in the kitchens, too. It wasn't anywhere to be found. He'd stashed it somewhere, probably out of the house. Perhaps he'd left it with an accomplice? Then when we'd given up all hope and decided to go to the police, he suddenly "found" it in the vegetable rack. Of course he'd hoped the hue and cry would die down and he'd be able to sell it or pawn it or something. Naturally, he was told to leave immediately.'

Bea wasn't sure the chain of evidence was foolproof. 'You think he killed the cats because he'd been given the sack? Why would he do that?

Surely he'd realize he'd never get another good job if that came out?'

'Why? It's obvious, isn't it? He lost his temper. He was furious at being found out and as a last gesture he lured the cats down to the kitchen and killed them before he left. Besides which . . . No, we don't need to go into all that, do we? What a nasty business! We were so grateful we got him out in time! We told the agency what he'd done and got them to strike him off their books. Hah! That will teach him! He won't get another good job easily. He'll probably have to change his name and flee the country.'

'I'm confused. Doesn't your mother believe that he killed her cats?'

'You can't always tell what my mother thinks. One moment she says it was the drains, and the next it's the electrics.'

'Drains? Electrics?'

'Manner of speech. The cats had been shoved under a drain cover at the back of the house. It rained heavily that night, the drain was blocked and the yard was flooded. Our housekeeper investigated, and there they were.'

'Had they been drowned?'

'No. Throats cut. They were put in the drain afterwards.'

'That's awful. Why didn't you call the police?'

'Mother was all for doing so but my brother agreed with me that, as Chef had been found out and blackballed, it was best to forget it.'

Bea suggested, 'Your brother doesn't like cats, either?'

Charlotte flushed. 'What? Well, I can't say that

he's enamoured of them in general, but that's entirely beside the point. He'd got his watch back and Chef has been sacked. If Mother wants another Persian cat then she can get one and it's up to the housekeeper to deal with the hairs it leaves everywhere and clean up its poo.'

Bea had not warmed to Charlotte. 'You really don't care for cats either, do you? They can be wonderful companions.'

'So they say. My mother says she prefers them to people at times. Even to her own family!'

Was Charlotte jealous of the cats because her mother loved them? Bea did not blame Mrs Tredgold for preferring the company of two warm little bodies who were responsive to affection to the sour outlook of this repressed woman.

It crossed Bea's mind to wonder if Charlotte had killed the cats herself. She hadn't sympathized with her mother's loss when they were found dead and there might even have been an element of 'So there!' when she commented upon it. It was not a pleasant trait in someone to triumph when their rivals died.

On the other hand, if Charlotte hadn't exactly been in love with the cats, it did not follow that she'd killed them.

As to the other matter if, as Charlotte had hinted, Chef had abused a schoolgirl, then he deserved everything he got.

Who to believe? And why did Bea feel that neither mother nor daughter had told her the exact truth?

Bea swung back to thinking she did not wish to help the Tredgolds. Not at all. She was sorry for Mrs Tredgold. A little. But she did not care for Charlotte. And as for investigating the death of two cats? Ridiculous!

Charlotte turned back to her papers. She produced a sheet of A4 paper and handed it to Bea.

'This is our address. As you can see, it's in a slightly more upmarket area than this.' She simpered, implying that anyone who lived in a mansion in Mayfair was worth six of a woman who ran an agency in a terraced house in Kensington.

Bea had an impulse to hit something but restrained herself.

Charlotte said, 'This is a list of staff we need to replace. We have a temporary man in to cook, with a boy to do the washing-up and prepare vegetables. They're both rubbish and need to be replaced as soon as possible. We also need another cleaner, who must come with good references. I am really too busy to be bothered with all this. So is our housekeeper and my secretary. She, my secretary, actually works for all of us but mostly for me because I contribute articles to a couple of magazines that you may well have heard of, nationally published women's weeklies, and so on.'

Charlotte gave Bea a sharp-eyed look to make sure she was properly impressed. Bea failed to react, having decided that she would never ever want to read anything which Charlotte was capable of producing.

'I have listed their terms of employment with starting salaries for all four posts. I do think it's time we also employed a butler to keep our staff in order, but . . .' She bit her lip. 'Well, my mother will come round to my way of thinking soon, I'm sure. I will speak to her again about it.'

Bea was intrigued. 'You want us to find you four members of staff?' Bea looked down the list. 'A chef. A kitchen hand, and a cleaner. Also, what is this? A chauffeur? I thought your mother was satisfied with the man who collected her this morning. By the name of Ahmed, is that right?'

'Edgar – that's my brother – doesn't like him and we have agreed to find someone else. Ahmed does understand the cars but he can be very diffi-cult. My mother says he has selective deafness, but I call it rudeness.' Her colour rose. 'There are times when I have asked him to do things for me and he has declined to . . . Well, never mind that! He was far too friendly with our old chef and we've been keeping an eye on him for some time. It is true that my mother has foolishly become attached to him and refuses to believe us when we tell her how, well, obstructive he can be. Matters came to a head last week when he deliberately disobeyed Edgar's instructions to take him to a meeting in the City and took my niece and her friend to a party instead!'

Ahmed didn't know which order to obey? Bea thought that a taxi could have taken Edgar up to the City in no time at all, but that young girls had a tendency to fall into 'adventures' and ought to be chaperoned around as much as possible. She placed the paper Charlotte had given her on to the table. 'I regret that we are unable to help you. One agency does not poach clients from another. If Ahmed has not yet returned for you, please allow me to call you a cab.'

'Don't be ridiculous!' Charlotte shoving the rest of her belongings back into her handbag. 'We will pay you well.'

'I daresay, but we are working at full capacity at the moment and—'

'My mother said you'd be difficult. She said that I wasn't to leave till I had signed a contract with you to find us some suitable staff. Oh yes, and she is prepared to give three sittings to your husband.'

Bea pushed back her chair. 'What was that?'

'She has commissioned your husband to paint her portrait.'

'I know nothing of that.'

'Why should you? She has been emailing him direct. Terms have been agreed. She will give him the first sitting tomorrow.'

So saying, Charlotte swept her bag under arm and strode out of the room. Bea looked out of the window on to the street and yes, there was Ahmed in the Mercedes. Some people had trouble working the catch on Bea's front door but not Charlotte, who sailed out and across the pavement and into the back of the car. Ahmed drove it gently away.

That went well, didn't it! How many times did I say I couldn't help them? Talk about selective deafness!

Bea turned from the window thinking that she could at least get herself some lunch now. Then she saw that although Charlotte might have removed her own shapeless handbag, she'd left her mother's behind on the table.

27

An oversight?

Bea might have thought so before she'd been exposed to Charlotte for an hour. Now, Bea had a nasty suspicion that it had been left for a purpose.

It gave her a bad feeling to realize that she'd been studied by the Tredgolds, both mother and daughter. They had sized her up and down and had formed a pretty good idea of how she would react under pressure. They'd taken precautions.

Bea felt she'd been manipulated by not one but two masters, and she didn't like it.

She'd been half amused and half impressed by Mrs Tredgold. She'd found her likeable. Not so Charlotte.

'I won't work for them!' Bea said it out loud, and then laughed at herself for sounding like a small child railing against the inevitable.

Had the Tredgolds really managed to nobble Piers? They would have guessed Bea wouldn't stand in the way of Piers getting another commission. How dare they!

'Grrr!' said Bea. She went to the back window to see if she could catch sight of her ex-husband. Yes, there he was. The garden seat was too short for his long legs, so he had fetched all the cushions from the shed, laid them out in the shade and gone to sleep there, with his empty coffee cup on the paving stone beside him. Winston the cat sat nearby in full sun, on guard.

She wouldn't interrupt him. No. Not yet.

She looked at that beautiful, stylish designer handbag on her table, and costed it at a couple of thousand pounds. Mm. Now any normal person, on finding something left behind by a visitor, would open it up at once to check that it belonged to the right person.

On the other hand, the Tredgolds were a tricky lot and Bea had a suspicion that the handbag had been left behind deliberately in order to check Bea's honesty. Hadn't they sacked their chef and a cleaner for theft?

Bea didn't touch the handbag. Charlotte had left various pieces of paper on the table when she left. Bea found a sheet of headed notepaper with the Tredgold's telephone number on it and dialled. An anonymous voice answered, the sort of voice you get at the end of the line when phoning the utilities. Not welcoming. Not accented in any way. Generic bureaucracy personified.

'The Tredgold residence. How may I help you?'

'My name is Mrs Abbot. Mrs Tredgold and her daughter visited me at my agency this morning and left a handbag behind.'

'I expect you have many visitors at the agency. It might be anyone's. Have you opened it to check whose it is?'

There it was. A suggestion for Bea to open the handbag and find . . . what?

Bea knew the answer to that one. 'I wouldn't dream of opening anyone else's handbag when I'm alone. I will get someone to witness it when I do. I will itemize the contents and ring you back. If it is Mrs Tredgold's, perhaps you will be so kind as to send your chauffeur here to collect it.'

'He is otherwise engaged this afternoon. Perhaps you would care to bring it over here yourself?'

'No, I don't care to do that.' Bea killed the call and went downstairs, where her girls were now all back at work. On the way Bea realized how hungry she was but decided that could wait.

She called Betty, her office manageress, into her own room, and shut the door behind her.

Betty was bright-eyed and unflappable, except when confronted by spiders. Fortunately Winston the cat loved to chase and kill spiders, so harmony ruled downstairs.

'Betty, two things. Did you try to tell me there was an application for a job this morning from a chef who claimed to have been unjustly given the push? I was on the phone at the time and didn't take it in.'

Betty nodded. 'I took his details and said we'd be in touch if we had anything suitable. We don't usually take on anyone who's been sacked from a previous job, do we?'

'No, we don't, but I have a bad feeling about this one. Was his last job with the Tredgolds?'

'Are they the people who made an appointment to see you and turned up late?'

'Indeed,' said Bea. 'They interviewed me, instead of my interviewing them. It left an unpleasant taste in my mouth. Betty, there may be more to this particular case than meets the eye. This chef of theirs won't be getting a reference from the Tredgolds because they've decided he's a criminal and sacked him for theft. At least, that's what they say it's about, though I have a nasty feeling there's more to it than that. I don't want to get involved with the family, but I'm thinking we might help the chef to another job. Can you get him to come in later this afternoon? Also, the Tredgolds left a handbag behind, and I want a witness when I check the ID. So will you come upstairs and we'll tackle the problem together? If what I suspect is true, then we'll need to take an inventory of its contents before I hand it back. And, before I touch it, I'm going to see if I can find some of those fine plastic gloves my cleaner uses when she cleans my odd bits of silver.'

Betty grinned. 'Got yourself involved with something criminal again, Mrs Abbot?'

'I sincerely hope not. But yes, possibly. So keep your mouth shut about it for the time being, eh?'

Bea led the way upstairs, found and donned some plastic gloves for herself and Betty, and opened the handbag with care.

Betty peered into it with Bea, then they both looked up at one another.

Betty said, 'That's odd.'

'Very odd,' said Bea. 'No hankies, no make-up, no comb.' She emptied the handbag out on to the table and pushed the contents around with her gloved forefinger. 'A pair of old spectacles, some used ticket stubs for the theatre.'

'No change purse,' said Betty, frowning. 'No pen or pencil.'

'Even worse, no credit cards. I would have expected a platinum card or two, at the very least.'

'No hairpins, no cough sweets, no diary.'

'No smartphone.'

'Yes, that's the clincher. No phone.'

'Just money,' said Betty. 'Fifty pound notes, aren't they?'

31

'Plus a cheque for two thousand pounds, made out to cash and drawn on the Tredgolds current account. That's the only thing with ID on it. There's nothing else to prove who it belongs to.'

Bea separated it from the wad of notes. 'The cheque is signed by squiggle squiggle Tredgold.'

Betty said, 'It's made out to cash so anyone could make use of it.' She squinted at the bank-notes. 'How much, do you think? Two thousand?'

'More. You understand we have to count it?'

'Do we photograph it as well?' Betty grinned. 'Then they can't claim we palmed some of it off? What fun! I wonder if it's marked with that stuff that comes off on your hands if you touch it, stuff that you can't wash it off. Smart water, isn't that what it's called?'

'We'll both count it, one after the other. Then we'll photograph it before we ring the Tredgolds and ask them to collect it. I think we have to make sure they count it out again in front of us and give us a receipt.'

'You don't want to return the bag to them yourself?'

'The less I have to do with them the better. They're far too tricky for my taste. I think this is all about testing my honesty.' She picked up a handful of notes and started to count. 'Perhaps they would have been pleased if I had chosen to help myself to some of the money or cashed the cheque, because then they could accuse me of theft and have me at their mercy. I think this is all about being in control. Three hundred and fifty . . . four. Four fifty, five hundred . . .'

Three

Betty tapped on Bea's door. 'That chef's arrived. Shall I show him in?'

Bea nodded. She'd been looking out through the French windows to where Piers had stretched himself out in the shade at the end of the garden. She'd told herself she really ought to wake him up or he'd be unable to sleep that night. She looked at her watch. She'd had a sandwich and a cup of good coffee. She'd rung the Tredgolds and told them to send someone with ID to check the contents of the handbag and to remove it. The voice on the other end of the phone had squawked indignantly but promised to send someone, soonest.

So now there was just one loose end to tie up. She wanted to find out whether or not the Tredgolds' chef had tried to steal from them because, if she liked the look of him, she might well try to get him another good job. And poop-poop to the Tredgolds!

'Mrs Abbot? I'm Kit Crossley.'

He was a tall man, broad-shouldered, lean. Late twenties? Mixed origin, part West Indian and part British? Born and brought up in Britain. He entered her office with an air of diffidence which verged on anxiety. But then, Bea considered that

33

being unfairly sacked might well undermine your faith in humanity. He looked reasonably intelligent and had capable-looking hands. He was well but casually dressed. He would probably be good in bed.

Um. Yes. Strike that thought.

'Thank you for coming in, Mr Crossley.' Bea waved him to a seat by her desk.

He sat, but he was not at his ease. He said, 'Mrs Abbot, you unnerstand I been done over? I did not steal nothing like they said.'

South London accent, comprehensive school education, no more than three – possibly four – GCSEs?

Bea liked that he'd said straight away that he'd been given the sack. 'Yes, I heard. I have been approached by the Tredgolds for a replacement chef. Let me be frank with you. I need to hear your side of the story before I can decide whether or not I can take you on our books.'

He nodded, hands clasping one another. He sent his eyes around the room, noting this and that but probably not interpreting them as well or as quickly as Mrs Tredgold might have done. 'I was fitted up. They searched the house from top to bottom when he, Edgar Tredgold, said he'd lost his watch. You'd have thought it was the Crown Jewels. I didn't give it no mind, knowing I hadn't seen it. I was in the middle of a good clear out, see, and then there was some loose tiles on the floor in the kitchen which I had a man in to repair, so we emptied out and moved everything, all the fridges and cold store stuff. That's how I can swear to you, hand on heart, it wasn't there that

34

day. And the next day there it was. Under a couple of bunches of asparagus that I'd had sent in the day before. I thought, that's odd. But I didn't think much of it because I'd got the lunch to prepare and I was in a hurry, so I rang through to Her Highness—'

'Who?'

'Sorry. Her. Charlotte. Madam. I said I'd found it, and the next thing I knew they was all down in the kitchen screeching at me that I was a thief and worse! I stood there with me mouth open, thinking they'd gone barmy pots. They wanted me out that day, that very afternoon, and me in the middle of doing lunch! Then they had another think because they was having a dinner party that night and they wouldn't want to be without a cook because what would their friends say! I mean, none of them can cook. I thought I was going mad, I really did. I looked to Mrs T, because I reckoned she'd stand up for me, but she walked out and left me.'

He shook his head. He repeated, 'I thought we was friends. Well, not friends as *they* unnerstand it, but . . . you know?'

He's very class conscious, isn't he?

He said, 'But we was friends, her and me. Real friends. We talked. You know? But she didn't say nothing when they accused me of theft. That cut me. Know what I mean?'

'So you cooked their dinner and left that night, or early next morning?'

'I did. I kept thinking she'd come down and tell me it was all a mistake. But she didn't. Then I cleaned up. I didn't want to leave anything they could get back at me for. Then I got my things together – I had a bedsitter in the basement where I kept a change of clothing, not much, because I like to get back home whenever I can – and I took a cab back to me mum's. I didn't tell her I'd lost me job. She's got enough on her plate with the chemo, you see. Next day I went straight back to Times Two and told them what had happened, but they said they couldn't help me, seeing as how the Tredgolds had said it was good I'd left or they'd have had to bring the police into it. I don't want to go back to restaurant work because of the hours and there's not much else going, seeing as I can't ask for a reference from Mrs T. One of my old friends in the trade – he's doing bar work now but we keep in touch – he said you was fair-minded and might help. So here I am.'

The French windows opened to admit Winston the cat, closely followed by a shambling, half-awake figure squinting at his mobile phone. Coming from the sunny garden into the dimness of the office, Piers failed to see anyone but Bea.

'You shouldn't have let me sleep on. I'll be fit for nothing tomorrow. Phew, I pong. I'll have a shower. You don't mind, do you? I'm trying to read my emails, but . . .? Is there anything to eat? I'm famished. Oh yes, and your cat says he needs feeding.' So saying, Piers stripped off his shirt and only then spotted that Bea had a visitor.

'Oh. Sorry. Didn't realize. Apologies all round. Come on, Winston.' Off he went back out into the garden and up the stairs to the kitchen.

Kit blinked.

Bea guessed he was making assumptions about Piers's appearance and his casual manner. She said, 'My ex-husband. Just flown in from the States. Jet-lagged. Moving back to his own place today.'

'Oh. Ah.'

She saw Kit re-evaluate her. From being an authority figure, old enough to be his mother, Kit was now wondering if she were still beddable.

Bea told herself not to blush.

She saw something else. Winston had not followed Piers but was sniffing at Kit's trousers. Kit put his hand down to let the cat inspect him. Winston made up his mind. This man had recently been in touch with other cats and smelled of good food, so was a possible candidate for providing the next meal. He butted his head against Piers's hand, asking for a caress.

Ah-ha! If Winston approves of Kit, he's no cat killer.

She said, 'How did you get on with Mitzi and Poppy?'

He didn't stiffen up. He was relaxed, half smiling as he rubbed behind Winston's ears. 'They keep the house clear of mice, I'll say that for them. They aren't supposed to come into the kitchen, but somehow I swear that Mitzi can give Houdini a run for his money. Can this cat of yours open cupboards? Mitzi can. And Poppy sits and waits for her to do so, and then they both wade in. They can't manage the fridge or the freezer, but any door with a handle, like to the old larder, is fair game. Those two can housebreak for Britain.'

He went on stroking the cat. 'Of course I turf them out whenever I find them in the kitchen. Sometimes two or three times a day. You may ask how they get in when it's a heavy swing door? I did wonder . . .'

Bea said, 'You thought someone might have been letting them into the kitchen to annoy you?'

He nodded. 'It sounds mad, but yes. I did wonder. There's nothing that someone wouldn't do to . . .' He shot Bea a look and decided not to complete the sentence.

'You suspected someone?'

'No, of course not.'

Which meant that he did suspect someone but had no proof. He made a shooing motion to Winston who understood petting time was over and padded off to see who he could bamboozle into feeding him. The girls in the office were usually good for the odd titbit.

Bea said, 'You heard the cats died the night you left?'

'What?' He shot upright in his chair, mouth open, eyes huge. 'Mitzi and Poppy?' Puzzlement. 'No! You're having me on!'

Bea shook her head. 'Their throats were cut and then they were put in the drain outside the kitchen.'

His warm colouring faded to pale. 'I don't believe it! No! Who . . . I mean, why? I mean, I was fond of them cats.' He searched her face for understanding.

Bea nodded. 'I believe you.' He hadn't known the cats had been killed. He certainly hadn't killed them.

He tensed. 'How could he? It must have been him . . . mustn't it?'

'Who?'

He gulped. Shook his head. Ran a hand across his face. Took a deep breath. 'No, I don't get it. Edgar, I mean. He's never liked me, but . . . No, I really don't think he . . . Then . . . Ahmed? He likes to wind people up, can't stand the cats but . . . No, I can't see that, either. Ahmed's by way of being a mate of mine and he wouldn't . . . Unless he was drunk? But no, I never seen him drink. Takes all that seriously. But if not him . . .?'

He rubbed his eyes. 'That's tough. How's Mrs T taking it? She loves – loved – those cats. She likes to be quiet of an evening. She don't go out much at night, nowadays. She's getting on, you know. She says – said – the cats were good company. Restful, she said. And they weren't that old. She must be going bananas.'

Mrs Tredgold's plea for Bea to find who had killed her cats began to make sense. There was something nasty in the woodpile at Tredgold House and it wasn't just the business of the cats being killed, or of their chef being falsely accused of theft.

Kit got up, saying, 'Excuse me . . .' He thrust open the French windows, stepped out into the garden and did some deep breathing.

Bea's internal phone rang.

Piers. 'Do you want something to eat? Shall I send out for some food?'

Bea said, 'Hold on a mo. I'm coming up.' Then to Kit, 'I fancy a cuppa. Would you like to join me? I've got to feed my ex.'

'I know about exes. Mrs T's is a bit of all right.' He rolled his shoulders. 'That's better.' His colour was returning to normal. 'Food. That's my cue, right? What you got? I could throw something together for you.'

Bea nodded. She'd hoped he'd say that. She'd always found people talked more freely when their hands were occupied, and she wanted to know more about Kit before she offered to find him another job.

She led the way out into the garden and up the cast-iron stairs to where a balcony gave access to both the sitting room and the kitchen.

There was Piers, damp from his shower, shoe-less and looking helpless. It was an act. Piers was perfectly capable of cooking for himself if necessary.

She said, 'Piers, let me introduce you to Kit. He's a chef, currently out of work. You'll be interested, Piers, because I believe you've been contacted by the people concerned. Kit, would you like to see if there's anything in the fridge or freezer that you can use to feed two hungry people while I make some coffee to keep us going?'

'Pleasure, though I haven't got me knives with me. But sure, I can cope.' He was quick and accurate in the kitchen. His diffident air vanished as he assembled ingredients, took a quick look at the oven and got to work.

Bea said, 'So Kit, where did you learn your trade?'

'I worked me way up. I allus wanted to work with food. I got a feeling for it. When I left school

I got a job in a restaurant, doing the washing-up, like. Then I moved on to another where I could do the veg, and I worked there till I got a better job. I kept me eyes open, like, and sometimes the chef would teach me a bit of this and that. I like to work with fish. I coulda gone on working in restaurants but the hours was terrible and I'd got this girl I was seeing and then me mum was peaky and I wanted regular hours so's I could get back to her most nights. She's got this council flat not too far off the Tube line, Elephant and Castle way. So the first agency I tried was Times Two, and they sent me to see Mrs T and we got on like a house on fire, and she gave me plenty of time off to visit me mum, although it's a live-in job, really. But she, mum, she's not so brilliant now though the treatment is working, they say.'

Bea noted that he hadn't mentioned a father. She said, 'When exactly did you start working for the Tredgolds?'

He counted on his fingers. 'Eight? No. Nine months ago.'

'There's a houseful of Tredgolds, is that right?'

Piers half-closed his eyes. 'Tredgolds. Where have I heard that name before?'

Bea was sharp with him. 'You've been booked to paint Mrs T's portrait.'

'What? No, I haven't. I've got enough commissions booked to keep me going for a year, and they're not on the list.'

'Charlotte Tredgold said—'

'I don't care what Charlotte said. I'm not in my dotage. I know what I've agreed to do and what I've turned down.' He thought about it.

Looked puzzled. Took his smartphone out and accessed his emails. 'Ah-ha. You're right. This came in this morning. Someone called Tredgold asking for my fees. Did I reply? Was I awake when I replied? Yep, I did. Told them I wasn't free. That's it.'

Kit turned the blender on and raised his voice. 'They'll offer you double your usual if they really want you.' He switched the blender off and dropped his voice to normal. 'Money's no object. "What I want I get," is their motto. Except for Mrs T, but she's no straightforward doll, neither.'

Bea said, 'Tell us about them.'

'Well . . .' He raised his shoulders to his ears and let them drop. 'The missus, now. Mrs T. She's all right. She's got all her marbles and no side to her, know what I mean? She owns the house, she has the money, and what she says goes. The rest of them have never earned a penny in their lives, unless you count the odd tuppence that Charlotte brings in with her articles for women's mags. As for her poems that she's so proud of, she says no one gets paid for poetry nowadays, which I don't know as is true, but that's what she says. Those two hear what they want to hear and if they don't want to hear it, it don't exist.'

He shook his head. 'I'm forgetting: there's the younger son, who's a sandwich short of a filling. He's some kind of scholar. He's all right when he's "with it," but most of the time nowadays he's away with the fairies. Lately, Mrs T's been getting tired. She wants to get out of that big house and find herself a smaller place. They don't like that idea. They've been shouting at her, making out she's past it . . . which she isn't, but it bothers her, know what I mean? I thought she was fond of me, sort of, not in the wrong way, you unnerstand? I thought she'd stand up for me when Edgar – who's a piece of shit, excuse my language, but he is – said I'd stolen his watch.'

His hands were a blur, throwing food into this pan, flipping it over, watching something boil in a pan and turning the gas down.

The cat, Winston, jumped up on to the table, where he knew very well that he had no right to be. Bea watched to see what Kit would do about it. If he lashed out at the cat, it would prove he didn't care for them, no matter what he'd said earlier.

Kit fixed Winston with a cold eye and lifted a forefinger at him.

Winston stared him out for a count of five, and then pretended he hadn't wanted to sit on the table anyway and jumped off.

Bea relaxed. Kit had handled the cat better than she ever had. When had she been able to turf Winston off the table with a look and a raised finger? She said, 'What were your duties?'

'I was hired by Mrs T to cater for her and if I had time over, to prepare meals and put them in the freezer for the others, who usually ate separate from her. If she had one of them up to her place for a meal, she'd give me good notice of it. Mrs T don't have much appetite, likes everything cooked fresh. Breakfast is muesli, a boiled egg with some of my oatmeal biscuits and fresh fruit on the side, with Lady Grey tea. Lunch is fish or chicken, grilled. No cream, lots of greens, fruit and cheese, with sparkling spa water to drink. For supper she has a sandwich and some of my homemade soup. I done hers fresh every day.'

'It's a variation on the Mediterranean diet, isn't it? Recommended for people who've had a heart problem, and for those who want to lose weight?'

'That's the one. I worked mornings from seven, finished at three or half past. When I'd sorted Mrs T's meals, I cooked for the rest and put the stuff in the freezer for them to take out and micro-wave. They wanted roast meat and two veg, pizzas and curries, and desserts with lots of cream and booze. Plus cakes and biscuits and sweet things, too. Every now and then they asked me to do an evening meal for them. They was supposed to pay me extra for that but mostly they "forgot" and Mrs T would say it didn't matter and make it up to me. Except for her, they could all do with cutting down a bit on the carbs, but that's their problem, innit?'

'Charlotte told me she was on a special diet.'

He grimaced. 'Must have started it after I left. Unless she meant the sherry and chocolate diet she's been on since the day I started.'

'So how many were you cooking for, apart from Mrs T?'

'It varied, see. As I said, there's Charlotte. A right bossyboots. Tried it on me, if you can believe it . . .?'

He looked to see if Bea did believe it. She'd witnessed Charlotte having a go at Piers, so she nodded.

He did an eye-roll. 'And she wasn't the worst.

That young . . .' He stopped, eyes down and then to the side.

Bea prompted him. 'There's a young girl in the house who perhaps doesn't quite know how to approach men?'

'She knows exactly what she's doing.' Grimly. 'She was furious when I told her I was old enough to be her father, and swore she'd get even with me. I even wondered if—' He stopped short.

Bea completed the sentence. 'You think she killed the cats?'

He frowned. 'No, I don't think . . . not even her! But I did think she might have planted the watch in my asparagus. But there, who'd believe me if I said anything against her?'

Bea sighed. She knew what he meant. And it rather looked as if it were not one but two people who'd made advances to him in that household. If you believed him. And Bea did. He was indignant and shamed and angry about it. Yes, it had happened all right. 'Go on. There's Charlotte and the granddaughter. Who else? Someone called Edgar?'

'Eldest son of Mrs T's. Looks down his nose at anyone who went to a comprehensive school. White scum.'

Bea told herself not to laugh. 'He's the one who accused you of stealing his watch?'

'Why would I? How could I sell such a thing? I mean . . . stupid!'

Bea nodded. 'Tell me about him.'

'Edgar lives at home during the week. At weekends he's off, fancies himself as a yachtsman, wears a blazer and a cap and has a little fancy beard, you know the type? Likes to be called "the admiral". Lavinia, that's his missus, lives there full time. Charity work, a bit of a cold fish, if you ask me. She and Edgar have the second-floor flat, all la-di-dah. She's terribly well connected . . .' His mimicry was brilliant. 'Daughter of someone who's managed to wangle himself a knighthood due to services rendered, if you know what I mean? She has money of her own, goes to all the charity events and sits at the top table where she can be seen. Eats like a sparrow. Looks a bit like a bird, come to think of it. But always remembers her manners.'

Bea smiled. She was enjoying this. 'And the girl who made a pass at you?'

'Their daughter, name of Petra. She's fifteen, coming up sixteen. Looks eighteen or more. Double trouble. I tell my mum what that Petra gets up to, and my mum – she's a right one, been round the block a couple of times – well, she reckons Miss Petra will be up the spout before she leaves school if she hasn't been there already. Not that she goes to school much. They don't know it, her parents, but I seen her bunking off with boys, different ones. What they see in her, I dunno. Money, I suppose. The current one sports a shaved head but he's well grown, know what I mean?'

Charlotte had given Bea the impression that her niece had been chatted up by Kit, or worse. Did Bea believe it? Er, no. Probably not. How very awkward for Kit, though, if that was being said about him.

She said, 'There's an ex-husband hanging around somewhere?'

'Coach house. Keeps his head down. Miniature railway enthusiast. Goes to all the meetings or conventions or whatever they call it. Pretends he doesn't hear when the others make fun of him. "Steam train Daddy," they call him. They treat him like a handyman or caretaker: do this, do that. He smiles and says he will when he's not too busy. I like him, sort of. He's always treated me right, and he's not as stupid as they make out, because he plays bridge with the old girl and she's sharp as a tack.'

He tasted something green in one of the pans and nodded. 'You want mugs or soup bowls for this?'

Bea plonked some mugs down in front of him, and he poured the mixture into them. 'My version of summer soup. One of Mrs T's favourites. You won't believe this, but Mrs T even had me playing bridge, making up a four in the afternoons now and then. Said I had a good head for figures, which I have. I get that from my mum, who used to work in a betting shop when she was fit. It wasn't often Mrs T asked me, mind you. Just now and then when the daughter-in-law wasn't able to oblige and they wanted a fourth.'

Bea counted on her fingers. 'So who played bridge? Mrs T, Edgar's wife, Lavinia, who is into charity work, and the ex-husband who lives in the coach house. Who usually made up the table? At a guess, it wouldn't be the daughter, Charlotte.' Bea sipped the soup and was pleasantly surprised. It was excellent. 'Yum, yum.'

Kit was already back at the stove, his hands flying between various pans. 'Never Charlotte! She fidgets and don't open her mouth except to criticize. Drives Mrs T crazy. No, the fourth is the second son, the one with his head in the clouds, lives on the third floor. Not quite the thing, but a good bridge player, I'll grant you that. There's initials for what he's got. OCD, ADHD, stress-related something or other? It was his wife that died, falling through a window, soon after I arrived. Accident, they said. It sent him doolally.'

Bea looked out of the window. She knew – and she thought Kit knew, too – that this piece of information was important. She told herself that she couldn't know, and there might be nothing wrong with the woman's demise.

Piers looked into the bottom of his empty mug. 'Any more of this?'

Kit was a whirlwind, marshalling plates, knives and forks, toast and greens and a mixture which made Bea sniff in appreciation. 'Enjoy!' He pushed the plates towards them and stood back, waiting for their reaction.

'Mm. What is it?' said Piers, round a mouthful.

'Mushrooms,' said Bea. 'Cheese. Out of this world, Kit.'

Piers eyed the pans which Kit was clattering into the sink. 'Seconds?'

'No. Fresh fruit salad for afters,' said Kit, his knife flashing over an apple.

Piers ran his finger over the last traces of food on his plate. 'If you're out of a job, will you come and cook for me?'

Kit grinned. Only now, with his expertise rated

48

high and his story believed, he relaxed. 'You couldn't afford me.'

Bea sighed as she polished off her last morsel. 'He probably could afford you but you wouldn't like his kitchen, it's tiny. Anyway, that's beside the point. You want your name cleared, don't you, Kit? And you're worried about Mrs T.'

He nodded.

'It sounds as if you should forget all about Mrs T and the goings-on in that place. For one thing, if the granddaughter has made up a story about you, they'll have to believe her even if they know in their bones that she made it up.'

'I know,' said Kit, wincing. 'Would a nice young white girl tell fibs about a big black man like me? Tell you what, though. I cook for you for a week for nothing, and you get me another good job.'

'Done!' said Piers.

'Hold on!' Bea was half laughing and half serious. 'You don't even live here, Piers, and there's no way I can guarantee to get Kit another good job. I admit I quite took to Mrs T and I'm sorry she's lost her cats, but I don't give a rush for the rest of that family, who don't seem to have more than a passing acquaintance with the truth and turn to bullying whenever anyone stands up to them. What's more, when Charlotte departed, she left an expensive handbag behind full of money, and I can't work out whether that was to bribe me or to entice me into crime. What a bundle of joy that family is! And you want me to tangle with this family of dodgy if not criminal minds? You must be joking!'

49

Four

Piers was unperturbed. 'You know you like a challenge. Besides which, I'd flown back expecting to start work tomorrow on a portrait for some French aristocrat or other and there's message on my phone to say he's not available this week so I'm free to take up the offer made by Mrs T to paint her. I can ask her to give Kit his job back, and it gives you a way into the household to find out what's going on.'

'She can't give Kit his job back after what her grandchild is reported to have said and I'm not going anywhere near them. You won't, either, if you know what's good for you.'

Her landline rang. She had an extension in the kitchen, so picked that up.

A smooth tenor voice. 'Mrs Abbot, this is Ahmed speaking. I have instructions to collect Mrs Tredgold's handbag but there's nowhere to park the car. Would you bring it down to me in the street?'

'No, Ahmed,' said Bea. 'I am not going to hand that bag over to you without proper authorization or without the contents being checked. There's a mews on the right just before the end of the street. Park your car in there outside the garage with the bright green door. Bring your

50

paperwork back here and we'll discuss the matter.'

She put the phone down and poured coffee. Kit rinsed plates and put them in the dishwasher, while shooting a glance at her. Yes, he wanted to know what was going on, didn't he?

Piers said, 'What? You've told him to park outside my place in the mews? Suppose I'd got my car parked there?'

Bea had allowed Piers to stay in her mews cottage after he'd had to leave his last place at short notice. Her car was garaged downstairs and he lived in the somewhat cramped space above it. For work, he'd rented a garret with a north exposure nearby.

Bea said, 'You mean you've actually bought a car?'

'No, but I might have done so. That's my parking space.'

'You've always said you don't need a car in Central London. Besides which—'

'I'm behind with the rent. I know. I'll transfer some money into your bank account today.'

Bea shrugged. She trusted him for the rent, and he knew that. He also knew that she normally rented out the mews cottage to business people on short lets. He was taking advantage of her good nature to live in her property, when he could easily have afforded to buy somewhere for himself. Ah, but he didn't want the bother of maintaining a house, did he? What's more, he enjoyed popping in to see her at different times of the day and cadging the odd meal. And it was – in a way that she did not intend to look at too

51

closely – a comforting thought that he was living locally and could be called upon for company, or to fix something for her with a screwdriver.

Which led her on to think about Mrs Tredgold's ex-husband, who lived in her coach house, and who was also useful with a screwdriver. Bea smiled to herself, thinking that she understood that relationship pretty well.

There was another ting on the house phone. It was Betty, ringing from the office downstairs. 'There's a man here, a chauffeur, says you told him to call.'

'Thanks, Betty. He's come for the handbag with the money in it. Send him up here, will you?'

Bea said to Piers, 'It seems Ahmed, the chauffeur, has arrived. Do you want to be off?'

'Not I,' said Piers, busy on his phone. 'I'm fed up with painting fat cats with sharp eyes and no morals. Mrs Tredgold intrigues me. I'm texting to ask when we can meet to discuss her portrait; terms and conditions, what she's to wear, what background she'd like. Or, given her age, does she want me to take photographs and work from them?'

Kit was cleaning the table. 'You want I should make myself scarce?'

'You like Ahmed?'

'He's OK. We're mates, sort of. He's Muslim. Vegetarian. I couldn't be doing with vegan, but vegetarian's all right. He likes Mrs T and Mrs T likes him, if that's anything to go by.'

Bea rather thought it was.

Betty arrived, shepherding Ahmed into the kitchen.

Ahmed was probably of Pakistani origin, clever-looking, thin-featured, and of medium height. Dapper. He was wearing a grey chauffeur's uniform and carrying his cap in his hand. He was ill at ease, a trace of perspiration on his forehead.

Ahmed recognized Kit and checked for a moment. He hadn't expected to see the chef here. Did they exchange a look of complicity? Knowledge of some kind? Or were they simply acknowledging one another's presence?

No, Ahmed was bewildered, eyes widened like a horse about to bolt. He addressed Bea. 'Mrs Abbot? I've been sent to collect a package from you.'

Ahmed was better educated than Kit. Aspiring second-generation Brit.

Bea said, 'Who sent you? Mrs Tredgold, or her daughter, Charlotte?'

Ahmed's eyes switched to Kit. Did he not know who had sent him? Why did he look to Kit for answers?

Instead of replying, Ahmed produced an unsealed envelope from behind the cap he was holding and held it out to Bea. 'My instructions were to hand this to you and return with the package by four o'clock.'

'Who are you supposed to give the handbag to?'

'I have to hand it in to the office and have it checked before I fetch Mrs Tredgold from her appointment in Wimpole Street, which is at half past four.'

Bea glanced at the clock on the wall. It was after three already. The time allowed was going to be tight. She repeated, 'Who will be in the office?'

He glanced at Kit again and shrugged. 'Whoever is there, I suppose.'

Kit ran the tap, refilling the coffee machine. 'He means it might be Her Highness, or it might be the secretary, or the housekeeper. It might even be Mrs T's ex, who steps in to help sometimes.' He switched the coffee machine on. Whatever reservations he might have had when he first saw Ahmed had disappeared. 'Relax, Ahmed. These people are all right. Kosher. Or whatever it is in your language. Coffee's on. You want something to eat?'

Ahmed shifted from one foot to the other. 'Look, I can't . . . if I don't get back in time . . . the smallest thing, and I'm out, and then what? I can't dump myself on my family because they live in the north. I don't have anywhere else to go, not like you. Mrs Abbot, please give it to me. I daren't be late.'

Kit folded his arms. 'Ahmed, come clean. What are you so nervous about? What they got on you? You being her favourite and all? Don't tell me! It's not that snotty little bitch again, is it?'

Ahmed shook his head violently. 'No, no. It's not like that. She hasn't, not for ages. And as if I would! No, never! No, not her.'

Bea added two and three and made a guess. 'Which bitch are you talking about? Old or young? Ah, the old one, is it? Charlotte Tredgold's made a pass at you? She's gone on a special diet to try to get you interested in her?'

He paled and stuck out his hand to rest against

54

the cupboard. 'How could you say that! It's not . . . Nobody would believe . . .!'

'I would, for one.' Kit clattered Bea's smallest cups and saucers on to the table.

Bea agreed. 'I would, too. Ahmed, would you please sit down and let us have a civilized conversation? I can see you're in a difficult position. Well, so am I. Did the Tredgolds tell you what was in the package you've been sent to collect? No? I thought not. It's money. A lot of it. Cash.'

Ahmed showed the whites of his eyes. 'You mean—'

'It might mean nothing,' said Bea. 'Let's have a look at the paperwork they gave you when they asked you to run this errand.' She opened the envelope and extracted a single sheet of paper. She read it through, shook her head and held it up for the others to see. 'This authorizes the bearer to collect a handbag containing three thousand five hundred pounds from Mrs Abbot. Today's date, signed with a squiggle.'

She looked at their bemused faces. 'Betty and I opened the handbag together, and counted out five thousand, five hundred pounds. There was also a cheque on a Tredgold account, made out to cash.'

Kit and Ahmed froze into immobility.

Piers gave a short laugh. 'They expect you to snaffle the money that's not accounted for in their note? Do they *want* you to pinch it?'

Bea said, 'Ahmed, Kit, what's your take on this?'

Ahmed sank on to a stool and put his head in his hands. 'Not again!'

55

Kit slung a tea towel over his shoulder. He poured out some thick black coffee into a small cup, and placed it in front of Ahmed, who gulped it down in one. 'Told you so.'

Piers's nose whiffled. 'What coffee is that?'

Kit poured out a second cup and set it in front of Piers, who picked it up, closed his eyes to savour the aroma and sipped it with an expression of bliss.

Kit looked at Bea. 'You don't like it so strong, missus? Shall I make you something else?'

Bea shook her head. 'Come clean, Kit. Do you think the money was placed in the handbag to see if Ahmed or I would help ourselves? Do I understand that they've tried this sort of thing before?'

'No,' said Ahmed, in a strangled voice.

'Yes,' said Kit. 'They tried it on Ahmed a coupla weeks ago. He was sent to the post office with a birthday card to post – which should have been for the secretary girl to do, but she's far too high and mighty for that sort of errand, isn't she? Anyway, the flap was open and the girl at the counter said it was too thick to go through the slot like that and she shook it and a second envelope fell out, addressed to Madame Charlotte with a hundred pounds cash in it, in fivers. That's what made the envelope too thick to go through the slot. He thought they'd made a mistake, couldn't understand how it could have happened. Mistake, my granny's boot! Ridiculous! He was meant to help himself, wasn't he? And then they'd have him on toast. What fools they take us for!'

Ahmed said, 'They want me out. But why? I

don't understand. If my face doesn't fit, why not just give me notice?'

Kit was grim. 'They'd have to give you your holiday pay. This way they don't even pay your wages up to the end of the month, right?'

Bea said, 'You've told me enough to realize that something very strange is going on in the Tredgold household. You, Kit, have been sacked on the flimsiest of grounds, and now Ahmed also thinks he's being framed for theft. I can't think why, but someone seems to be trying to draw me into the Tredgold net, too.'

'And me,' said Piers, staring at his smartphone. 'I'm commanded to present myself to the Tredgolds tomorrow morning at nine, and not to be late.' He put the phone down. 'Why me? Why at such short notice? I'm always booked months ahead.'

Bea said, 'I don't like this. Not any of it.'

'Neither do I,' said Kit, pounding some dough into submission.

'Nor me,' said Ahmed.

Kit said, 'Mrs Abbot, what's going on at the Tredgolds, it's criminal. Nobody's job is safe for more than a few months. I've seen it, Ahmed's seen it. They got me out in the end. Who's next?'

Bea said, 'There was someone else, wasn't there? One of the cleaners. Was that long ago? Found with a diamond ring in her purse?'

Kit and Ahmed looked at one another and looked away.

'Was that it?' said Kit. 'Thing is, one minute she was there, and the next she was being shown out of the door. We were told she'd been taken

poorly and not to gossip. We did wonder, but . . .
Well, we knew she was skint, although I wouldn't
have thought she'd take that route. I thought she
was all right, but there it was and how can you
tell?'

Ahmed said, 'That was two weeks ago. She
used to clean for Mrs T up at the top. Mrs T was
fond of her, and I would have said she was fond
of Mrs T. And then . . . *pfftt*! She was gone.
There's such an atmosphere. We don't know
what's going to hit us next.'

Bea said, 'You think there's some kind of purge
going on, and I agree that the Tredgold manage-
ment skills don't seem to be marvellous, but—'

Kit said, 'Ahmed, tell her about the physio,
and what happened to him.'

Bea said, 'You mean there's been other false
accusations of theft?'

Ahmed said, 'Mrs T said this physio did her
more good than any doctor, but . . . You tell
her, Kit, if you think it'll make any difference.
Sorry, Mrs Abbot. I've got to get back with the
package, and I'm due to collect Mrs T from
the dentist after. She'll be on the fidget if I'm
not there on time.'

Piers said, 'Surely you can phone her if you're
a few minutes late?'

'She has an old-fashioned phone with big
letters on it for emergencies, but she never
switches it on. She says she's not all that sure
how to work it, though I've shown her several
times and I'm pretty sure that if there was an
emergency, she'd use it. Or get someone to use
it for her. You don't understand the Tredgolds.

They mean what they say. If I'm not where they want me to be, on time, then I get my wages docked.'

Piers said, 'They can't do that! I mean, London traffic, congestion, nobody can be sure how quickly they can make any journey.'

'They make the rules, not me.'

Bea said, 'Why do you stay when they're so difficult to work for?'

Kit smiled. 'They pay us double what we'd get anywhere else.'

There was no answer to that. Bea fetched the handbag and a printout of the photographs she and Betty had taken of the cash and cheque. There was also a list, which she and Betty had signed, stating exactly what they had found in the handbag when they opened it. Bea handed the money, the papers and the handbag to Ahmed, and fished out her smartphone.

'Stand there. Hold everything up in front of you. I'll take a photo of you and text it to Charlotte. That will prove that you picked up the handbag with all the money intact. Right?'

'You'll let me take it?' Ahmed wasn't sure what he'd got himself into, was he?

Bea said, 'I have a feeling that anyone who has anything to do with the Tredgolds is at risk so let's take all the precautions we can, shall we?' She took the picture. 'There now, that should be proof that neither you nor I have robbed them.'

'Why didn't I think of that?' Kit kneaded something – pastry? – on a board. 'But I don't suppose it would have saved me if I had taken a photo of the watch in the vegetable drawer. It's my word against theirs, and who do they believe? Not me.'

Bea said, 'You two keep saying "they" framed you. Who do you mean by "they"?'

Kit sighed. 'Truth is we don't know. We've talked about it, dunno how many times. Charlotte, maybe? Though it's not exactly her scene, is it? I mean, all that poetry stuff. She writes about "true love", though what she knows about it I couldn't say. Edgar? More likely. And yet. Dunno. The only thing for certain is that anyone Mrs T likes gets the chop.'

Ahmed grunted agreement and put his cap back on.

Kit said, 'Come back later, Ahmed, right? You knew the physio, and how he tried to make a fuss. Why don't you phone him to come over here and tell Mrs Abbot what happened to him? That would make three of us in trouble. Mrs Abbot, you'll have to help us if you get the physio's story, too. Won't you? I mean, we can't all of us be round the twist, can we?'

Ahmed was already removing himself. 'I have to take Mr Edgar and his wife to the theatre in St Martin's Lane this evening. After that I'll be free till I have to collect them at half ten.'

Bea was about to say that she didn't want to interfere, but Kit got in first. 'Get the physio to join us here for supper, right?' Kit rolled out his pastry . . . or whatever it was.

Ahmed didn't say he would, and he didn't say he wouldn't, but shot off like a rabbit to his warren.

Piers said, 'I'll see him out,' and went after Ahmed.

Bea was half amused and half annoyed. 'Really, Kit! You take too much on yourself. How many times do I have to say that I want nothing to do with the Tredgolds? I will see if I can get you another good job, but if you feel you've been sacked unfairly you can always consult a solicitor.'

'No, I can't do that,' said Kit, cutting rounds out of his dough and laying them on a greased tray. 'The moment we squeak about anything, they threaten us with all sorts. "Take it like a man!" That's what the admiral says. "We won't bring the girl into it if you go quietly." And who's going to take our word for it against that of a fifteen-year-old with great big baby blues?'

Ah-ha. That was what Charlotte had been on about, wasn't it? Bea said, 'But you said you didn't—'

'Of course I didn't. Wouldn't. Apart from anything else, got me own girl. Bright as a button. Been going with her nigh on a year now, thinking of moving in together if Mum don't get no worse. Besides, there's something about miss which gives me the creeps.' He bunged his tray into the oven and twiddled knobs.

'You want me to wave a magic wand and make the whole nasty business go away? Well, I can't.' Bea looked at her watch. This business had occupied far too much of her busy day and she needed to go downstairs to the agency and see what was happening there.

Only here came Piers, dragging his tote bag

61

into the kitchen. He unzipped the bag and proceeded to stuff dirty clothing into the washing machine.

Bea said, 'What the . . .!'

'The washing machine in the mews is broken.'

Bea almost shrieked. 'When did that happen, and why didn't you tell me so that I could have had someone look at it? You've been away three whole weeks and—'

'I forgot. I was going to do a big wash the day I went but things happened, and now I haven't any clean clothes there, either.'

Bea raised her arms and screamed, silently.

Kit was amused. 'Home from home. I'll make us a fish pie for supper, shall I? And the Welsh cakes will be five minutes. Me mum's recipe. She's proper Welsh. She misses Cardiff, but when she goes back it's not the same as she remembers, and she's better off in the flat with folk around as knows her.'

Bea's phone rang. It was Betty, asking if Bea could spare a minute. 'We've a client in some distress, and she's asking for you personally.'

'Not one of the Tredgold ménage?'

'No, no.' Betty mentioned the name of one of their oldest clients, and Bea said she'd be right down. 'And,' Bea said, fixing Kit and Piers with a cold eye, 'no funny business while I'm gone. No talking to the Tredgolds. Do not, even by an inch, indicate that I am going to have anything whatever to do with them. Understood?'

'Of course,' said Piers, in a soothing tone. 'You will make up your own mind what to do.' And to Kit, 'Do you mean genuine Welsh cakes? I remember having some when I was staying with friends in Wales years ago. Like nothing else, are they?'

Bea fled.

Wednesday early evening

She was so busy that afternoon that she forgot all about the Tredgolds till it was time to shut down the computers and see the staff off the premises for the night. Only then did she remember her awkward visitors. She shook her head and wondered in vague fashion how the Tredgolds and their staff, present and past, were getting on. Having drawn a blank with Bea, Charlotte would have tried another agency, wouldn't she? Good riddance.

As for Kit, who'd said he'd cook for her for a week if she got him another job, she'd been firm with him, hadn't she? She supposed she might well try to find him something else but the lack of a reference was going to make it difficult. He would have taken the hint and gone back to his mum's place by now, wouldn't he?

She also hoped Piers had removed himself and his bits and pieces. He was a good companion and could be amusing but Bea was wary of letting him back into her life again. She had never got over his tomcatting around in the days when they'd been married, so long ago. Ah, well. Water under the bridge. She wasn't denying that every now and then something in her responded to him. He was an attractive man and could still work his magic, if she let him. But she would not. Self-preservation insisted.

She took one last look around before leaving her office. Some time ago she'd shut the French windows leading from her office into the garden because there'd been an irritating breeze which had ruffled papers on her desk, and some neighbours had been chatting outside with no consideration for those who had to work for their living.

Checking that the French windows to the garden were locked and the grille over them had been closed, she froze.

Sitting in a cosy little group at the bottom of her garden, happily taking advantage of the late afternoon sun were . . .

Not one, not two, but three large men!

Five

Wednesday early evening, continued

Bea was outraged!

The garden was her sanctuary. Nobody else went into it unless she issued a specific invitation to that effect. Surrounded by high brick walls, it was a suntrap. A small pond invited birds to drink and water lilies to bloom. There were large pots filled with annuals on the flagstones in the centre and flowering shrubs around the perimeter, while a couple of small trees with interesting foliage provided some shelter from the sun.

The men had dragged garden chairs out of the shed and made themselves very much at home.

Bea stepped out into the sunshine and the men turned their heads to greet her. They were all three relaxed, quite at home, each with a can of beer in their hands.

She wanted to box their ears!

But, while Piers was acting as host and Kit was all smiles, what could she do about the situation?

She bared her teeth in an attempt at a smile. 'Were you waiting for me to finish work?'

Kit and the stranger struggled to their feet to offer her their chairs. Bea declined the honour, making the point that they were invading her territory.

Piers didn't bother to stand but lifted his beer can in a salute. 'Bea, this is Andy, Mrs Tredgold's physio, and does he have a tale to tell!'

Andy was a chunky man in his mid-thirties, with a decent tan. 'Nice to meet you, Mrs Abbot. Ahmed rang me just as I was treating my last client for the day. He said you wanted to meet me. I've heard so much about you that I dropped everything to come. May I fetch you another chair?'

A slight accent. Australian? He looked dependable. His good manners softened her attitude, and she nodded agreement. He scrambled to get another chair out of the shed for her, and placed it where she indicated, in partial shade.

Bea said, 'You've heard about me?'

'One of my clients, Lord Rycroft, twisted his

ankle, soon put to rights. His wife's expecting, you know? I understand you helped him with some family problem. He was full of your praises. As a matter of fact, Mrs T knows him, too, from some art gallery event they both go to.'

Kit said, 'Small world, innit?'

Bea struggled to be polite. 'You do understand that I can't get you your jobs back?'

Piers said, 'Ah, but you haven't heard Andy's story yet.'

Kit looked at his watch. 'I'll put the veg on in half an hour, supper at half six, right?'

Bea told herself to relax. She'd hear Andy out, and pack the whole boiling lot of them off. It had been a long and tiring day, and she was looking forward to a quiet evening all by herself.

Andy cleared his throat. 'Well, it's like this. Mrs T has dodgy joints but, like a lot of older people, she won't do the exercises to keep herself in trim. So she used to have me visit her once a week. If her knee was all right, we'd tackle her shoulder. We'd chat away, get her nicely loosened up and I'd bill her once a month. She said it was keeping her going and better than taking pills from the doctor. When we started she used to make sure her housekeeper or the cleaner was there to act as chaperone but after a while she didn't bother. Sometimes one of them would be there to offer me a cup of tea, but often not.

'Mrs T and I always had plenty to talk about because, like me, she followed the football. Manchester United, that was us. She had her opinion on the new man they'd brought in, and so did I and, well, we begged to differ on that subject. One day I mentioned I'd placed a bet on a big horse race that was being run that afternoon and she said she'd never yet had a bet on a horse race, and she rather fancied the idea. She got out her handbag and gave me a fifty to put on the favourite for her and said I should keep mum about it, or her family would get in a flap because they were that strait-laced you wouldn't believe. I thought she was a great old biddy and why shouldn't she have a little flutter if she wished to do so? It wasn't as if she wasn't flush with money, or would miss the odd hundred or so.'

Piers said, 'Did she win?'

'Yes, she did. I gave her her winnings the following week and, don't you know, she had the newspaper right there, looking up the runners for the next big race. She won on that, too. Right canny, she was. Studied form, and all that. Every time after that, she'd hand me a fifty and tell me to put it on such and such a horse, and most of the time I put my money on what she'd picked out, too. We did all right, both of us. I mean, we didn't win all the time. You can't expect that. But by the end of the year we'd come out on top and had a lot of fun.'

Kit asked, 'Why didn't she set up an account with a bookmaker?'

'I told her she could do that, but she said it was more fun this way, because she could discuss it with me and we'd look forward to it together. She was right, you know. It *was* a lot more fun that way.' He sobered up. 'I don't reckon her family know what it is to let their hair down and have fun. Not good clean fun, if you know what I mean?'

Piers said, 'Only, it all came to a sticky end?'

'She must have got careless, let the family suspect what she was doing. Maybe she'd left the sports section of the newspaper around, marked up with her picks. I don't know how it happened, but six weeks ago I got there to find the son and daughter upstairs, shouting at Mrs T for wasting money. To listen to them, you'd think Mrs T had become a gambling addict who was about to mortgage the house and all. They knew it was me who'd been placing her bets and they said I was a bad influence and wasn't welcome to come any more. Mrs T told them it was none of their business, and that if I had run errands for her, then that was her responsibility, not mine. They weren't best pleased, said they'd call a family conference and told me to leave without treating her.'

'And you did?'

He shrugged. 'She's an old lady, and being shouted at like that, it wasn't good for her. She was in tears though trying to hide it. I didn't know what to say, or to do. I didn't want to leave her like that, but what choice did I have? So yes, I left. I collected my bag and got into the lift – and went home. That was the last I saw of her. I swear to you I didn't touch the vase. I may be a clumsy lout, but I'd have known if I'd knocked it over, wouldn't I?'

'What vase?' said Kit.

'There was a great big blue-and-white jar thing that sat on the floor by the middle window in the sitting room. Ming, they said. Priceless. She told me that her uncle had picked it up somewhere in the Far East and she thought it was a Victorian copy and she'd never liked it and wished she could lose it, but she supposed it was an heir-loom and you couldn't get rid of an heirloom much as you'd like to do so.'

'So what happened to it?'

'Dunno.' He lifted his hands, helplessly. 'When I left that day, it was in its usual place or I'd have noticed, wouldn't I? They rang me the next day and said I'd smashed it, deliberately, when I left because I'd been hoping to get money out of her by turning her into a gambling addict. They said the vase was worth a hundred thousand pounds. I said I hadn't done it. They said I'd been seen to do it, that I'd pretended to leave but Charlotte had seen me sneaking back and she'd heard a crash and got back up there just in time to see me getting into the lift and leaving. I said that if that were so, they should bring in the police and they said it would be her word against mine, and who would believe me? I said, "What about Mrs T?" and they asked if I really wanted to drag an elderly lady into court when she was so distressed at my having abused her trust and all that.

'I hadn't done it, but what chance did I have if Charlotte said she'd seen me? They said they'd send me a bill for the vase and well, I panicked; I haven't that kind of money and they're rolling in it. I could see what it would look like if I went into court and said I'd been helping Mrs T bet on the horses. I'd be found guilty and they'd force me to sell my house to pay the bill! I said

I couldn't pay. They said, all right, they'd pretend it was an accident and try to get the insurance to pay up for it. They said they didn't want a scandal so if I promised not to go near Mrs T again, they'd not pursue the matter any further. And that was that. I've got other clients. I'm good at my job. But I'm still angry at what happened. And, tell the truth, although you'll think I'm going soft I'm worried about Mrs T.'

Kit said, 'But that vase is still there. I saw it, on the day I was given the push.'

The more Bea heard about the Tredgolds the less she wanted anything to do with them, but she had to ask one question. 'Andy, you and Kit keep saying that "they" told you this and "they" told you that. Who do you mean by "they"?'

'Charlotte and her brother organized the showdown, and it was he who rang me next day and told me about the vase.'

'That's the eldest son, Edgar?' Piers was interested. 'Is that the one whose watch turned up in the artichokes?'

'In the asparagus,' Kit corrected him. 'Yes, that's him. Goes around sniffing like there's a bad smell in the room.' He turned his empty beer can over and over in his hands. 'Poor Mrs T. Poor old duck. First her favourite cleaner gets the chop. Then Andy gets shot out and her arthritis will be playing up without him to keep her going. Then I go and who's going to see to her food now? She can't be doing with all those carbohydrates the others like to eat. Who's going to look after her food and see she gets a little treat now and then? And, I've been thinking, would it be right to get her another cat or two?'

'What for?' said Andy. 'Two's enough, right?'

The others stared at him. Kit said, 'You hadn't heard, man? It's the last thing . . .' He got up and strode around, relieving his mind by muttering something under his breath.

Andy had an uneasy half-smile on his face. 'Now what have I said?'

Bea told him. 'The cats were found under a drain cover the day after Kit had got the sack. They'd had their throats cut.'

Andy rocked back in his chair, making it creak. 'What . . .! You're joking!' And then, 'No, I can see you're not. But who would . . .? Mrs T must be going spare! She loved those cats. I know they were always underfoot and I'm not a great cat lover myself, but once you'd paid them a little attention, they'd just sit and watch and . . . I can't believe it! What is going on there?'

Kit said, 'You tell me!'

Andy said, 'But . . . who would . . .? That last day, I took another collar up for Mitzi, not that she'd keep it on for long. That cat could wriggle out of a collar like greased lightning and it didn't really matter because they're both microchipped and anyway, they never leave the premises.' He stared into space. And then, quietly, 'We've got to do something.'

Kit gestured widely. 'What can we do?'

Piers yawned. And stretched. 'Kit. Andy. You reckon Mrs T is next for the chop?'

Piers was enjoying this. Bea thought he was treating it like a game. She didn't think it was a game, and if it *had* been a game then it would have been the old nursery rhyme of 'Oranges and Lemons', and the bit where they get to 'Here comes a chopper to chop off your head'.

Kit exploded. 'What are you saying?'

Andy said, 'No way!'

'I think so,' said Piers, annoyingly calm. 'Anyone from outside the family circle who gets close to her is targeted for dismissal. Surely you can see that bit by bit she's being isolated until . . . Well, my imagination is working overtime and it tells me she's next for the chop.'

Bea said, 'This stops right here! Piers, I agree with you that what we've heard is disturbing. What can be done about it is another matter. If we went to the police claiming that three people employed by the Tredgolds have been dismissed on flimsy grounds, which proves there's a conspiracy to kill Mrs T, they'd laugh us out of court.'

Kit said, 'We can't go the police, anyway. They'd get that hell-child to testify against us, saying I made a pass at her. Which I swear to you I didn't.'

Piers yawned. 'Come on, Bea. You can work something out. Remember I've been summoned to the Tredgold mansion tomorrow to start painting Mrs T's portrait? You're good at sorting out baddies. Tell me what to look out for and what to say to Mrs T when I get there.'

Andy said, 'That's it, Mrs Abbot. You've got a reputation for helping people in trouble. That's what I told Mrs T ages ago when we were gossiping about this and that. Not that I gossip much, but she asked me one day if I knew of someone who might help a relative out of a difficult situation. And I said, "There's Mrs Abbot. You know about her because of what she did for the Rycrofts. You can trust her." That's what I said.'

'Many thanks,' said Bea, through her teeth. 'So that's why I had the pleasure of a visit from her this morning, is it? That's why she interviewed me, instead of asking me to find replacement staff for her?'

'Well, yes,' said Kit. 'That fits. She knows she can trust you. You can talk to her, explain that we've been stitched up and—'

'You're too close to the problem to see what's really going on,' said Bea. 'Yes, I had the pleasure of spending some time with Mrs T this morning. And yes, I hear what you two have had to say. But the problem is that the woman I met this morning wasn't at all like the woman you tell me about, who stood back and let you take the blame for something you hadn't done. The woman I met knew exactly what she was doing when she came here. She bamboozled her daughter into giving us a private conversation. She didn't waste a minute on the niceties. She didn't ask me to find you another job, either of you. She made friends with my cat and asked me to find out who killed her kitties, and then she left, exactly at the time she had arranged to leave. There was no sign of the tears and distress which you two have told me about. So which woman is the real Mrs T?'

There was silence while they thought about that. Piers said, 'There's a third personality. What about the woman who emailed me to start painting her portrait tomorrow? And what about the handbag with all the money in it?'

Bea said, 'At a guess, that wasn't Mrs T. She herself didn't try to bribe me but played on my sympathy for an older woman in trouble. I think the handbag scheme was thought up by someone else, someone with a corkscrew mind, and it was a bit hit-and-miss. For a start, I'm not even sure who was meant to be entrapped by it. Was it me, or was it Ahmed? He thought it was him, didn't he?'

'What handbag?' asked Andy.

Kit told him. 'One of Mrs T's, full of fifties and a cheque made out to cash. There was a note saying the amount was about half what was actually there, which means Mrs Abbot or Ahmed could have half-inched the stuff and there would have been no comeback . . . except that we know it was a trap.'

Andy said, 'I don't see the trap.'

Bea knew the answer to that one. 'If I've understood what's happened to you two, then I don't think there needs to be a foolproof, take-it-to-the-police proof of a crime. The mere threat of prosecution is enough.'

Piers pointed at Bea. 'You think Mrs T knows that her faithful friends are being knocked off one by one, and she is not prepared to do anything about it? If it's someone in her family, then why doesn't she put a stop to it?'

'I don't know.'

Kit slammed his fist down on his knee. 'It's that something Edgar, isn't it? He's never liked me. Mrs T won't stand up for me because he's her son. I don't like it, but I suppose that's understandable.'

Andy shook his head. 'If it's a family matter, she can't do anything about it, can she?'

Bea said, 'The woman I saw this morning was on top of the situation. If her son is trying to do her down then I think she must have had a plan in mind to stop him. Otherwise, why try to get me and Piers involved?'

Piers said, 'Well, she has asked you to find out who killed her cats.'

Kit nodded. 'It's the daughter, Charlotte, innit? A right cow, pardon my French, but she is.'

'Could be,' said Andy. 'She was the one who found out I'd got Mrs T into a betting habit but it was the son, Edgar, who shouted loudest at the old dear, and it was he who rang me next day to give me the sack.'

Piers said, 'Perhaps they're both in it together?'

Bea said, 'But why? She may be getting on, but there doesn't seem much wrong with her brains. I looked her up on the internet when she first made the appointment to see me. There's articles about her being Lady Muck to this and that charitable organization. She inherited family money and her husband left her a whole lot more. She pays the wages for the household, yes?'

Kit and Andy nodded.

'She supports the family in the manner to which they are accustomed. The only problem Charlotte mentioned to me was that some of the family wanted Mrs T to employ a butler but she didn't like the idea.'

75

Kit said, 'She don't like being shouted at. It makes her cry.' He reddened, looked down at his hands. He was embarrassed at having displayed tenderness for his old employer.

There was another long silence.

Bea said, 'I'm so sorry. I don't see what can be done. If, as you think, the family are trying to isolate her then I must tell you that the woman I met is perfectly capable of dealing with whatever they throw at her. I'm sorry you two have lost your jobs. Kit, I'll see if I can find you a placement. Piers, if you want to go and paint her, then you must do so, though I would advise against it. And now, gentlemen, I am going to throw you out. It's been a long day and I haven't finished yet. Piers, have you found your key, because if not, I'll lend you my spare and you can drop it back through the letter box tomorrow?'

She stood up and they followed suit. Slowly.

Kit said, 'I'm cooking you supper.'

'Thanks for the thought, but I can manage. Shall we go through the office? You can go up to the street that way.'

Piers said, 'I've got my stuff in your tumble dryer, so I'll go up and out through the kitchen, if you don't mind.'

She gave him a look but said nothing more as she ushered Kit and Andy through the house and up the outside stairs to the street. She shut and locked the door to the agency and put the alarm on for the basement.

She took the inside stairs to the kitchen to find Piers packing his dried clothes into his tote bag. He opened his mouth to say something, and she

76

held up her hand. 'Not another word. Have you your key now?'

He nodded, and removed himself, shutting the front door rather too sharply behind him. Bea put that alarm on as well.

Peace reigned.

She drew in a deep breath. She still had to put the garden chairs away, but she was all alone with nothing to do except throw some supper together and look forward to the twice-weekly phone call from her ward, who was away at boarding school but liked to ring and complain to Bea about this and that.

Bea was certainly not going to worry about Mrs T. That lady was perfectly capable of dealing with whatever problems her nasty family had in mind for her.

Bea shut out the mental image of Mrs T driven to tears.

However, a prayer or two might be in order. Yes. Probably.

Dear Lord, I have no idea what's going on there, but even the most capable of women find it hard to deal with family members who are putting pressure on them to . . .

To do what? Hand control of her money over to the son and daughter?

Bea shrugged. It was not her business.

Kit's fish pie smelled heavenly, but Bea was feeling disagreeable and she told herself she didn't fancy fish pie that night. Also, it was big enough for three or four people. Who did Kit think was going to eat it? Piers, perhaps? Or did Kit think she'd invite him to partake as well?

She popped it on the side to cool. It could go in the fridge when it was cold and she'd reheat it when her ward arrived for the weekend.

Kit had left a colander full of broccoli florets and some neatly chopped rounds of carrot. Presumably he'd intended to cook those to go with the fish pie. Well, she didn't fancy those, either. She dumped the lot in a Tupperware container, put the lid on and shoved that in the fridge. She ferreted around in the freezer and found a box of frozen chicken drumsticks. She'd cook them up with some onion, a tomato or two and lots of mushroom. With rice. And perhaps a pinch or two of curry powder?

The phone rang as she was busy at the stove.

Her hands stilled. She guessed who it would be.

No, she couldn't possibly know who it was, but she wasn't going to answer it. The woman could leave a message if she wished to contact Bea urgently.

The caller clicked off.

Bea tested the rice. Brown rice was good for you. Her nerves were stretched, waiting for the phone to ring again. She drained the rice, gave one last stir to the chicken mix and reached for the plate which she'd kept warming on top of the stove.

The phone rang a second time. The caller was not giving up, was she? This time she'd speak. Yes.

'Pick up, Ms Abbot. I know you're listening.' It was Mrs Tredgold. Of course.

Bea didn't move.

An irritated sigh. 'I need to know how you've

got on. You've had Kit round, and maybe Andy, too? Are you any closer to finding out what happened to my cats? I'm leaving you my personal phone number. Please ring when you have any news for me.'

There followed a phone number. Not a landline number, but that of a cell phone. The number was repeated and the call ended.

According to Ahmed, Mrs Tredgold didn't know how to use a cell phone. She'd given Bea a number which was too long to be that of a landline.

Bea took her plate to the central table and reached for a fork. She picked up the daily paper which she'd not had time to read and tried to interest herself in what was happening in the wider world.

She finished the chicken dish and peeled herself an apple for afters. Did she fancy a bit of cheese with it? Possibly not. A cup of tea? Yes.

In two days' time, on Friday, her ward Bernice would arrive home for the weekend. Bernice was an extremely bright but rather spiky young teenager, who would inherit a lot of money one day but was finding it hard to blend in with her peer group.

Mrs Tredgold needs your help.

No, she doesn't. She's perfectly capable of sorting out whatever it is that's happening in her family. They sound most unpleasant.

She cried.

Nothing to do with me.

Are the family isolating her so that they can have their wicked way with her money? Are they

79

*going to trump up various charges, saying she's
no longer capable of dealing with her own
affairs? Perhaps they'll try to make out she's got
Alzheimer's? They'll lock her away and take over
her money.*

What an imagination you have!

Bea slammed down the newspaper which she
was trying to read, fetched a pad and pencil from
the side, replayed Mrs Tredgold's message and
wrote down her mobile phone number. Just in
case. And sincerely hoped that she never had to
make use of it.

She tidied up in the sitting room, tried on the
bracelet Piers had brought her. Yes, it was rather
nice . . . Not that she usually wore bracelets, but
perhaps she'd make an exception this time.

And went upstairs to bed.

Six

Thursday morning

Bea didn't sleep well.

As she was putting the kettle on for her first
cup of the day, she heard Piers turn the key in
the lock on the front door.

She hadn't been expecting him. No, of course
she hadn't. She'd told herself several times how
good it was to be alone in the house, to wake up
at the hour of her choice, and not to have to
worry about what anyone else wanted to eat. It

was pure chance that she had turned the house alarm off before he came.

Piers sang out, 'It's only me.'

She muttered to herself, 'Who else would it be?' while opening the dishwasher and taking out the mug that he liked best. She said, 'Coffee's on.'

'Ah. Home from home. Apologies for calling so early. I think I must have left my blue sweater in the tumble dryer.'

He opened the dryer and pulled it out.

She raised her eyebrows. 'You left it on purpose.'

He nodded, put a couple of slices of bread into the toaster and depressed the lever. 'I can't stop worrying about Mrs T.'

Bea was silent, unloading everything else from the dishwasher.

He said, 'Yesterday she sent me a text, ordering me to report for duty at ten thirty today. This morning there's a message saying, "Due to unforeseen circumstances, please present yourself at noon." Any ideas?'

'None that don't give me the creeps.'

'How can you be so calm about it? Perhaps the Tredgolds have lost yet another staff member? Who else works for them? There's a housekeeper and a secretary person. Is that right? I assume there must be cleaners who come in by the day. A gardener, perhaps? And didn't you say there was a temporary chef and kitchen helper? Which of them has got the chop now?'

'Look, the people who've got the sack were all dear to her, right? She was upset when they were sent away but she didn't stand up for them. In other words, she knew exactly who had engineered their dismissals but she was not prepared to do anything about it. Which means it must be someone she cares for even more than those who'd got the sack.'

Piers squinched up his eyes. 'There's an alternative way of looking at it, isn't there?'

'Yes,' said Bea. 'Not love, but fear. She may be afraid of whoever it is. Would you like some porridge?'

He shook his head. He got the marmalade and butter from the fridge, collected his mug of coffee and set about eating breakfast.

She thought about making porridge for herself and abandoned the idea. She looked out over the garden. The birds were twittering. She must replenish their nut and seed containers. The flowers that bloom in the spring were coming along nicely. She must get some more plants for the bed under the left-hand wall soon. Something bright. Yellow flowers always made her feel more cheerful.

Piers said, 'You're wearing my bracelet. I'm glad you like it.'

She looked at it as if she had forgotten all about it. 'Am I? I suppose I am. It's beautiful. Thank you.'

'I thought of having our initials engraved on it. Would you like that?'

As in a wedding ring? Don't push your luck.

She didn't reply and eventually he said, 'What shall I do about Mrs T? I can't turn my back on her and refuse to attend.'

'She left me her mobile phone number, after telling Ahmed she didn't know how to do so.

82

Perhaps she's recognized that she needs help but can't bring herself to ask for it outright.'

'You said yesterday that you thought she was in control of what's been happening.'

'I've changed my mind. It looks to me as if Mrs T was in control up to a certain point in time, but that that control is slipping away from her.'

Piers made a second cup of coffee. 'Family problems are usually about money. You think someone in the family wants a bigger slice of the cake?'

Bea shivered. 'There's been a case recently where an older person signed a Power of Attorney only to find himself not just sidelined from handling the money but shoved into an old people's rest home so that his heirs could take over the estate.'

'Surely the family have first to prove that their mother is losing the plot? Mrs T is still very much on the ball.'

'But she's vulnerable. If two or more of the family said she was becoming forgetful, the doctors might say she was no longer capable of managing her affairs.'

Now it was Piers's turn to shiver. 'Do you think that's what she's afraid of?'

'I don't know.' Bea looked at her watch. 'I ought to get started, open up the office. Got a busy day ahead.'

'I'll put the breakfast things in the dishwasher.' He stretched and yawned. 'You think we should keep well out of the Tredgold affair?'

'That would be the wise thing to do, wouldn't it? But no. I agree that we can't walk away from this. I will return her call. I'll say that I'm at the end of the line if she needs me but that I can't honestly recommend anyone for a job in her household at this moment. You will present yourself at noon, ready to discuss the portrait?'

'With eyes and ears open. I could bear to know what the "unforeseen circumstances" are which have caused them to defer my visit. I'll ring you when I find out, shall I?'

Thursday noon

He rang at one, while Bea was making herself a sandwich for lunch.

He said, 'Is this a good time to speak?'

'Yes. Where are you? Still at the Tredgolds?'

'No, I'm sitting in a cafe with a view of a specialist's rooms in Harley Street. When I arrived at the house Mrs T apologized for cancelling our meeting but said she'd got toothache. She asked if I would drop her off at her dentist's as she was unhappy about the filling she'd had done yesterday. I said I hadn't a car but would take her in a taxi. The daughter was hovering. She said that if I'd take Mrs T they'd make sure someone would come by to collect her after her appointment. I don't think that's going to happen.'

'She's given you the slip?'

'The address the daughter gave me was that of a dentist, sure. I summoned a taxi and we rode off to Harley Street, but Mrs T asked the driver to stop a hundred yards before the number I'd been given. She said there was a shop she wanted to pop into beforehand, since she was early for her appointment. She told me to leave her. I took the taxi round the corner, paid it off and walked back to see her enter one of these high-class, discreet buildings which has a plate outside. It is not that of a dentist. The name on the plate outside is that of a famous psychiatrist. That was three-quarters of an hour ago and she hasn't come out yet.'

Bea said, 'Ah-ha. She's getting herself checked out for signs of mental distress. If given a clean bill of health, she can tell the family that any attempt to get her sectioned will fail and to get lost. Am I right?'

'Possibly, yes. What you wouldn't have guessed at is that Mrs T put an envelope in my pocket while we were chuntering along through the traffic in the taxi. She said it was a little something for my trouble, since she's decided to defer having her portrait painted for a while. I thought she might have tipped me a fifty or maybe even a hundred, but the only thing in the envelope is her passport.'

That needed some thinking about.

Bea said, feeling her way through a maze of possibilities, 'She trusts you, but she doesn't trust anyone else in the house? She's given it to you to hold for her, so that her daughter can't get hold of it and prevent Mrs T leaving the country if she wishes to do so?'

'It looks as if she's planning to run away, and who can blame her?'

'She's not the running away type. She doesn't have any luggage with her, does she?'

'No luggage. No handbag. I paid cash for the taxi out of my own pocket.'

'She gave her passport to you as insurance? She gave it to you because you have an international reputation, and would make a fuss if she disappeared? Am I being fanciful?'

'I can't think of any other reason.'

'She really doesn't have a handbag?'

'She has a couple of pockets in the jacket she's wearing. I suppose all she needs to run away are her passport and her credit card. She doesn't need to carry a wallet and she doesn't wear make-up. If she asks me to meet her at the airport and hand over her passport, what should I do?'

'Do? Nothing. She has every right to go where she pleases.'

'Well, yes. But perhaps not now the police are involved.'

'What!'

'Yes, there's something else you should know. The real reason why my appointment was put back this morning. Ahmed, the chauffeur, took an overdose and died last night.'

Bea felt for a stool and let herself down on to it. 'You're joking! Why, he was with us till . . . what? About six?'

'He took Edgar and his wife to the theatre, returned to his quarters and downed a handful of sleeping tablets. The alarm was raised when he failed to collect the theatregoers at the end of the performance. I'm told Edgar was livid about Ahmed's no-show. He had to bring his wife back by taxi and, on his return, he went straight to Ahmed's room to give him the sack. And found his door locked. He roused everyone, including the housekeeper, who located the spare key, let herself in and there he was, all neatly laid out in bed, not quite dead but dying. They carted him off to hospital and pumped him out but it was no good. They couldn't bring him round. On his bedside table was a number of fifty-pound notes and an empty bottle of sleeping pills. Apparently there was a text message on his phone to Mrs T, saying he was sorry. Verdict: suicide. Reason: because he'd stolen the money and was going to lose his job. The police were sympathetic, the body has been removed and no one's going to raise any questions about it, are they?'

Bea said nothing. Loudly.

Piers said, 'Ahmed told us he was afraid of being sacked, but he wouldn't have stolen that money, would he?'

'No, he wouldn't. And would he have texted Mrs T? Does she know how to read a text? I'm not sure she does. Piers, I'm in shock.'

'Yes, so am I. I liked him.'

'You say the police were satisfied?'

'They'd been and gone by the time I arrived. I was assured that everything was straightforward. He'd stolen that money, he'd been warned about his timekeeping. He was going to be found out. Suicide.'

Bea wondered if it would make any difference if she told the police about the earlier incidents of attempted entrapment experienced by Ahmed and by herself. She did still have the photo on her phone showing how him holding the notes and the handbag, didn't she?

87

Her brain was in a whirl. Poor Ahmed! If she'd had any idea . . . he could have confided in her, if he was so worried . . . but no, he hadn't been that concerned, had he? Not to the point of taking his own life.

What on earth was going on at the Tredgolds? She said, 'How did Mrs T react?'

'She told me, and the police, that she hadn't seen Ahmed after he brought her back from the dentist yesterday afternoon. She was hollow-eyed. Monosyllabic. Shocked. Her hand trembled when she took my arm to help her into the cab. She said she didn't want to talk about it.'

'She's fighting back by getting someone to give her a clean bill of mental health? And then what will she do?'

Piers voice rose. 'She's coming out now. I'll wave to her, show her I'm still here and at her disposal. Shall I suggest bringing her to you for a visit? No, that's no good. It's the first place they'll look for her. I'll ring you later.' He cut the call.

Bea looked across the central unit to where Ahmed had been standing in her kitchen. He'd been worried about getting the sack, yes. His family lived up north. He'd been well paid for his work, but it was not long before the Tredgolds had tried to trap him into stealing money from them. He'd refused to take the bait. Charlotte had made a pass at him and he'd declined. He'd acted in honourable fashion. What should he have done to protect himself? Go to the police? No, he couldn't. He'd have been sacked all the quicker, if he'd done that.

He'd told Bea and Piers that he was due to take

two of the Tredgolds to the theatre. He'd said he'd be free after that until he collected them at the end of the show. Kit had suggested that Ahmed contact Andy the physio and then return to Bea's for supper. It had seemed to Bea that Ahmed had been tempted to do so. He'd rung Andy and urged him to visit Bea. And then what?

Had there been anything about Ahmed's movements and actions to indicate that he was seriously considering suicide?

N-no.

Well, perhaps he'd let his fears about being sacked get the better of him when he was alone? Perhaps he had family back home who were relying on him to send them money every month and he had become paranoid about getting the sack? Wouldn't that be enough to tip him over into suicide?

No. He'd been worried, but not frantic.

He'd talked freely to Bea and Piers about his situation. He'd shared his concerns with them. That wasn't the behaviour of a man about to commit suicide.

He'd left a suicide note. Um. You couldn't get round that.

But it was *all wrong*!

Bea wished, oh how she wished, that she'd been more encouraging when Kit and Ahmed had spoken of their problems at the Tredgolds. Perhaps, if she'd been more helpful, if she'd even said that she would look into the matter, Ahmed wouldn't have taken his own life.

No. Stop right there. There was no point beating

herself up for Ahmed's suicide because it was *not* suicide.

If it wasn't suicide, then he'd been murdered.

There. It was out. Murder. For reasons unknown.

No, not unknown. There'd been a concerted course of action to separate Mrs T from anyone outside the family. The cleaner. The physio. The chef. And now the chauffeur.

Yes, but why go to the lengths of killing Ahmed? Surely it would have been easier just to give him the sack?

Mm. Bea had heard that criminals often start in a small way and build up to bigger things. Had someone lost patience with the softly, softly approach and gone for the jugular? There'd been an earlier attempt to get rid of Ahmed, hadn't there? Attempts to entrap him with money had failed. So, instead of making another attempt, they'd written him out of the plot.

Which meant . . . Bea wasn't sure what it meant, except that it didn't bode well for Mrs Tredgold's life expectancy. If someone had murdered once, they could do so again. Bea could imagine a scenario in which Mrs T might be found with an empty bottle of sleeping pills beside her, and everyone would say, 'How sad, but of course she was so depressed at being let down by so many people.'

The phone rang. Bea picked it up.

Piers said, 'You won't believe where I am now. In a penthouse flat in Docklands, overlooking the Thames. Mrs T has prepared a nice little bolt-hole for herself. Fully furnished, all mod cons. There's good security downstairs, but no one to cook the food for her. Can you magic up a housekeeper of some sort, to live in? Or perhaps Kit would come and look after her for a bit?'

Bea was sarcastic. 'And a couple of cats to sit on her lap, I suppose?'

'You've got it. Mum's the word, of course. This is a secret hideout. She's had to move in rather more quickly than she'd expected. She's ordered some food to be delivered but forgot the milk, so she says would you bring some when you come over?'

'What! I can't just drop everything and—'

'She wants you to deliver some letters to the people at the old address. You're to observe their reactions and report back to her. Today. I'll expect you over here in half an hour, right? And don't forget the milk. She can't drink her tea without it. I'll text you the address and how to get past security.'

Bea said, 'Don't tell me! You've started painting her—'

'No, no. Preliminary sketches only.'

'She intrigues you so much you'll do whatever she asks, so long as you can get her image down on paper?'

He laughed and put the phone down.

Bea screamed, more or less silently. She reviewed her workload. She had two interviews scheduled for that afternoon, but neither of them should be too difficult for Betty to handle. She'd sorted out a couple of jobs for which Kit might be suitable. Had he left her his email address? She couldn't think straight. Yes, she was sure Betty would have the details.

Would Kit love to go back to work for Mrs T again? Yes, of course he would.

On the other hand, considering what had happened to Ahmed, would it be wise for Kit to do so? Probably not.

Her smartphone beeped to tell her a text message had arrived. Bother the Tredgolds!

She wished they'd never heard of her, or she of them. They were altogether too much!

And now Mrs T wanted Bea to find her a new cook-cum-housekeeper. Just like that! And what about the replacement staff which Charlotte wanted for the old house? Were they now not required?

Bea rummaged through her mind. A cook-housekeeper who liked cats. Now there was somebody who rang a bell. Now who . . .? And would she be free?

There was a commotion in the big office. Betty shouted something. The door to Bea's office was thrown open so hard that it rebounded against the wall.

Charlotte, red-faced, shot into the room with someone who must be her elder brother, Edgar, on her heels.

Charlotte looked around and, not finding anyone but Bea there, screeched, 'What have you done with her?'

Bea stood up. 'Miss Tredgold?'

Edgar shook his fist in Bea's face. 'Where is she?'

Charlotte strode to the French windows and threw them open. 'She's in the garden, right?'

Edgar shouted, 'I'll search upstairs, shall I?'

Bea said, 'Are you looking for your mother? But why here?'

Charlotte took a good look around the garden and came back inside. 'She's not down here. Yes, Edgar, you'd better search upstairs, except . . . No, on reflection, she couldn't climb those stairs, could she?'

Bea said, 'Miss Tredgold, I do not understand why you think your mother should be here. I have not seen her since yesterday and I am not expecting her, either. I must ask you to leave.'

'Not so fast,' said Edgar, brandishing his fist in Bea's face again. 'My mother had a private conversation with you yesterday. You went off with her, didn't you? Leaving my sister out in the cold? I demand to know what she said to you. If you refuse, we shall have no option but to go to the police and register my mother as a missing person. I shall inform them that you were the last person to see her, and they will come here to question you, and they will not be so easy to fob off. If you persist in denying your part in my mother's disappearance, they will have you under arrest in a trice. And then you will be only too happy to talk, won't you?'

Bea told herself to keep calm. 'Mr Tredgold, you must do as you think best. Certainly you should inform the police that your mother is missing if that is the case. I have no problem telling you what she said. She wanted me to find out who killed her cats—'

He screeched, 'What!'

Bea said, 'And I declined to help her. Now, if

93

you please, I have work to do and must ask you to leave.'

'Not without giving us some satisfactory answers.' Charlotte seized a chair and seated herself. Leaning forward, she placed her hands on her knees. 'What do you mean by saying she asked you to find out who killed her cats?'

'Just that. I declined. I want nothing to do with the matter, and I want nothing to do with finding you any new staff, either.'

Charlotte narrowed her eyes. 'She went off this morning with your husband or boyfriend or whatever he is. He'll know where she's gone. Where is he now?'

Bea shrugged. 'My ex-husband doesn't have to answer to me for his every move. Try his mobile phone.'

Charlotte frowned. 'We have. When he sees who it is who's ringing, he cuts the call. So where is he?'

Bea stood up. 'He rang me this morning to say he'd dropped your mother off, as she requested, in Harley Street. She'd told him to take the taxi on. And that's what he did. He has his own place, you know. He doesn't live here. And no, I am not going to give you his address unless he gives me permission to do so. Now, I really must ask you to leave, or do I have to call the police to evict you?'

Prompt on cue, Betty appeared in the doorway, mobile phone in hand. 'Shall I ring the police for you, Mrs Abbot?'

Edgar seemed to find the room too warm for his health. He wiped a handkerchief round his neck. 'Come on, Charlotte. There's more ways of killing a cat than . . .' He started, realizing how inappropriate that had sounded. 'What I mean is, Gordon will know where she's gone. Or Hubert. She wouldn't leave them without a word, would she?'

Charlotte tried to stare Bea down. When that didn't work, she made a virtue of necessity and got to her feet. At the door she turned to say, 'This is not the last you've heard from us, Mrs Abbot. And yes, I hold you to our contract to supply us with another chef.'

'And another chauffeur.' That was Edgar.

Bea said, 'I have not signed a contract to supply you with any staff, and I do not intend to do so. Just go, will you?'

They left.

Betty saw them off and returned to Bea's office. 'There are some clients we can do without?'

'Yes,' said Bea, 'unfortunately Mrs Tredgold is not one of them. Do you remember we had someone come to us recently for a housekeeper's job? She has to live in and has a cat. Can we find her details?'

Seven

Thursday afternoon

Bea didn't bother getting her car out because public transport was quicker in London traffic.

Instead, she took the Underground and, after a couple of changes, surfaced at Canary Wharf. It always gave her a thrill to emerge into daylight and find herself surrounded by the astonishing buildings that had sprung up as the Docklands area reinvented itself. Old warehouses had been turned into spectacular apartment blocks, skyscrapers of different shapes and colours abounded, and the ancient, working docks had been turned into modern marinas.

The scenery was something of a contrast to Mrs T's slightly stodgy – though no doubt worthy and indubitably Grade II listed – surroundings in Mayfair.

The pace of life here was faster than in Kensington or Belgravia. People here were constantly on the move, smartphones in hand. Time was money. Brains were at a premium.

People worked long hours. They made a lot of money, or crashed and disappeared, burnt-out by thirty.

Piers had said Mrs T had a penthouse suite on top of one of the renovated buildings. There was a security man on the door, and Bea had to produce ID before she was shown to a lift and wafted up.

She stepped out of the lift into a square hall with doors leading off it to left and to right. Ahead of her was a wall of glass giving on to a wide balcony surrounded by a hip-high brick wall. Above that, Bea could see nothing but sky and a plane crawling across it on its way to Heathrow airport. She caught her breath at the view. How many skyscrapers could she see from here? Wow!

She saw that there was an open door leading

out on to the balcony. Piers was sitting there in a comfortable wooden chair, sketch pad in hand. 'Did you bring the milk? She's inside. First door on the right.'

Bea opened the door indicated to find herself in an office, bare as to walls but fully operational. A printer chattered softly to itself. Mrs T was there and working on a computer.

Now why was that surprising? Bea felt she ought to have anticipated the set-up.

Mrs T looked up. 'Can you make a cuppa for me, dear? I did ask Piers to put the frozen stuff in the freezer. Can you check that he did so? When men get an idea into their heads they forget everything important, like food. Back through the hall. The kitchen's the second door on the left.'

Bea did as she was told. The kitchen was fully fitted and looked rather like the interior of a spaceship. Anything less like the image Bea had formed of Mrs T would be difficult to imagine. The brand-new kettle burbled but didn't scream.

Bea checked the bags which had been dumped on the central unit, located the freezer and shoved packets of frozen food into it. She found a pack of biscuits and broke it open. Mugs were brand new, still in their packaging. Ditto cutlery. Tea towels? There were no tea towels. Well, Mrs T couldn't be expected to think of everything. Or perhaps she had thought of them and they were arriving on the morrow?

Bea took a mug of tea out to Piers, who was absorbed in sketching the view. She waved the mug in front of him. He looked at it as if he'd never seen such a thing before and shook his head. Bea put it on the floor beside him and hoped he wouldn't knock it over.

Bea took a second mug of tea to Mrs T, who swivelled away from her desk and nodded her thanks. She looked tired but pleased with herself. Her stick lay within her reach. 'Thank you for coming. Now, do you have any news for me about a housekeeper?'

Bea said, 'I have someone who may be suitable on my books, yes. She's worked as a housekeeper and cook for a diplomat and his family for five years. They have relocated to the Middle East but she has a cat whom she couldn't take with her, so she is currently free and looking for a new position. She likes to live in provided she can bring her cat with her, which makes her difficult to place. How do you feel about having another cat about the place?'

'Excellent. I've always had cats. Yes, tell her to come this afternoon if she can. Warn her that nothing is finished yet. The balcony will eventually have toughened glass panels around it to over a man's height, and the garden is being delivered tomorrow. It comes already planted up, I understand; clipped hedges to ring the balcony, some shade trees, and a few raised beds. She will bring a litter tray for her cat, won't she? Excellent. I was a little afraid you'd offer the job to Kit.'

'No, I wouldn't do that. You'd be afraid he might get hurt.'

'How well you understand me. What do you think of my running away?'

'Surely it's not "running away" but a "strategic withdrawal"?'

'No, dear. I'm tired. I'm running away and leaving them to fight among themselves.'

'What I don't understand is why you don't go to the police?'

'What could I say? What would I accuse my nearest and dearest of doing? What proof do I have of anything? If they'd queried Ahmed's death . . . but they didn't. If I'd said I was afraid for my life, they would laugh and suggest I see a doctor.'

'Which is what you did today. I trust he gave you a clean bill of health?'

'And a nice fat bill into the bargain.' She eased her back. 'Let's go and sit down in comfort next door. The view, as Piers has already informed me twice, is spectacular.'

She seized her stick and made her way back through the hall and into a huge sitting room, furnished with pieces old and new. There were some good watercolours in gold mounts on the walls and Chinese silk carpets had been strategic-ally placed here and there on the shining wood floors. There were two modern low coffee tables and some comfortable chairs near a large tele-vision set. And a card table with four chairs round it at the far end.

Bea hung on her heel to take in the fabulous view inside and out. 'This has not been put together in a day. It took time to buy this place and fill it with things you liked. How did you manage it without letting the family know what you were doing?'

'I have an old friend who helped me find this place, decorate it and arrange for the furniture to be delivered and put in place. He bought the computer and all the other office equipment for me, and had a man come in to install it. My husband liked me to keep up with modern technology and although I find it something of a bore, I have managed to keep up with it, more or less. Over the past few months I've been sending favourite pictures and pieces for repair or cleaning, and when they were ready to return I had them sent here instead of back to the old place. I chose the paint for the walls and the blinds for the windows, though I must confess that I can't abide the pink I selected for my bedroom. That will have to be changed. The place is not finished yet. I thought I had plenty of time, until Ahmed died and I panicked.' She settled herself in a high-backed reclining chair and leaned back.

Yes, she did look her age and more today.

Bea located a footstool and carried it over for Mrs Tredgold, who put her feet up with a sigh. 'Thank you, my dear. It is pleasant to think that I judged you correctly. I have not always been a good judge of character. I suppose I should apologize for dragging you and Piers into my affairs but I was clutching at straws. I thought I could arrange to retire gracefully without causing too much upset in the family, but Ahmed's death . . .' Her eyes starred with tears. 'I feel responsible. He was a good man.'

'You don't believe he committed suicide?'

'No. And yet, he'd left a text message for me on his mobile phone which said just that. It had been saved but not sent. Also there was a bundle of notes on his bedside table.'

'You think he was framed for theft and poisoned?'

Mrs Tredgold looked off into the distance. 'It's all so terrible. I try to feel anger about what's been happening but I can't hold on to it for long. Half the time I'm so confused I don't know right from wrong, and the rest of the time I'm so afraid I can't think straight. This is where you come in, my dear. I want you to act for me, if you will.' Her eyes went out of focus. More or less to herself she said, 'I used to be so strong.'

'They made you doubt yourself?'

They made her cry, but we won't mention that.

'I wanted to spend my last few years in peace and quiet and they wouldn't let me do that.' Mrs Tredgold leaned back in her chair and sighed. 'Where did it all go wrong? I married twice, you know. My first was someone I'd known from childhood. He drank, I flirted with other men, we quarrelled. We separated at the end of our second year of marriage and divorced. Fortunately there were no children. We lost touch for years.

'Then I met Marcus, my second husband. He was older than me, quick tempered, attractive and a brilliant financier. He'd made one fortune by the time he was thirty and doubled it, quadrupled it by the time he died. He was a ball of fire, never still, travelling here and there, making more and more money. He wanted me to go with him but I was torn because I'd produced three children in short order and didn't like leaving them.

'They were so sweet when they were young. Edgar was mad about the sea, always wanting to mess around in boats. Charlotte was a little tomboy and Hubert was, well, he always had his head in a book. How could I leave them? And yet I felt I must. Employing nannies seemed the answer but that way my babes were never taught how other people live. They were told that they were special, that it didn't matter if they never picked up their clothes because there would always be someone else to do it for them, and that if they frittered away their pocket money on trifles there would always be more to come.

'Marcus saw nothing wrong in that. He was turning his millions into billions. Our children were not gifted that way but he said that didn't matter as they would never have to earn their living. He said that if they didn't learn how to handle money they could always employ someone to do it for them. He said that if they didn't want to go to university, they didn't have to do so. Well, that's not quite true for Hubert. He did study and work at his heraldry and eventually drifted into work in that direction. It hardly paid enough to keep his car on the road but that didn't seem important. I think he's the best of the three. At least, that's how he used to be.'

'And now?'

Mrs Tredgold avoided that question. 'When Edgar was thirty Marcus developed heart trouble. Everything possible was done but . . .' a sigh, '. . . these things happen. Marcus planned to put his money in a trust fund for the children, but when they heard about that there was a major row. Didn't we think they were mature enough to deal with money for themselves? How demeaning was that? And so on. Actually, I wasn't at all sure they were clever enough to handle large sums of money but I was overruled. My husband left them ten million each, with the rest coming to me.

'They got through the lot in double quick time. Edgar bought a yacht. Hubert bought a small magazine running articles about heraldry . . . It's never lost too much, rather to my surprise. Charlotte was guided by friends into buying different loss-making companies; a perfume factory here, a vineyard there. I lost count how many, they all lost money. They didn't think that mattered. They had more than enough to last them out, they thought. The boys got married. They made good choices. I liked both the women and thought they'd be sensible and help to look after their husband's finances. Charlotte has had three on-and-off affairs with married men. It would make me sound mean if I said I don't think they were ever consummated but . . . well, there it is. She's managed to sell a few articles about this and that, poetry and wine. A reasonable combination, you'd think, but not bringing in any money. It's all about kudos, isn't it? Being seen to be "special".'

Bea said, 'So they ran through the money and never left home?'

'It's a big house. It was easily divided into flats, and it's in such a good area. Running hot and cold water and servants on tap. Why would they ever bother to leave? And of course they could keep an eye on dear old Mum to see she didn't fall into bad company and fritter away the fortune which would come to them all in due course.'

Bea said, 'It worked out well enough?'

'For a long time, yes. I had my own friends. I learned how to play bridge and I met up with Gordon again, after all those years. The children didn't like it, of course, but we didn't want to get married again or to live together. We were just good friends. He had his interests and I had mine. I sold him the coach house for a pittance, and that caused a ruckus or two, but when they found out that Gordon had inherited a small estate in Devon and had a good pension from his job . . . He was an engineer, you know, bridges and things . . . Well, they thought that as he'd never married again, he'd leave his money to them, too. They weren't very nice to him but they weren't actively rude. It worked for a long time.'

'What changed things?'

'I'm not really sure. Perhaps it was the bad bout of flu I had over a year ago. I was in hospital for nearly a month and nearly died. When they visited me I could see the calculation in their eyes. I survived but I could no longer cope with the bickering that went on between them. I didn't want to dress up and sit through lengthy charity dinners and meetings any more. I resigned from all my commitments and began to think of finding myself a nice retirement home where I could be quiet and perhaps just have one maid to look after me. I told an old friend what I was thinking about and he said it was a brilliant idea and that he'd look out for some place for me. And he did. This place. I bought it, but was in no hurry to move in. It was a hobby for me to decide how I'd like it decorated and furnished. I did tell the family I wanted to downsize, and there was the most almighty row. That was when it all came out – how they'd got through all the money and were starting to worry about the future.

'I didn't know what to do. I couldn't leave them in the lurch, could I? I told them there was no hurry for me to move out and things calmed down. And then Stefanie died. That's Hubert's wife. A dreadful thing, and he was never quite the same afterwards. I was shattered. My back began to play up. Someone recommended Andy, the physio, to me and he did me so much good. I perked up nicely for a while and didn't think so much about leaving the big house.

'Andy and I had such fun together, betting on the horses and honestly, if I did lose a fiver here or there, it was nothing to what the children . . . but least said, I suppose. I was sorry when Andy stopped coming, and no one would tell me why except some stupid story about his making a pass at Charlotte, which was obviously nonsense, dear, because dear Andy was as gay as a lark. And then my nice cleaner, June, left. She'd stolen something, they said, but . . . I thought I must be losing my grip. I liked her. She'd been with me for ever. That's when I began to doubt my ability to judge people. Some days I even wondered if I were jinxed.'

'And they started to shout at you again?'

'Yes. Not Hubert. He drifted around, a lost soul. I was so worried about him. He wouldn't talk to me or anyone, but I could see he was losing ground. Charlotte and Edgar did start shouting, yes. And then there's Petra, Edgar's daughter.

I'm so afraid she's mixing with the wrong sort, but what do I know?'

Mrs Tredgold was silent for a while. Then she pulled herself more upright in her chair. 'When Kit stole that watch, I was shocked. I could have sworn he was as honest as the day. And the next day, my poor cats . . . I didn't know what to do. I wanted to scream. I couldn't believe it. For the first time I allowed myself to wonder if I were being targeted and if so, what could I do about it? That's when I remembered Andy talking about a Mrs Abbot who had helped another client of his. I did a spot of research and learned a bit about you and Piers. I told Charlotte that we should go to you for replacement staff. She said she'd contact you herself but I insisted on going with her, and I must say, dear, that you impressed me. Then Ahmed died . . . Was it only last night? I can't believe it was only last night. And yes, that was the last straw. I didn't stop to think, I just ran away.'

'I don't know how long you'll be able to hide before they find you. Your son and daughter have already visited me at the agency, looking for you. How secret is this place, and how soon will they track you down?'

'I understand that, but with your help, my dear, I may be able to divert them until I feel more secure. I want you to give them each a file of letters. The first is a certificate that I am sound in mind and body. That should put paid to their wish to rush me into a locked ward somewhere. Then they are each to have a copy of my will, which leaves my whole estate to charity.'

106

Bea smiled. 'Cat's Protection Society?'

'Of course. Next, I am putting the old house on the market with vacant possession. And yes, I can do that. The children have never paid me any rent or taken care of any bills so they are not tenants but my guests.'

Bea drew in a deep breath. 'You surprise me.'

'Yes, dear. I dare say. When you've hit them with that, you can give them another letter which says that I will divide the money I get from the sale of the house equally between those who slept in the house the night that my cats were killed.'

Bea blinked. 'That includes Ahmed.'

'Correct. I want Ahmed's family to have a share. Rough justice, you might say.'

'It excludes Kit?'

'True. I'm fond of Kit and when this is all over, I hope to employ him again. But don't tell him that yet, right? Now, there is a sting in the tail. I will divide the money from the sale of the house between those who slept there on the night the cats died, with the exception of the person who was responsible for their deaths. That person is to get nothing.'

Bea sat back in her chair, considering the ramifications of this caveat. 'Your family will work out that their share will be larger if they can find out who killed the cats, so they'll be happy to point the finger at whoever did the dirty deed?'

'That's right, dear. You know, I was brought up to believe in people. It's been a nasty shock to find out that people I trusted, like Andy and Kit and June, had stolen from me.'

'And an even nastier shock to discover that

they hadn't, but were framed by someone in your immediate circle?'

Mrs Tredgold winced. 'Yes. I didn't want to believe it at first. I didn't believe it for a long time, but it was wicked to cause them to lose their jobs.'

Bea warned, 'It may not be the same person who was responsible for everything bad that's happened.'

'I understand. That's why I am focusing on the cats' deaths. Will you deliver these papers for me and get them to sign statements saying they slept at the house the night the cats were killed?'

What she says she wants is too complicated. Surely what she really needs is an investigation into the affairs of her family? She says she wants one thing but what she really wants is to get enough dirt on the family to stop them hounding her . . . isn't it?

'You don't want to go to the police?'

Mrs Tredgold shook her head. 'No police. I can't prove anything, and this way the baddies will be punished and the good rewarded.'

Is this a sensible way of going about it? Perhaps not. But if it gives her peace of mind, I suppose it's worth doing.

Bea said, 'Who is to decide if these people are speaking the truth or not?'

'You are, dear. And Piers, too, if he likes to get involved. He's taken some photos of me on his smartphone which he can work up into a portrait at a later date. I'm not sure I have the energy for multiple sittings, but something in pastels will do me nicely.' She closed her eyes and leaned back in her chair. 'I'm afraid I get tired rather more quickly than I used to do.'

Bea put her hand over the frail, freckled hand of Mrs Tredgold, and pressed it lightly.

'I'll do what I can.'

Without opening her eyes, Mrs Tredgold said, 'The papers are all on the printer in the office. Oh, and do tell the daily staff that they will get a bonus when the house is sold. They have served me well in the past and may have something to tell you about the cats. They are the key to the puzzle, you know. The cats.'

'I don't like to leave you alone.'

'I feel safe here. No one, absolutely no one knows I'm here. Wonderful!'

Bea wasn't so sure about that. What about Mrs T's 'friend'? What about the people who'd decorated and moved the pictures and the furniture in? Then there must have been people who'd hung curtains and blinds and set up the office? One invoice, one telephone message going astray and the rest of Mrs T's household would be able to guess what was going on. How long could this hideout remain a secret?

Mrs T seemed to drift off to sleep.

Bea collected the paperwork from the office and Piers from the balcony.

They left the flat together. Going down in the lift, Bea told Piers what Mrs Tredgold had asked her to do.

'She told me her life story. Looking back, I can see she set out to charm me into helping her. And succeeded. I only hope I don't come to regret it.'

Piers said, 'She told me it would be the first time in her life that she'd spent a night alone. She says she's going to enjoy it. I'm not so sure that she will, but what can we do?'

Bea got out her phone. 'I'll see if the housekeeper can get over here soonest. With her cat. Mrs T said it would be all right to bring her cat up there, but cats can take against people. I can only hope they get on together.'

Bea was lucky. Her client was free and liked the idea of living in Docklands. She promised Bea to get over there straight away. Perhaps Mrs Tredgold would not have to spend the night alone after all.

On the Underground going home, Bea and Piers read through the paperwork together.

Piers said, 'It might be a good idea to get an independent view on who might have been sleeping there on the night the cats were killed. Who can we trust to speak the truth about it?'

'How about Kit? He doesn't stand to gain or lose anything. Betty will have taken his details when he applied to us for a job so I'll phone him when we get back and see what he has to say. Then we can compare any statements the others make against his testimony.'

Piers rubbed his eyes. 'I'm still jet-lagged. How about I treat us to a meal somewhere? Steak and a glass of wine do you?'

Bea nodded. She didn't feel like cooking, either. She immersed herself in the wording of the documents Mrs Tredgold had prepared. 'I wonder how she got her will done so quickly. All properly signed and witnessed, too. I suppose if you have so much money, you can get people to come to you instead of you going to them. I do hope Mrs T takes to the new housekeeper. Do you think Mrs T knows how to use a microwave, and will she be able to make up a bed for herself?'

Piers yawned. 'She had plenty of ready meals delivered. I made up her bed for her, while she stood over me, saying I was an idiot because I don't know how to do hospital corners. She'll be all right, though I suppose it will feel a bit strange, after living in that big house for so long. Perhaps this "friend" of hers will drop by to keep her company.'

Bea had been thinking about this 'friend' of Mrs T's. She wondered who it might be.

Piers said, 'She wants to be portrayed in pastels. I don't work in pastels. I told her so. She smiled and said that if I thought about it, I'd see she was right. The worst of it is that she probably *is* right. Heaven send I don't make a mess of it.'

Bea relaxed. It had been a tiring day. So yes, it would be a good idea to go out for a meal. In fact, she relaxed so far over supper that she forgot all about ringing Kit till after they'd had supper and returned home, when she noticed it had grown dark enough to draw the curtains.

She fed Winston and told Piers it was time for him to depart and to make sure the alarm was on before he left for the night. Then she went down to her silent office – it always felt strange and shadowy after her staff had left for the day – found Kit's details and was fortunate enough to get him on the phone straight away.

He greeted her with eagerness. 'How's things? How's Mrs T? Is she all right? You won't believe it, but Mum and I've had that Edgar round here today, demanding to know what I've done with Mrs T! Has she really taken off into the blue? Is she all right, do you know? I'm dead worried about her.'

'She's quite safe, and yes, she's in hiding. She's worrying about you, Kit. She knew you were sacked unfairly, but she didn't know what to do about it, or even who to trust. Now she's in a safe place and trying to figure out what to do next. She's putting the house on the market and—'

'What? Well, good for her.'

'And when it's sold there's going to be a bonus for all her staff, you included.'

'That's a flaming relief. The way I was shot out, it's not going to be easy to get another good job. I was telling my mum about it, and we was wondering about going to the police or maybe a solicitor about what happened to me, but then there's what Petra would say, which isn't true, but what could I do against that?'

'Mrs T's working on it, Kit. She wants me to find out who killed her cats. I'm to start off by finding out who had been sleeping in the house that night. I need to make a list. Can you help?'

Eight

Thursday evening

Kit thought about it. 'Who slept in the house that night? Well, there was Mrs T at the top, of course. Next down is Hubert, poor creature. He prowls around most nights looking for his wife, the one that died in that nasty accident. Sometimes he goes outside into the back garden and sits there in the cold, looking at the stars. I saw him earlier that night, when I was clearing up the kitchen preparing to leave. Mebbe twelve, half past? I thought he might say something about being sorry I was going, but I don't think he even knew about it. So yes, he was there that night, though whether he was in his bed or not, I couldn't say.'

'That's Mrs T up top, and Hubert, next floor down. Who comes next?'

'Edgar, the one that likes to call himself "the admiral", and his missus. They was both there. It wasn't a weekend when he'd have been down on the yacht. He come downstairs for something, can't remember what, after the dinner party that I'd cooked and served up for them. He looked a bit taken aback when he saw me cleaning down the kitchen at midnight but he didn't say nothing.'

'What did he come down for?'

'Ah, I remember now. Whisky. He said he'd run out. Dunno about that. I did see him checking the front door was locked and the alarm on. But when I let myself out – that's after he'd gone upstairs again – I saw the alarm wasn't on for the basement. Though why he bothered I don't know because that daughter of his knows more about fixing alarms than I've had hot dinners. Did she come back that night? Dunno. Might have. My guess is she didn't, but I can't swear to it.'

'Did she often stay out all night?'

'How would I know? I liked to get home to

Mum, no matter what time. Ahmed thinks she's more often out than in, but he can't prove it. The thing is, her parents aren't strict enough with her. She tries, does Lavinia, that's her mother. But the admiral's weak and lets her get away with murder. It takes balls to bring a child up right nowadays, don't it?'

'Petra might have had a sleepover with a friend from school?'

Kit laughed. 'A "he", not a "she". Her current bit of rough. I've never seen her with a girl but she's got the boys flocking around her.'

'Is she so attractive?'

'N-no. It's not that. Sexy, yes. Oozes it. Stinks of it. And it's the money. Throws it about. Tickets for gigs, gifts of the latest apps or high-heeled boots or whatever. She's always overspending her allowance and asking her parents for handouts. Mostly she gets them.'

Bea wondered if Ahmed had chauffeured a boy or girlfriend with Petra to any place recently, causing annoyance to Charlotte, who had wanted him to do something for her. Bea had assumed it had been a girl, but maybe not?

Bea said, 'So Petra may not have slept there that night. Who's next?'

'Charlotte. She come in late, watched me cleaning the floor in the kitchen, didn't say nothing. Not a word. Munched biscuits, then went up to bed. Her lights went off as I was leaving.'

'You can tell?'

'Staff don't go in and out by the front door. Oh dear me, no. Staff has rooms in the basement and the family keep their cars in a garage which

114

is on the same level, under the garden at the back of the house. Staff and cars use a service road at the back of the property. Once you're above ground you can look back and see whether or not there's lights on in the house. Mrs T and Charlotte, they turned off their bedroom lights as I was leaving. There was a couple of lights on where the admiral and his missus sleeps and in their hall. The lights on the stairs are kept on all night. Hubert: dunno. His lights were on in every room, but he might well have gone to sleep with all his lights on. He can't tell night from day nowadays.'

'You had a room in the basement. Who else did?'

'Ahmed, of course. I thought of knocking on his door to say goodbye but I didn't because I thought he'd be asleep and what was the point of waking him?'

Bea thought of telling Kit what had happened to Ahmed but decided not to do so until she'd gathered more information about his death.

Kit continued, 'Then there's the housekeeper. She's got her office and bedsit with a tiny kitchen and shower room on the ground floor at the front where she can keep an eye on deliveries and that, but she's also got a room down in the basement that she uses for, well, dunno, really. Storage and stuff? There is a bed there, but . . . Well, I've never been in there so I don't know. I can't tell you if her lights were on or not. Didn't look. I've never known her sleep out, though. First up in the morning and first to bed, that's her.'

'That's the lot? What about Gordon, Mrs Tredgold's first husband?'

'He's in the coach house, not in the main building. Was his lights on? Dunno. Didn't look.'

'That's the lot who slept there on your last night? So which of them do you think killed the cats?'

Slow, heavy breathing. 'I've been going over and over that. I know it wasn't me. Sometimes I think it's this person and sometimes that. Sometimes I think it's the admiral, because he never liked me and he must know he got me the sack on flimsy grounds. Then I think that fitting me up for stealing his watch is his style but I can't see him taking a knife to two cats. He's fumble fingered. He'd make a right mess of it. Yet perhaps he did it in the bath and cleaned up after himself?

'Next? Well, it's not Lavinia. She wouldn't. She's the county type, hunting, shooting, fishing. Not that she does any of that but if she had to kill something it would be done neatly and I suppose you could say killing the cats was done neatly. But why should she? I can't get my head around that. Charlotte, now. She can be vicious. Sometimes I can see her doing it . . . and then I think that's nonsense, because why would she?'

'So you've come to the conclusion that it was Hubert, dazed with grief and half out of his mind, and that he can't be considered accountable for his actions?'

A sigh. 'I think he needs treatment, yes. I heard Mrs T has tried to get him to a shrink but he refuses. Tell the truth, I think he's getting worse and he'll end up topping himself or trying to, and then he'll be locked up for his own good, won't he?'

'Did he love his wife so much?'

A long silence. Kit cracked his knuckles. 'I suppose he did. They were always together. Even looked alike, a bit. Both dark haired. Wrapped up in their work. Money didn't mean much to them. They wanted a car that would start in the mornings, they wanted food they could heat up in the microwave, they went to the gym together twice a week. Perhaps it's the gap in his life that's sent him crazy. I've heard him walking about at night, recently, talking to himself. It's like a raw wound that doesn't heal. Ahmed and I spoke about it, of course. Ahmed says Hubert's blaming himself for his wife's death because he let her go up the ladder to try to rescue the cat instead of him. He's not good at heights, you see. It seems to run in that family, not liking heights.'

'No children? No pets? How were they with the cats before all this happened?'

'They didn't seem to feel the need of children or pets.'

'How was Hubert with the cats before all this happened?'

'Dunno. I didn't take no notice. Why don't you ask Ahmed? He keeps his eyes open, and he'll know more about who slept at the house that night than I do.'

There was no help for it. Bea had to tell him. 'I'm afraid that's impossible. I'm so sorry to tell you this, Kit, but Ahmed died in his sleep last night.'

'What? Pull the other one. I'm seeing him Sunday, his day off. Unless they change it, last minute, which they sometimes do. He likes Mum's cooking, says it's pretty good.' He took a deep breath. 'You don't mean it. No, of course you don't. I mean, why would he . . .? Are you trying to say he had a heart attack or . . .? No, that's not it. Not his throat cut! Tell me it wasn't that!'

'No, Kit. He took some sleeping pills. I'm told there was a suicide note saying he was sorry and a bundle of notes he shouldn't have had, on his bedside table.'

'That's not fair—!'

'No, it's not right, is it? He told us he was taking the admiral and his lady to the theatre, which he did. You asked him to phone Andy, the physio, and to join us for supper. He did phone Andy, but he didn't go out again. He seems to have had a drink and fallen asleep. He failed to wake up in time to fetch the admiral and his wife from the theatre, so they came home by taxi, got the housekeeper to let them into his room and found him in a coma. He was taken to hospital but died. The official line is that it was suicide.'

'I don't believe it!'

'Neither do I. Neither does Mrs T. She thinks that if I can find out who killed the cats, I'll find out who killed Ahmed as well. She's made this new will, which says anyone who slept in the house the night the cats were killed will get a share of the sale of the house. Ahmed's share will go to his family. It was his death which caused Mrs Tredgold to run away.'

'I could murder someone. I could! If I only knew . . . Well, that's torn it. Hubert wouldn't do that. I mean, why would he?'

'Suppose Ahmed challenged him about killing

the cats and threatened to expose him? Suppose he laced the drink which Ahmed took that evening. I know he didn't drink alcohol. What did he drink in the evenings, anyway?'

'Some special herbal tea. He makes it up every morning, keeps it in a thermos, cold. Drinks it when he feels like it. I suppose someone could put some pills in it, but it wouldn't be Hubert. He doesn't know anything about what Ahmed drinks. Probably doesn't even know which is his room.'

'Agreed. I think it was premeditated murder.'

'Ahmed's family! He's putting his young brother through uni. And his mother has arthritis. His father's dead two years. Ahmed was the bread-winner. There's cousins, but . . . I'd better ring them. But what can I say to them? I don't under-stand what's going on.'

'Neither do I,' said Bea, but Kit had already put the phone down.

Bea felt draggingly tired as she made sure all the doors were locked and put out the lights in the agency rooms. She pulled herself up the stairs to find all the lights still on throughout the ground floor. She checked to see if the alarm had been switched on there and found it had. She made herself a hot drink, fed Winston for the last time that night and made her way slowly up the stairs to bed, thinking she wouldn't even bother to shower but have a lick and a promise and fall into her lovely big bed . . .

Only to find it was already occupied.

Piers hadn't even bothered to undress but fallen flat on his face on her bed, fully dressed. Fast asleep. She pulled on his arm. He was too deep in dreams to stir. She started to laugh and stopped lest the laugh turn to tears. She was too tired to do more than tug off his shoes and pull a fold of the duvet over him.

Had he planned to sleep in her bed? No, probably not. He was still jet-lagged, and it had been a rough day.

She rescued her nightgown and slippers and took herself off to the guest room next door. She'd have it out with him in the morning.

Friday morning

Someone clunked a mug down on Bea's bedside table. She realized it was time to wake up. She didn't want to wake up. She might not have her eyes open yet but she already knew that a large black cloud was hanging over the day.

'Budge up,' said Piers, pushing her across the bed so that he could lie down beside her.

She budged. His arm went under her shoulders and she rested her head against him. He smelled of her shower gel. He'd slept in her bed and used her shower. She couldn't think why she wasn't mad at him. Maybe it was because she wasn't really awake yet, or because he'd always brought her a cup of tea in the mornings when they were married?

He put the mug in her hand and closed her fingers around it. 'Milk, no sugar, right?'

She drank. Nodded. Tried to open her eyes. Sighed gently. Wanted to return to the land of Nod.

He said, 'I phoned Mrs T. Her new housekeeper

answered. Scots. Capable. Cat in tow. I heard the cat mew. Mrs T had a good night, no interruptions. She wants to know if we've delivered our pieces of paper yet. I said that we were going to do it this morning.'

Bea thought about that. 'Me, yes,' she said. 'Not you.'

'Yes,' said Piers. 'Two of us. I may not be much of a bodyguard – I would probably fall flat on my back and crawl away if someone so much as snarled me – but I'm not letting you go back into the lion's den alone. Drink your tea.'

'Kit thinks it was Hubert who killed the cats, but that he wouldn't have killed Ahmed.'

'Nothing wrong with having two strings to your bow. Is your tea all right?'

She sipped. It was fine. 'What do you mean by sleeping in my bed last night?'

'I didn't mean to. I was so tired I couldn't think straight. I seem to remember wanting to ask you something, I went upstairs to find you, only you weren't there. I went out like a light. I used your little electric razor to shave this morning. Hope you don't mind. Grovelling apologies and all that.'

He didn't sound apologetic. He sounded amused and more than a little pleased with himself. He'd been trying for some time to get back into her life. He thought he was succeeding. She would shoot him down in flames when she felt a bit stronger.

He moved off the bed. 'Breakfast coming up. The full English?' He walked out before she had a chance to decline.

* * *

121

By ten o'clock she'd checked that the office could manage without her for a while and was on the road. Or rather, she and Piers were in a taxi on the way to the Tredgold mansion in one of London's most expensive streets. All the buildings were detached and gated. Alarm systems bristled. Chauffeurs drove silent, expensive cars up and down, tinted windows protecting the identity of those within.

They paid off the cab.

'We're out of our league here,' said Piers. 'No hoi polloi, by request. Just a few pedestrians – probably staff – walking dogs and babies in buggies.'

Bea surveyed the mansion, set back from the road. In many ways it resembled a castle. There was no moat or portcullis but instead wide, gilt-tipped, electronically operated gates barred the way to a spacious courtyard in front of the house. The gates were defended by modern technology with speaker systems and remote controls, and spy cameras were lodged here and there to observe anyone who managed to get past the gates.

The postman would have to leave letters and packages in a large box attached to the gates, which could probably only be accessed from the courtyard with the aid of a special key. The milkman wouldn't deliver at all.

The house had been put up by a Victorian magnate with money to burn. It was not pretty. Built in red brick, extra wings stuck out here and there and the roof line was uneven. What it lacked in symmetry, it made up for in bulk.

Bea counted five storeys above a basement

whose windows were partially below ground. An imposing coach house was linked to the main house by more wrought-iron gates, backed with wooden cladding.

The only sign of life was a flourish of red geraniums in huge lead planters on either side of the imposing front door.

'It reminds me of Alcatraz,' said Piers. 'Not that I've ever been there.'

Bea shivered. Yes, perhaps Mrs Tredgold had come to view this enormous house as a gilded cage rather than a home. Bea located the intercom on the gate post. She announced her name and said that Mrs Tredgold had asked her to call with some paperwork for the family.

The gates swung open and they stepped inside. The gates closed behind them. For a moment Bea panicked, wondering how they would ever get out again . . . And told herself not to be so dramatic.

They mounted three steps to the front door which opened to let them through into a hall floored with red-and-black tiles. Ahead was a smoothly graded, uncarpeted staircase which led up to a landing lit by a stained-glass window, turned back on itself and disappeared into the upper regions. As they entered the sun went behind a cloud and the hall was enveloped in shadow.

A young woman with short blonde hair had let them in. She was dressed in a functional white shirt over a black skirt. Was this the 'secretary' whom Charlotte had mentioned? The woman said, 'This way,' and threw open a door on the left.

'Come in, come in! What are you hanging about for?' Charlotte was in good voice.

Bea and Piers entered what was clearly the main drawing room of the house, a long room with a marble fireplace and a lot of heavy but expensive pieces of antique furniture. Four tall windows, draped and lined and fringed in a multitude of layers, looked on to the courtyard. Gilded mirrors reflected wallpaper designed by William Morris, while patterned carpets had been laid on floorboards which glistened with polish.

It was a chilly room intended for formal reception purposes and yet Charlotte was seated at a round mahogany table, working at some papers. An open laptop and an empty chair opposite hinted that she'd been interrupted in the task of dictating notes to the girl who had let them in. Did Charlotte actually use this room to work in? Did it give her a sense of worth to be surrounded by this evidence of inherited wealth?

Charlotte had told Bea she wrote articles for some magazines. Was that what she was working on now?

Charlotte gestured to the girl who had let them in. 'You may go, Mercy. But stay close. This won't take long and I need to get my article off today.'

The girl disappeared and Charlotte twitched a finger at Bea. 'Explain yourself.'

She did not invite Bea and Piers to take a seat, which left them standing in front of her like naughty children summoned to the headmistress's study to account for their misdeeds.

Bea and Piers knew how to counter that move. Piers faded into a chair in the background and took out his sketchbook. Bea took the secretary's chair and laid her papers down. 'Mrs Tredgold has asked me to deliver some letters to you. She—'

'So you lied to me yesterday. You have seen her?'

'Yes, I saw her last night, but—'

The door behind them shot open and the would-be admiral Edgar Tredgold charged into the room shouting, 'Call the police!'

'Hang about, Edgar,' said Charlotte. 'They've come to—'

'To try to pull the wool over our eyes, as they did yesterday?' He shook a finger at Bea. 'I knew you'd done away with her. All that fake innocence! You don't fool me!'

'I wouldn't dream of it,' said Bea. 'After you'd left my house, Mrs Tredgold rang and asked to see me at her new address. She—'

'Where is she! I demand to know what you have done with her.'

'She gave me these papers, which she asked me to deliver to everyone living here. Here is yours, Mr Tredgold. And yours, Miss Tredgold. I think they are self-explanatory.'

'Tush!' Edgar seized the papers Bea had handed him and tore them across. 'Her address! Now!"

Charlotte declined to take her papers. 'Yes, what have you done with her? We want answers and we want them now!'

'If we don't get them,' said Edgar, 'we are definitely going to call the police.'

Bea kept her cool. 'The first of the papers is a copy of the will Mrs Tredgold has just made, leaving everything to charity—'

'What? What, what?' That was Edgar. 'Nonsense! Absurd! That does it! We'll have to get her sectioned.'

Bea continued as if he had not spoken. 'The second is a certificate that she is in full possession of her senses. The third is to say that she has put the house on the market so you should make arrangements to leave straight away—'

Charlotte thrust back her chair. 'She can't do that!'

'And the third is to say that the proceeds from the sale of the house will be divided equally between those who slept here on the night the cats died, excluding the person who did the deed, of course.'

Shock, horror! Edgar's hand shook as he sought for some reading glasses and put them on, only to realize he'd torn up the papers he'd been handed. 'What was that? What?'

Charlotte sat with her mouth open, looking stupid. Then she picked up her copies of the papers and read through them one by one. Edgar strode up and down, trying to fit the torn sheets together. 'She can't, she can't!'

'I suppose she can,' said Charlotte. Colour drained from her face. She attempted to get to her feet and fell back into her chair. Her eyes switched behind Bea and her expression hardened. 'I didn't call you, Mercy. We can manage without you. Go and tell my sister-in-law not to go out yet as she'll be getting a visit from Mrs Abbot shortly.'

The door closed behind Bea. Had the pale girl been eavesdropping? Was her name really 'Mercy'?

Edgar shouted, 'Mother can't do this to us!' He drew up another chair and leaned over the table to face Bea. 'You can see she's half out of her mind, she needs to be with her family, she's not been herself for some time and now . . . We must speak to her, today! *I* must speak to her today! What she's proposing is out of the question. If she wants to downsize because of her age, well, that's understandable, but this is over the top and it's got to stop!'

Bea said, 'She has requested that if you wish to communicate with her you do so through her solicitors, who are the people who drew up her new will.'

His eyes were wild. 'She doesn't realize – the yacht, the expenses!' He narrowed his eyes and drew back in his chair. Thinking. His eyes switched to and fro.

'Yes,' said Charlotte. 'This is a shock. Where will you go, Edgar? What will Lavinia say to this? And Petra?' She started to laugh, a harsh sound.

'And you, Charlotte?' said Edgar. 'You trusted your latest inamorata to make you a fortune and—'

'Enough!' said Charlotte. She looked down at the papers, and up at Bea. 'It says here that whoever killed the cats is not eligible for a share of the sale of the house, which will be divided between the rest of us. Is that correct?'

Bea inclined her head. 'She wants you to sign an affidavit stating that you spent the night of the cats' decease in this house.'

A look passed between Edgar and Charlotte. There was a pause full of unspoken questions.

Someone was counting on their fingers? How many people were going to get a share of the loot?

Charlotte felt her way forward. 'Well, of course we know who killed the cats. That's right, isn't it. Edgar?'

'Yes, of course.' His tone lacked conviction.

'I'm all ears,' said Bea.

Charlotte patted her hair. 'Oh, I don't think I should give him away. What do you think, Edgar?'

'Do we have an option?' Edgar, hedging his bets.

Charlotte shook her head, mournfully. 'I suppose we really do have to say, although it goes against the grain, it really does.'

Bea said, 'I shall need proof, of course.'

'Proof?' Charlotte licked dry lips. 'Oh, I expect we can find some proof for you. Bloodstained clothing, that sort of thing. I'm pretty sure that Mother won't want to prosecute. What do you think, Edgar?'

Edgar followed her lead. 'Absolutely not. She wouldn't.'

Bea said, 'Are you planning to blame Kit for the cats' deaths?'

Calculation. Kit hadn't slept in the house that night and wouldn't be eligible for a share in its sale. Therefore, there was no point in accusing him of the cats' death. 'Er, no,' said Charlotte. 'It would be most convenient, but no.'

'Then you've settled on Ahmed?'

A longer pause, while Charlotte considered the pros and cons of blaming Ahmed. She said, 'No, I'm afraid not,' with some regret. 'I'm afraid it was poor, dear Hubert. He's been out of his mind with grief since his wife died. Such a tragedy.

128

For him, and for us who have seen him drift away into Never Never Land. Mother ought to have had him put away a long time ago. As it is, I expect she can find him some nice secure unit where he can live out his days without hurting anybody else.'

Edgar had finally caught on to her lead. 'And, as he was responsible for the cats' deaths, he's not eligible for his share of the sale of the house.'

'So sad,' said Charlotte. 'We shall visit him now and then.'

Bea brought her eyebrows down from her hairline. 'You mentioned bloodstained clothing. You have that and the knife, I suppose?'

A tinge of colour in Charlotte's cheeks. 'I put the knife in the bin, and the clothes, too. I'm afraid it's all gone out with the rubbish.'

'A pity,' said Bea, getting to her feet. 'I have to be sure that I have the right person.'

'We have already told you that it is Hubert. Surely that's enough. It will be enough for my mother, I'm sure. You tell her it was Hubert and that wraps it up.'

'No,' said Bea. 'Hubert may or may not have been responsible for the death of the cats. I don't know whether he was or was not, although I intend to find out. If it was Hubert, then that is what I will tell Mrs Tredgold. If it was someone else . . . Well, time will tell.'

'You stupid woman,' said Edgar, 'You stupid, stupid—!'

'Hush, Edgar,' said Charlotte, smiling with big, white teeth. 'I am sure we can convince Mrs Abbot of the truth sooner or later.'

'If she can't take our word for it . . .!' Edgar was getting on his high horse. 'How dare you, Mrs Abbot or whatever your name is! How dare you question our word! You have simply no idea of the respect due to your betters.'

'Now, Edgar,' cautioned Charlotte.

'Typical!' He was working himself up into a right royal rage. 'And typical of Mother to pick a third-rate detective to do her dirty work for her. How she came to select such a—'

'Edgar!' Charlotte cracked the whip and he subsided. Charlotte wasn't finished, either. 'Mrs Abbot, I don't think you have any idea what the consequences would be of your attempting to act for my mother. I am sure, when you have thought about it, you will realize that you have strayed into deep waters, waters which could easily close over your head if you didn't make a strategic withdrawal. I daresay you are very capable of dealing with clients of the middling sort but you could never afford to be sued for exerting undue influence on a pensioner, which is what you are doing.'

'Yes, we could sue her, couldn't we?' said Edgar. 'Only . . .'

Only, thought Bea, he probably hasn't the readies to pay a top solicitor's bill.

Charlotte said, smoothly, 'I am sure Mrs Abbot will see sense when she's thought about it. Now, you mentioned that we are to sign an affidavit stating we slept the fatal night here? I will sign that. You will, too, Edgar.'

'What? Oh. Yes, I suppose so. I'll sign for Lavinia and Petra as well, shall I?'

Nine

Friday morning, continued

'I regret,' said Bea, 'each person must sign for themselves. Piers and I will witness your signatures.'

Charlotte read hers through and signed. Bea and Piers witnessed her signature.

Charlotte said, 'Now you sign, Edgar.'

Edgar had torn his paper up. Patiently, Bea extracted another form from her bundle and handed it to him. He scowled, but scribbled some words on the paper, thrust it at Bea and shot out of the room, saying he had work to do even if Bea didn't.

Bea glanced at the affidavit and held back a sigh. Edgar had written that he, his wife and his child had all slept at the house on the night in question. She showed Piers what Edgar had written. Piers shrugged and signed as a witness. Bea did the same. They were, after all, acting as witness to Edgar's signature but not to the truth of what he had written.

Bea gathered her papers together and stood up. 'Now, where shall we find Mrs Lavinia Tredgold?'

Charlotte looked behind Bea to the doorway. Her lips pinched in, but all she said was, 'Mercy will take you to her.'

The pale young woman who had admitted

them to the house was indeed waiting by the door. She signalled that they should follow her down the hall and into another, much smaller and less pretentious sitting room. Here the windows looked not on to the street but on to a garden at the back of the house. It was not an interesting garden. There was a collection of shrubs of roughly equal height around the perimeter and a scrawny man, presumably a gardener, attending to an immaculate lawn in the centre.

The young woman called Mercy said, 'Mrs Tredgold junior will be with you instantly.' She went out, closing the door behind her.

Piers said, 'Little pitchers.'

Little pitchers have big ears.

Bea nodded. She agreed with Piers that Mercy had been listening in on everything that had been said next door. So why wouldn't she go on doing it now? Bea would like to have known what position the girl had in the household, and whether or not she, too, had slept in the house on the night the cats had been killed, but it seemed more important to speak to members of the family first.

The door opened and a slender woman of perhaps forty years of age entered the room. She was another pale blonde but this one wore her hair in a French plait which was not particularly fashionable, but which advertised her as being above fashion. She had probably been a Sloane Ranger in her youth, and still wore the string of pearls which had once been de rigueur for that set. She was dressed expensively but not showily in cream and green and wore little or no make-up. She looked intelligent but tired, as if she had not slept well.

Bea's first reaction was to wonder what this woman had seen in Edgar to marry him, and her second was to wonder why she'd stayed with him.

'I'm Lavinia Tredgold. I understand my mother-in-law has been in touch with you. How is she? Is she all right?'

Lavinia was the first person to ask about Mrs T. Bea liked that. 'Yes, she's well and safe. She wants to keep her new address secret for the moment but has asked me to give you some paperwork which will explain everything.'

Lavinia waved them to a couple of comfortable, chintz-covered armchairs and took another herself. She sat with her knees together and her feet placed gracefully to one side. No one was going to take a photo up her short skirt, were they?

Bea handed her the papers one after the other, explaining them as she went.

'This is a copy of the will Mrs Tredgold has just signed, leaving everything to charity.'

Lavinia's lips curved in a smile. 'Excellent. Just as she should.'

'This is the statement giving her a clean bill of mental health.'

Lavinia looked surprised for a moment. Then she said, 'Good for her.'

'The house is going on the market . . .'

Lavinia held up her hand to stop Bea. She read the papers through with care, then laid them down on her lap and looked off into the distance. She would have a lot to think about. For one thing, her home was about to disappear. She did not appear distressed, but rather, abstracted.

Bea said, 'Ms Tredgold asked me to get a statement from everyone who slept here on the night the cats were killed. I believe you did so. Is that correct?'

'What? Oh, yes. But . . .' She stood up and went to look out of the window. Was it going to rain? The gardener had moved on to the far side of the garden, but Bea didn't think Lavinia was seeing him.

Piers shot Bea a look of enquiry.

Bea shook her head and shrugged.

At last Lavinia turned away from the window. 'Apologies. There's a lot to think about. It had crossed my mind once or twice that my mother-in-law was unhappy about . . . Well, I knew she wanted to downsize. I wish her well. I really do. She has every right to dispose of her money as she thinks fit. Yes, I would be happy to sign your paper. I did sleep here that night.'

'Do you know who killed the cats? Whoever did it will not be allowed a share of the money from the sale of the house.'

Lavinia shook her head. 'I've thought about nothing else for days. I tried to talk to my mother-in-law about it but she cut me short. I wondered if, perhaps . . . but then I thought not. I really have no idea who did it.'

'Not Hubert?' said Bea.

Lavinia shook her head. 'He'd have said if he'd killed them. He wouldn't have hidden them. No, it's not Hubert.'

'Was it your daughter?'

134

Lavinia drew in her breath. Suddenly she looked a lot older. 'How ridiculous!' But there was a lingering, agonizing doubt in her eyes which told Bea that Lavinia did in fact think her daughter capable of doing such a thing. Lavinia rallied. 'Anyway, she didn't sleep here that night, so she couldn't have done it.'

'Are you sure?' Bea remembered Edgar stating that Petra had slept there.

'Yes, of course I am sure. She had a sleepover. Edgar came into my room at just after midnight worrying because Petra wasn't in her bed. I reminded him that she was having a sleepover with a friend.'

'Can you give me the name and telephone number of the friend's house?'

'I'll have to look it up, but yes, of course.' She reached for her handbag just as the door was flung open and Edgar strode into the room.

'Lavinia, I need a word. You haven't signed anything yet, have you?'

Lavinia shook her head. 'No. I was just looking for—'

'There's no need for you to do anything. I've already signed for three of us, which includes you and Petra.'

Lavinia looked startled. 'But Edgar, you know that Petra wasn't—'

'Shut up, woman! Shut up!'

Bea said, 'Mr Tredgold, as I have already told you, each member of the household must sign for themselves.'

'What?' The meaning of her words slowly filtered through to his brain and he changed tactics. 'Very well. I need a word with my wife, in private. Would you kindly . . .?' He gestured to the door.

Bea retreated to the hall, followed by Piers.

Edgar raised his voice. 'And shut that door behind you!'

Piers pulled the door closed, holding the handle down . . . and then slowly, quietly, pressed it open a couple of inches so that they could hear though not see what was being said inside the room.

Lavinia was saying, 'Edgar, she was out. She had a sleepover. You know she did.'

'I know nothing of the kind. You stupid woman, you can never see beyond the end of your nose. God knows why I've put up with you all these years. We all three slept here that night. Understand? Do I have to spell it out in words of one syllable?'

'I told Mrs Abbot I'd give her the phone number of the family who—'

Something fell sharply to the floor. Had he struck her handbag out of her hand? 'You were mistaken. Petra slept here that night. She had a sleepover the night before, remember?'

'No, I—'

'Are you so stupid you can't add up one and one? Everyone who slept here that night gets a share of the sale of the house. We need that money. Get it?'

'But that's—'

There came the sound of something soft being struck. A slap? Edgar had hit her?

There was a muffled cry from Lavinia.

Bea and Piers looked at one another. Ought

136

they to interfere? But perhaps he hadn't really hit her? They couldn't actually see what was happening inside the room, could they?

Edgar said, 'Hah! Now you remember, don't you?'

'I . . . Edgar, no! You promised me, remember, after the last time . . .!'

This is not the first time she's been hit?

Edgar's voice, closer to the door: 'You can come back in now, Mrs Abbot. And you, whatever-your-name is.'

Bea and Piers trooped back in to find Edgar, smiling widely, and Lavinia standing at the window with her back to them, blowing her nose on her handkerchief.

Edgar said, 'My wife has remembered how it was now. A simple misunderstanding, soon corrected. Right, Lavinia? You really are getting absent-minded, aren't you?'

'What's she done now?' A young girl appeared in the doorway. Was this Petra? Cut-off jeans, skimpy top, long dark hair and an expression whose default position was sulky.

'Some days,' said Edgar, smiling broadly, 'your mother has difficulty remembering her name, doesn't she? I blame the booze, myself.'

Bea switched her eyes to Lavinia, who remained at the window, looking out over the garden. Bea didn't think Lavinia was a drinker. A victim of abuse, yes? A drinker, no. The cheek nearest Bea looked suspiciously red. On the floor, some distance away, was Lavinia's handbag. Had Edgar knocked it out of his wife's hand?

'Mommy dearest!' said Petra in a sharp voice. 'What have you gone and done now?'

Edgar said, 'She got muddled about which night you slept over at your friend's house, and I've had to remind her what's what. You know where you were, don't you? This is Mrs Abbot, who's acting as a messenger for Granny. The house is being put on the market and everyone who slept here the night the cats were killed gets a share of the sale. Mrs Abbot wants us to sign an affidavit saying we did sleep here the night the cats were killed. I've signed for us three, but your mother had one of her "moments" and forgot that you were here. If I hadn't put her right, she would have lost you your share of the sale of the house.'

'Stupid Mummy!' Petra lifted her upper lip so that her incisors showed in a sneer.

Lavinia turned round. She was very pale, except for the mark on the side of her face. Tears glittered on her cheeks. She said, very quietly, 'Mrs Abbot, I am prepared to sign that affidavit. I did sleep here that night. And that's all I have to say on the matter.'

'No need for that,' said Edgar. 'I've seen to it already.'

'No,' said Bea. 'She's right. Everyone must sign for themselves. Mrs Tredgold, do you have a pen? Allow me to lend you mine.' Bea took her bundle of papers over to a small table in the window, sorted one out and invited Lavinia to sign.

Which she did. Slowly, taking her time about it.

'Now Piers and I sign as witnesses,' said Bea. She signed, and Piers did the same.

Bea produced another of her forms. 'Now, would you care to sign, Miss Tredgold? This is a legal document and may be produced in court at any time. Do be careful what you put your name to.'

'Are you dumb or something?' Petra seized Bea's pen, glanced over the paper, wrote that she'd slept in the house the night the cats died, and signed her full name.

Bea and Piers signed as witnesses.

'There, now,' said Edgar. 'That wasn't so hard, was it?'

Lavinia stooped to pick up her handbag and check that nothing had fallen out. She said, 'I'm done here,' and walked out of the room. Her heels tapped on the tiled floor in the hall, and then they heard her going up the stairs.

Petra threw herself into a chair and sprawled there, legs wide apart. Her gaze was first on Piers, and then on Bea. 'You run a small-time domestic agency, or something? Supplying servants to order?'

'I try to place them, yes.'

'For a fiver here or there, I suppose? You do realize you're well out of your comfort zone here? You can't possibly understand people like us.'

Bea didn't reply. She remembered Mrs T speaking of her children's sense of entitlement. Petra seemed to have it, too.

Petra was annoyed that Bea refused to rise to her challenge. 'Haven't you heard it's polite to answer when you're spoken to? Who pays your bills, eh?'

Bea felt her colour rise. 'Not you, Miss Tredgold.'

Petra swung her foot, grinning. 'You think you can get money out of poor old Granny? Well,

139

you can't. We won't let you. She's nuts, you know. The sooner she's locked up and we can get on with our lives the better.'

Bea seethed but refused to reply. Instead, she put her papers in order ready to leave.

Edgar was all smiles. 'Oh, come now, Petra. That's putting it a bit too strong. Granny is showing her age, that's all. We all make mistakes. She's making more than usual, that's all. She'll see reason soon.'

Petra shrugged. 'I don't like being cheeked by the hired help. You should tell Mrs Abbot to mind her manners when she talks to me, right?'

Bea ignored her. 'I think we're done here. Now, we have to find Mr . . . Gordon?'

Edgar said, 'What do you want him for? He doesn't live in the house and he's not entitled to a share when it's sold.'

Bea held up her papers. 'It says here that I should get a signature from everyone who lives at this address, and the coach house seems to be included. Now, how do I find him?'

Petra said, 'Through the servants' quarters, of course. Where you will feel right at home.'

Bea walked out of the room into the hall, fuming.

Piers came after her, carefully closing the door behind him.

Bea said, 'Another minute and I'd—'

Piers interrupted her. Loudly. 'What an amazing place this is. It reminds me of a National Trust property, though I can't recall which.'

She nodded. He was right to warn her of listening ears. Someone was at the top of the stairs at this very moment. An older woman?

140

Who was she? The sun came out, and the woman was silhouetted against the light from the window behind her . . . and then she stepped aside into the shadows.

Piers investigated a series of doors on the far side of the hall to see if they would open. The first and second didn't. Then he found one in an unobtrusive corner under the stairs.

'This way, I think.' They went through the door into a tiled corridor, the floor of which was covered in some sound-absorbing material. Doors opened off at intervals, but an open door at the far end let them in to a large kitchen with fitments that looked industrial. Some serious cooking was done here, but by whom? No cooks were in evidence.

However, a further half-glazed door hinted at daylight beyond. Piers half closed his eyes. 'If my bump of locality hasn't deserted me, the way to the coach house leads this way.'

He tried the outer door and it opened.

What had perhaps once been an open space between the mansion and its coach house had been closed off at either end with high gates and covered over with a glass roof. The coach house presented a blank wall to their view, broken only by a door and one small window.

Piers tried the door in the coach house and it let them in to a small lobby. To their right was another door – leading into the garage? – which proved to be locked. To their left lay some wooden stairs, and from above came a low thrumming sound.

Up the stairs they went to find that the interior

walls on the first floor had been gutted to provide one enormous room. A deep shelf at hip height provided the base for a working display of model trains. The walls had been decorated with blue skies above and appropriate country and town scenes below. There were miniature ramps, hills and mountains, all beautifully crafted from plaster of Paris and painted. There were tiny villages and stations and station masters, signal houses and gates and goods depots and turntables and . . . how many trains were on the go? Three? Five? There were two passenger trains, and a goods train and . . . Was that a maintenance engine of some sort?

'I've died and gone to heaven,' said Piers.

'Hello?' A burly man with longish silver hair and a small, well-kept beard was working at a central table, taking apart – or perhaps he was putting together? – a coach from a passenger train. He raised his eyebrows, looking from Bea to Piers and back.

'Forgive us intruding. I'm Bea Abbot. Mrs Tredgold has asked me to—'

'Ah, yes. She did say.' He was clad in an old plaid shirt over jeans: both stained with engine oil, as were his well-worn trainers. He gave the impression of wearing a station master's cap and sporting a whistle, although in fact he had neither.

'You are Gordon?' Bea held out her hand.

He put down the model carriage, wiped his hand on a piece of cloth and shook her hand. A firm clasp. He had bright blue eyes and lines of humour around eyes and mouth. Bea liked him at sight.

142

'I'm Gordon, yes. Mrs Tredgold's first husband. Long an ex. I understand you are in much the same situation with . . . Piers, is it? The famous portrait painter?'

Bea had to laugh. 'Yes.'

Piers also laughed but switched his attention to the trains. 'This is . . . wow! May I look around? I promise not to touch.'

'Sure,' said Gordon. 'In fact, do me a favour, will you, and take a look at that section at the far end? I'm not happy about the gradient on that corner.'

He drew out a collapsible chair, offered it to Bea, and seated himself on a tall stool.

Bea said, 'You've been in touch with her last night or early this morning? You know where she is and how to contact her? In fact, you are the "friend" who organized her escape?'

'"Escape"?' He repeated the word with his head on one side. 'Would you call it that?'

'Tactical withdrawal? I've just seen Edgar reducing his wife to pulp. He used the same tactics on his mother?'

'He didn't hit Marcia, no. But yes, he shouted at her and threatened her.'

'Why didn't she leave long ago? And I'm not talking about Lavinia, who, sadly, seems to me to have become accustomed to her treatment.'

'Marcia and I are old friends. Yes, I thought she ought to have got out from under before this, but she kept thinking they'd come round to her way of thinking. Nonsense, of course. Edgar and Charlotte can't see beyond the end of their noses. And then, when Marcia did start to plan a new

143

life for herself, that overdeveloped conscience of hers came into play. She felt guilty about leaving them, would you believe? One minute she wanted to put her cards on the table and clear the air, and the next she was saying they'd be lost without her. Which they would be. Lost, I mean.'

'Finally, she ran away.'

'Mm. Yes. You could put it like that. She saved herself. Not before time, eh?'

'And Lavinia?'

He picked up the carriage which was minus a set of wheels and looked it over. 'Lavinia has tried very hard to be a good wife and mother. Marcia tried very hard to be the same. Both have put others before themselves. Edgar underestimates both. Meanwhile, I "play with my trains". If they want me, they know where to find me.'

Did Gordon mean he was on stand-by to help Lavinia, as well as Marcia?

Bea said, 'Edgar hasn't started on you yet?'

'No grounds. Marcia sold me a long lease on this place so he can't get me evicted, and I'm useful in lots of ways about the house.'

'You keep your head down and let them say about you what they like?'

'Something like that, yes. No one takes much notice of what poor old Gordon does . . . except Marcia, of course. I'm no millionaire, you see. I'm just an engineer who frittered away a fortune in my youth but earned an honest crust when I followed my bent into building bridges. Now I'm retired, I have enough money to live on with care, but not enough to lend anything to anyone, which means I'm no one of any importance to the Tredgolds.'

Bea said, 'You are a bystander, an onlooker, someone who sees everything and keeps his own counsel. So what did you think of Ahmed's death?'

'No one asked me. The police didn't visit me. Nothing had taken me into the house that morning and I didn't even hear about it until the police had departed.'

'What would you have said if they had got round to interviewing you?'

'It stinks. I liked Ahmed. They say he'd written a suicide note on his mobile but not sent it. What I think is that anyone who found him could have keyed in the word "Sorry", and left it there to be found by the police. It makes me angry to think what happened to him and Kit. And to June, the cleaner, who was a really nice woman. But who am I to have an opinion on the matter?' Gordon shook his head. 'I see, I hear, I say nothing.'

'Until Marcia asked you to help her.'

'There is that.'

'You will help Lavinia, too, if she asks?'

'Possibly, but if Edgar found out, my life wouldn't be worth living, would it?' He looked around him, at the humming trains which were clicking over the points, diving into tunnels and re-emerging into the light. 'I can't move all this overnight, can I?'

'You are thinking of doing just that?'

'You have quite an imagination, Mrs Abbot.'

'Yes, I do. Who killed the cats?'

He shook his head. 'I know that I didn't. Nor

145

did Hubert, poor chap. Day and night, it's all one to him. Often he sits out in the garden all night looking up at the stars. It seems to calm him. If I find him out there, I bring him in and let him doss down here.' He jerked his head to where another flight of stairs continued up inside the building. 'I've a one-bedroom flat upstairs but he's welcome to sleep on my sofa.'

'Did you bring him in the night the cats were killed?'

He nodded. 'I did. Marcia – Mrs Tredgold – said she wanted affidavits from everyone who slept in the house that night, but I'm not sure she got that right. I mean, Hubert wouldn't know what you were talking about and if he did, well, him and cats . . . that's difficult. I'm willing to vouch for him, if you'll accept that.'

Bea hesitated. 'I didn't accept Edgar trying to speak for the rest of his family, so I can't accept you speaking for Hubert.'

Gordon said, 'Well, I tried to warn you. He's up top, probably asleep. You want to go up?'

Bea decided she didn't need to disturb Piers, who was happily watching a train climb an incline in the far corner of the big room, so she climbed the stairs by herself.

On the second floor she found herself in a room perhaps half as big as the one below. It was furnished as a sitting room with no two pieces matching in colour or age. Books and magazines spilled from a coffee table on to the floor. Two mugs, each containing half a cup of tea or coffee, were on the floor among the papers. The carpet needed a good hoover, but otherwise everything looked well-cared-for. Half-open doors to the rear gave Bea glimpses of a small kitchen, a bedroom, a bathroom and a storeroom.

A couple of dormer windows in the sloping roof flooded the big room with light, allowing her to locate a tall, thin figure sitting slumped in front of a television set. The television was not on.

'Hubert Tredgold? I'm Mrs Abbot. Your mother asked me to have a quick word with you.'

He was a gaunt, grey man who looked fifty but was probably much younger than that, clad in a grey sweater and jeans. There were no shoes on his feet and he had a hole in one black sock. His features were fine-drawn as if he'd recently lost weight. He looked what he was, a scholar, out of his depth in everyday life. Over-conscientious, perhaps? A worrier?

He peered at Bea with a puzzled air. Then some cog managed to click in and he struggled to his feet. 'My mother asked you to . . .?' He seemed puzzled, but willing to have the matter, whatever it was, explained to him.

Bea said, 'You mother has moved out, as you probably know?'

'Has she?' He rubbed his forehead. 'Oh, that's right. She did say. I'm afraid I'm not quite . . . What was it she wanted me to do?'

Afterwards, Bea thought that was the point at which she ought to have given up. But she didn't. She said, 'It will only take a few minutes. She asked me to tell you she's made a new will leaving everything to charity, and that she's putting her house on the market.'

'Good, good. I do realize I have to move on soon. I'm not sure where I should go, but no doubt it will become clear. I really ought to be getting back to work at the office.'

'Yes, of course.' Bea crossed her fingers. 'Now your mother wants you to have a share of the sale of the house to help you buy something elsewhere, provided you are willing to sign a paper saying you slept in the house the night the cats were killed.'

His eyes went blank. No one at home.

His eyes rolled up in his head, his knees bent, and he collapsed.

Ten

Friday noon

Gordon appeared from the stairwell, saying, 'Oh, dear. I did warn you.'

He pushed Bea aside, and got Hubert's head down between his knees. 'There, now. Take a deep breath. That's it. There's nothing to worry about. You've been under the weather, feeling a bit tired. Some kind of virus, no doubt.'

Piers appeared, looking a question.

Gordon said, 'Hubert's had a nasty turn. Help me get him on to the bed, there's a good chap.'

Bea had dropped all her papers when Hubert collapsed. She picked them up, took a seat and occupied herself by putting them in order while

148

the two men half carried and half steered Hubert into the bedroom.

What was going on? Gordon had warned her that Hubert was fragile, but surely he was more than just fragile, he was in need of medical attention? How had it happened that his mother hadn't seen to it?

There were soothing noises. Hubert was being encouraged to take a little nap.

Piers came out to join Bea, shaking his head and shrugging his shoulders. He didn't know what was going on, either.

Finally Gordon joined them, shutting the bedroom door after himself.

Bea said, 'I think you'd better explain.'

'You hadn't been told? No, I see you hadn't. Well, the fact of the matter is that if anyone had something against the cats it would be Hubert, but he didn't kill them. I'd spotted him wandering around the garden the night they died, about midnight, maybe a touch later. It looked like it was coming on to rain, not that he'd notice, so I asked if he'd do me a favour and give me a game of chess. To get him inside, see. And he came.'

'Through the house, or through the covered courtyard?'

'The courtyard. It's locked at night but I have a key. I know the cats were all right when I brought him in, or rather, one of them was. I think it was Mitzi. She was chasing moths around the garden. I don't think Hubert had seen her, and I certainly didn't draw his attention to her at the time.'

Bea said, 'Kit left about that time, didn't he?'

'That's right. I saw the lights in the kitchen go off as we came back through the courtyard. I got Hubert upstairs, sat him down on the settee, gave him a whisky and he went out like a light. I put a blanket over him and went to bed myself. Hubert suffers from insomnia, you see. He doesn't want to take pills but if you can get him to drop off then he's asleep for hours. He didn't stir at all that night. I'd have heard him if he had.'

'What's his problem with the cats, then?'

'You've not been over the house, have you?'

Bea shook her head.

'Marcia has the top flat in what used to be the servants' quarters. It isn't that big, but it suited her. The next floor down is where Hubert and his missus lived. Nice woman in the same line of business, research, genealogy and that. No money, but that never worried Hubert or Stefanie. Their flat is the same as Marcia's but bigger because it has a wide balcony to one side, which acts as a flat roof to the rooms below.

'Hubert wasn't a gardener, but his wife was. She fixed the balcony up with plants in tubs and grew more stuff in the little conservatory she'd had built there. It's not that big, more of a greenhouse really, but there's room enough for a couple of chairs and a table among the pots. She used to sit out there a lot. It faces south and she loved the sun. Because Marcia's flat is smaller, one of her windows lies directly above Hubert's conservatory. Maybe four feet above, maybe five. Marcia doesn't have a balcony, get it?

'Somehow or other one of the cats got out of

the window in Marcia's flat, dropped on to the conservatory roof and couldn't get down. Hubert and his missus heard it and went spare. They got out their stepladder and tried to coax the cat down but couldn't make it see sense. Hubert's not got a good head for heights, you see.'

Bea said, 'Same as Charlotte?'

'Same as Charlotte. So Hubert's wife went up the ladder and tried to crawl up the glass roof to get the cat. Only, the glass shattered and she fell through. Cut an artery.'

'She bled to death in front of him?'

'He blames himself because she went up the ladder and not him.'

'It was an accident,' said Piers. 'Or was it? How did the cat get up there?'

Gordon rubbed his eyes. 'Accident. Of course. You couldn't rely on the glass breaking like that. You couldn't rely on Stefanie cutting an artery cut as she fell. As for the cat, it fell with her but, being a cat, it landed neatly and fled to live another day.'

Bea said, 'Edgar and Charlotte say Hubert killed the cats in retaliation, but you don't believe he did?'

Gordon wiped his face with his hands. 'It's a convenient theory.'

'Lavinia says Hubert wouldn't have killed Ahmed.'

'The two events might not be linked. There's different sorts of nastiness around.'

Piers put into words what Bea had been thinking. 'Why isn't Hubert in hospital?'

'At first he seemed to be coping all right. He

151

was shocked but able to function. Marcia arranged for him to see a therapist. He went once, said he didn't need to go again. He made plans to go back to work but never got there. Every day he seems to slip further away from reality. Marcia made another appointment with a different therapist but Hubert refused to go. Now it seems he can't even step out into the street.'

'He needs treatment,' said Bea.

Gordon nodded. 'It's all arranged. He's been spending more and more time with me. He says he likes to see the trains go round. The "hum" seems to sooth him. There have been times when he's not wanted to go back to his own place at night and I've let him stay. Marcia's arranged for him to see a third therapist tomorrow and I've agreed the consultation should take place here. I'll have him stay with me overnight so that I can keep an eye on him. He can have my bed and I'll sleep on the settee. Now, he's only got the clothes he's wearing. Would it be possible for you to go over to the house – I've got his keys – and collect a few things for him? Shaving things, underwear, shoes, a jacket and so on?'

Piers had been at his sketchbook while they'd been talking, but now put it away. 'We'd be glad to. As for these papers Mrs Tredgold asked us to get signed, I'm sure she won't want us to insist in Hubert's case. I wish she'd warned us to be careful when we spoke to him.'

Gordon sighed. 'She's had a lot on her mind and to be fair, I think he's deteriorated in the last couple of days.'

'Are you sure you can cope with him?' said Bea. 'What about food for tonight?'

'I have some here and can always raid the freezers in the big house if I run short.' He produced a bunch of keys and showed them which would let them in and out of the coach house, into the kitchen across the courtyard and up into Hubert's apartment.

Bea followed Piers down the stairs and into the courtyard where she took a deep breath of clean air. The coach house had been scented with oil, and the constant thrum of the engines had given her a headache.

They let themselves into the kitchen. It was still deserted, but from behind a closed door in the corridor beyond came the murmur of voices and the sharp *ping* of a microwave oven. Perhaps that was the staffroom, and they were on their lunch break?

Piers hesitated. 'Do we need to see the staff now?'

Bea checked her watch and shook her head. By the time they'd got Hubert's things back to Gordon it would be time to go home. She didn't want to be late as her ward was coming back from school for the weekend.

They went through the door into the hall. That was quiet, too. And not well lit. There was a feeling of tension in the air. Behind closed doors people were talking. Or arguing. Or being abused?

They took the stairs to the first-floor landing and the reason for the poor light in the hall was revealed. There was a stained-glass window

153

ahead but it looked out, not on to the garden, but into a sunroom which had been built out over the staffroom below. It was fitted up with garden furniture as it was south-facing and got a lot of sun. There were blinds at both internal and external windows which could be lowered at will. Today was a grey day and the blinds were up. No one was in the garden room.

Bea said, 'I think this must be Charlotte's domain. I wonder if she finished the article she was writing . . . or rather, which she'd been dictating to the young woman who let us in? I can't believe that girl's really called "Mercy", can you?'

He shrugged. They turned to the right and took the stairs up another floor, where there was a layout identical to that of the floor below. Here the blinds had been pulled down inside the sunroom, even though the day was so dark and dreary.

'Edgar and Lavinia's rooms?'

Bea wondered if Edgar were still shouting at Lavinia, or worse. And what about that girl, Petra? A nasty piece of work. Her sense of entitlement was huge.

Another turn and another flight of stairs. Here the air was lighter, because the window on the landing looked straight out on to a wide balcony with a conservatory on it. Exactly as Gordon had described it. This must be Hubert's floor.

Piers found the right key to let them into Hubert's rooms.

Bea cocked an ear. There was a chugging noise coming from somewhere in the flat? Was someone playing a radio? No, surely not.

Piers opened the first door on the right. A sitting room, clean and tidy, with French windows that led out through the conservatory on to the balcony outside. There were no mugs, no daily papers, no books lying around. No cards on the mantelpiece. There was a tall plant in a tub in one corner, which looked as if it were dying from lack of water.

Hubert's wife had had green fingers, hadn't she? But Hubert was letting her plants die.

Piers went to the French windows and struggled with the lock, so that they could access the conservatory, and through that go out into the open air on the balcony.

The place was a suntrap. Or would be, when the sun came out. The wall around the balcony was built of brick to a height of four foot with toughened glass panels above, taking it to well over a man's height.

Piers turned his back on the wall to study the roof of the conservatory. Two panels seemed to have been recently replaced, as they looked brighter than the rest. A glisten of broken glass could still be seen between the tiles on the floor of the conservatory.

Bea looked up and up. The conservatory had an ornamental cast-iron strip running along the ridge where the roof panels joined. Behind rose the wall of the house with a sash window directly above it. Presumably the cat had jumped down from that window on to the top of the conservatory and then been unable or unwilling to descend the steep slope of the window to the gutter and safety.

Or someone had opened the window and

155

dropped the cat on to the conservatory in a fit of petulance. Perhaps it had soiled a carpet or committed some other misdemeanour?

There were shrubs in planters set around the balcony. They, too, were dying from lack of water and care.

There was a jumble of bamboo chairs inside the conservatory, thrown up against one another. Their cushions had been removed, possibly because they'd been shredded by some of the broken glass from the roof?

Bea shuddered and Piers nodded. 'It's good that Gordon's taken Hubert in. This place stinks of death.'

They returned through the conservatory into the lifeless sitting room, and thence to a corridor, which bisected the flat.

The chugging sound was louder here. Some kind of music? Bea looked her astonishment at Piers. He could hear it now, too.

He tried doors. A dining room on the left was rigid and tidy. Closed windows. Airless. Next came a kitchen with a selection of breakfast things on the central unit. Sliced bread had been left out and was hardening. There was a group of mugs, each half full of cold tea or instant coffee. Hubert had been existing on bread and coffee? Had no one in the house thought to check on him?

Finally, they came to an open door through which light streamed into the corridor. This was the master bedroom, containing some old-fashioned, heavy brown furniture – which Bea supposed was rather like Hubert himself – and an imposing four-poster bed. The bed had been slept in and was unmade. An expensive brocade cover had been thrown back over the sheets. Half of it trailed on the floor.

The bed also contained a fake blonde, somewhat on the chubby side, who was painting her toenails. She was plugged into headphones and nodding her head in time to the chugging sound they'd heard earlier.

The girl was wearing a sleeveless cropped top which barely contained her breasts, the tiniest of denim skirts and no pants, as Bea and Piers could observe from where they stood in the doorway.

Some movement must have caught the girl's eye for she started, said 'Oops!' and spilt the bottle of nail varnish over the brocaded cover. She unhooked herself and killed the music. 'Hello, who are you? I was expecting Hubert. Do you know where he is?'

In flight from this little madam, perhaps?

Bea said, 'I'm Mrs Abbot. We've been asked to fetch some overnight things for Hubert. More to the point, who are you?'

The girl dabbed at the coverlet with a tissue and swore, because the varnish was not going to disappear that way. 'I'm Carly. I'm supposed to be getting together with Hubert. Has he gone away? Auntie won't be pleased. She said I was to be his muse or something. Coax him back to life, that sort of thing. But I can't do it if he's not here.'

She wriggled her toes. Half of her toenails were painted blue and half not. She tried to get another brush full of varnish out of the bottle, but there was only a trace left. Her face screwed up. She looked as if she were going to cry. 'Now what am I going to do?'

'Yes, indeed.' A new voice, slightly sibilant. Bea and Piers were edged into the room as an older woman pushed them in from behind. 'Just look what you've done now! Oh, Carly! How could you!'

The woman would probably be in her late fifties, an ash-blonde with severely disciplined hair in a long bob, no make-up and an expensive white blouse over a black skirt. She swung Carly off the bed, exhibiting good muscle control, and swept the coverlet off it too. 'I'll have to have this dry cleaned, and the cost will come off your wages, Carly.'

'It wasn't my fault,' whined Carly, who perhaps wasn't as old as she'd tried to make out. 'I was waiting for Hubert, but he's not here and these people startled me and—'

'What was that?' Again, the slight sibilance. The woman swung round on Bea and Piers. 'Who are you? How did you get in? This is private property.'

Bea said, 'Mrs Tredgold asked us to deliver some letters to the family but we got held up at Gordon's place. That's where Hubert is. Gordon asked us to collect some things of Hubert's as he plans to keep him there tonight. And you are . . .?'

'How extraordinary!' She was not pleased by this news. Her eyelids fluttered as she considered the pros and cons of the arrangement. 'He should have let me know. I'll tell the girls they can come in and clean up in here, if Hubert's going to be away for the night. He'll be back tomorrow?'

Bea shrugged. 'I have no idea. What did you say your name was? Are you the housekeeper here, because if so—'

'Don't get back on the bed, Carly! There's no point your staying if he's gone out for the day. Come back tomorrow, same time. And for heaven's sake, put some pants on. He's not one of the lads from the pub.'

Carly felt under the bed for some flip-flops. 'Keep your hair on,' she said, but in subdued fashion. The newcomer was clearly top dog in their relationship.

Bea repeated her question to the older woman. 'Are you the housekeeper, because if so, I have some paperwork to give you from Mrs Tredgold.'

'I'm Ms Andrews, yes. I think you may have met my daughter when you arrived. Some paperwork? What do you mean?'

'I think these are self-explanatory,' said Bea, handing them over.

Carly stamped her feet into her flip-flops. 'What about Hubert? Auntie, didn't you say he was the easiest—'

'That's enough.' Auntie cracked the whip. 'Carly, get your skates on. Mrs Abbot, you won't mind if I oversee you collecting some things for Hubert? I am responsible for everything in Mrs Tredgold's absence.'

'Yes, of course,' said Bea. 'Would you care to read the papers she's sent you now, while I'm here, so that if you have any queries, I can deal with them straight away?'

Ms Andrews made her way over to the window.

She read through the papers quickly, returning only once to reread a particular paragraph. Her face showed nothing of what she was thinking, or rather, the muscles around her mouth tightened . . . and that was all.

She said, 'I suppose it was only to be expected. The family were pressing her rather . . . but she shouldn't have . . .' She tightened her mouth further. 'Well, Mrs Abbot, no doubt I will have some queries when I've thought through what this means, but for the moment all I can say is that I can see this is going to be most upsetting for the family. And, if the house is to go on the market straight away . . .'

Bea noticed that the woman's hands were trembling though she was making an effort not to show distress.

But she is distressed. No, not so much distressed as angry. Yes, really, really angry. She's hiding it well but she's almost vibrating with the effort of concealing it.

I suppose Mrs Tredgold selling the house means the housekeeper will have to look for another live-in job. Do I offer to help her? N-no. I don't think so.

Mrs Andrews reread one of the papers. 'The house goes on the market straight away? I shall have to get the house ready to be shown round. I assume someone will tell me sooner or later who I am to contact about it. Then I will need to know what arrangements the family will make for their removal. This is all very difficult. I imagine I shall be instructed to stay on until the house is sold, but there is nothing here to say that is the case.'

160

Bea said, 'I expect the solicitors will know. You have their address there.'

'Possibly.' Ms Andrews held up one sheet of paper. 'Lend me a pen and I'll sign the affidavit for you now. I did sleep here the night the cats were killed. I don't take time off, like some people.'

'What's that?' Carly shrugged herself into a man's leather jacket. It was far too big for her. Was she 'borrowing' Hubert's clothes?

Mrs Andrews said, 'Nothing to do with you, Carly. It's just that everyone who slept here on the night the cats died will get a share of the eventual sale of the house.'

'That's me, too,' said Carly, eyes shining at the thought of a windfall.

'No, it isn't,' said her aunt, squashing that one straight away.

'Ooooh!' Carly pouted.

Her aunt gave her a look and Carly flounced to the door.

Ms Andrews called her back. 'Give me your keys, Carly. That's my spares you've got, and I shall need them.'

Carly reluctantly handed over a bunch of keys. 'Can I go now?'

Mrs Andrews nodded, at the same time answering a bleep from her smartphone. 'Yes. Yes, Lavinia . . .?' She listened for a moment, her eyes flickering this way and that. She said to Bea, 'Will you excuse me?' and walked out of the room without another word.

'Well!' said Piers, folding up his sketchbook. 'The plot thickens. Is Ms Andrews really arranging for Hubert to get together with that piece of jailbait? Fifteen if she's a day.'

'Yes, it's bad. The girl seems willing but I wonder if Mrs T realizes what's going on. As for Hubert, I wouldn't have thought he'd be interested, but he's in a vulnerable condition and if she climbed into bed with him, who knows what might happen?' Bea looked at her watch. 'I'm not waiting for Ms Andrews to return. Can you find some sort of bag to put Hubert's things in? I'll start with the bathroom which is probably . . . ah, yes, this door leads to it.'

Piers opened the doors of an old-fashioned Victorian wardrobe, which was one of a pair of monumental pieces of furniture. 'This is all women's clothing. His wife's? Stuff he can't bear to get rid of? Oh, and look! There's a lady's manicure set, hairbrush and hairspray still on the dressing table.'

'Mm?' said Bea. She stared at an empty bathroom cabinet, then returned to the bedroom, to find Piers standing on a chair to get at some tote bags from a high shelf.

'There's no shaving things. There's no toothbrush and no brush or comb. The shower has been run recently, there are used towels on the floor, but no toiletries.' She looked under the pillows. 'No pyjamas, though I suppose he might not bother with them.'

'Conclusion?'

'He slept here last night, ate some breakfast and then moved out. The question is, did he take his toiletries with him, intending to sleep somewhere else tonight, or—'

'You think someone came and got them for him later?' Piers clicked his fingers. 'Gordon came. Gordon is planning to take him somewhere today. Gordon doesn't trust anyone, not even us. He sold us a line to get rid of us, giving him time to think what he'll do next. You think he plans to remove Hubert to a hospital?'

'Probably. In which case, we can help by doing as he asked. We'll collect a selection of clothing and whatever else we think might be needed. We'll take it back to Gordon and see what he has to say for himself.'

Piers opened the doors of the second wardrobe, while Bea explored the contents of a couple of large chests of drawers, and took out some under-clothes, shirts, T-shirts, a pair of jeans, ditto some trainers. Finally she packed a rainproof jacket.

She opened the top drawer of the dressing table and found a collection of photographs of a happy, laughing couple. All in silver frames, all face down. So sad.

Piers took one last look around. 'Shall we pop up to Mrs Tredgold's rooms while we're here? I want to see if the window over Hubert's conservatory roof is easy to open or stuck fast with paint.'

There was still no sign of Ms Andrews so they locked the door to Hubert's flat, and took the last flight of stairs upwards. On the top landing they found a door into Mrs Tredgold's apartment. Piers tried keys till he found one that let them in. The air inside smelt fresh and clean. Perhaps a window had been left open somewhere?

This top flat was, as they'd been told, smaller than the one immediately below it. The first door

163

on the right let them into a sitting room with windows on two sides. The window looking out over the garden was open a crack. The one on the left, directly over Hubert's conservatory, was firmly closed and latched.

Piers tried it. It was a sash window. Sash windows in old buildings tend to stick, and eventually the cords fray and break. Modern windows use a different system. This window moved upwards smoothly and stayed where it was put.

Piers leaned out and beckoned to Bea to do likewise. She did so, with care. The crest of the roof below was no more than four feet below. Maybe five.

Someone who was annoyed with a cat might well pick it up, dangle it out of the window and drop it on to the conservatory roof. And then close the window. The cat couldn't climb up the wall to get back in. The only way out of the situation was down . . . but the conservatory roof was steep and slippery, so it had mewed for attention. Hubert and his wife had emerged to see what they could do to help, climbed up and . . . bingo! The roof collapsed.

Piers said, 'It looks like misadventure to me. No one could foresee someone climbing on to the conservatory roof, or that it would collapse.'

'Someone might have intended to kill the cat by dropping it out of the window?'

Piers drew the window down and latched it. 'Who killed Cock Robin? Or, in this case, the cats?'

'"I, said the sparrow, with my bow and arrow. I killed Cock Robin." Or, in this case, the cats? But who is the ultimate target?'

Eleven

Piers repeated her question. 'Who is scheduled to die next? I suppose it's Mrs Tredgold.'

'Why did Ahmed have to die?'

'Perhaps that wasn't intentional? Perhaps someone set him up as a thief? He took some pills but might not have died . . . but even if he didn't die, he would have been sacked, wouldn't he? Kit didn't die. The physio didn't die. The cleaner didn't die. By the way, where is the cleaner? Or cleaners? Oughtn't we to have a word with them?'

Piers turned on his heel to look at the sitting room. It was nicely furnished with what looked like family pieces. No sign of modern fashions. There was a slight air of neglect, a trace of dust here and there. A small television set stood on a side table; a much smaller one than Bea might have expected from someone so wealthy.

They went through the rest of the rooms quickly. Again, they saw some nice pieces of furniture, a number of books on shelves and on a coffee table. Nothing which screamed that this was the home of a woman who could buy and sell Windsor castle and have some change left for Buckingham Palace.

'Look,' said Piers, bending over to inspect

165

where an empty space on a side table showed that something had been removed. 'There were photographs of the family here, don't you think?'

Again, the bedroom was nicely but not extravagantly furnished. Bea inspected the dressing table. 'There's no hairbrush. I suspect there's no toothbrush in the bathroom, either.' She checked the en suite. The bathroom fitments hadn't been updated for some years but were perfectly adequate. There were no toiletries in evidence there, either.

She said, 'Gordon strikes again? He came back for the things she couldn't take with her yesterday?'

Back in the bedroom she pulled open the doors of fitted cupboards. 'Clothes are excellent, but not showy. Shoes, ditto. Mrs T lived frugally, seeing no need to show off her wealth. She fled with nothing but the clothes she stood up in.'

She said, 'Gordon has some explaining to do. Shall we go?'

As they left the flat, Piers said, 'There should be a lift, right? Let's see if we can find it.' Looking closely at the opposite wall, he located a door with an unobtrusive set of buttons beside it. Hey presto! The lift arrived and they were gently lowered to the ground floor.

There was no one in the hall, though they could hear someone hoovering on one of the upper floors. There was no one in either the kitchen, or the staffroom next to it.

They went across the courtyard and into the lobby of the coach house.

Bea put a hand on Piers's arm. 'Listen!'

166

They listened. The thrum of engines had ceased. The building had a listening air.

They went up the stairs and found the trains had been stopped in their tracks. There were no lights on and the huge room seemed dark. Piers went on up to the top floor and Bea followed him.

Doors hung open. Half-empty mugs still sat on the table. Of Gordon and Hubert there was no sign.

Piers said, 'I thought Gordon was on the level, but he got us out of the way so that he could spirit Hubert away.'

'I suppose he didn't know who to trust.'

'Which tells us something about the state of affairs in the household.'

'I suppose when you're frightened, you imagine an enemy behind every closed door.'

Piers shook his head. 'Gordon didn't seem frightened to me. He seemed to me to know precisely what he was doing. Let me show you what I mean.'

He led the way downstairs and turned on the lights. 'This layout was the creation of a meticulous mind. Look how the gradients are never too steep for the trains, and how the various points intersect. The tools he keeps on that central stand are immaculate. They are placed just so, in orderly fashion. There is no evidence of haste, or of waste. This was a well-thought-out project, which took time and skill to prepare. The man who built this is not one to take chances or to act impulsively.'

Bea nodded. 'Agreed.'

'We know he helped Mrs Tredgold find and

create an alternative home. We know that it took months to do. We know he's been in touch with her today. If Ahmed had not died, I suspect Mrs Tredgold would not have wished to move so quickly . . . which leads me to wonder what other plans those two have been hatching.'

'To get Hubert safely to a therapist?'

'She couldn't take him with her yesterday because—'

'She fled with just the clothes she stood up in. But she rang Gordon and asked him to fetch one or two things from her flat and rescue Hubert. I don't know what they intended to do with him: a hospital? A care home? But, judging from what we see here, Gordon intends to return.'

'He does if his pyjamas are under his pillow. I'll just take a look, shall I?' Piers shot back up the stairs to investigate and returned, nodding. 'Yes, they're here. So what do we do now?'

Bea looked at her watch. 'We report to Mrs Tredgold and have some lunch. My ward, Bernice, will be coming home this afternoon for the weekend. We have to get back in time for that.'

Piers brightened. 'I could manage a steak-and-kidney pudding, with spinach and mashed potatoes. Or a chicken pie, with carrots and baked potatoes. Or—'

Bea held up her hand and he stopped.

A key had turned in the lock of the door below, and someone – a woman – called out, 'Hello?'

'Hello!' said Bea, going to the head of the stairs.

A spry-looking woman in her forties hove into view. She was wearing a T-shirt and jogging trousers and carried a bunch of keys in her hand.

'I'm Maggie,' said the newcomer. 'You must be Mrs Abbot, right? And her partner? Mr Gordon rang to say he was expecting you, and that you were bringing him a suitcase or something. Is that right? Ah, I see it is. Thanks. He said he had to go out but he'd be back later. Gives me time to have a bit of a clean around. When he's here, he doesn't half get in the way, but that's men for you, isn't it?'

Maggie picked up the dirty mugs and took them out to the kitchen, where there was a sink full of dirty dishes.

Bea said, 'When will he be back?'

'Dunno, love. He didn't say. I hope it's not too soon. I'm all behindhand, what with the goings-on at the big house and all. I've got a good two hours' work to do here and that means I'll get caught up in the rush hour going home.'

'What goings-on?' said Piers.

'What's it to you, eh? We've been told, I dunno how many times, not to gossip, and look where it landed my friend June, eh?'

'Where did it land her?'

'Out on her ear, that's what. I need this job so if you don't mind pushing off, I can get on with things.' She ran hot water and clattered dishes.

Bea said, 'I run a domestic agency and I'm always looking for good workers. Do you think you might ask June to contact me if I left you my card?'

Maggie's hands slowed. She took a dish out of the sink and dried it. Thinking.

She said, 'It's true June could do with another job. Her husband's a waste of space – why she ever married him, I don't know. Her daughter's worse than useless and the grandchildren all need shoes and that. It's a never-ending battle, innit?'

'It is,' said Bea, fishing a card out of her handbag and handing it over. 'Do I understand, like Kit Crossley, June wasn't given a reference from the Tredgolds? I'm going to try to find Kit another job.'

'My lips are zipped. Right?' said Maggie, whose sharp eyes saw further than most. She took the card and read it. 'You're telling me that Kit's been to see you?'

'He says his mum's doing as well as can be expected. He cooked us lunch. He believes he was wrongfully sacked. I'll help him if I can.'

Maggie stowed the card away. 'June got the same treatment as Kit, if you know what I mean. I'm flaming furious about it, because she never, ever did what they said.'

'Am I right in thinking she used to clean Mrs Tredgold's rooms? And possibly Hubert's, too?'

'Zip!' Maggie drew her hand across her lips. And then nodded.

Bea said, 'Mrs Tredgold asked us to speak to everyone here. She wants them to know she's putting the house on the market, but that everyone who worked for her will get a bonus when it's sold.'

Maggie's hands stilled in the washing-up water. 'That's like her. She's all right, is she? I mean, we worry about her, we really do. That business of the cats . . .!'

'Yes, she'd like your opinion on that.'

A moment's thought, and then, 'I really must

170

get on. So much to do and I've got to get back to feed my crew. Lazy lot that they are – they'd live on junk food if I let them.'

'Understood,' said Bea. 'We'll be on our way, then.'

A new voice broke in. 'What, are you still here? Maggie, have you been gossiping?'

A cut-glass voice, educated but sharp. The younger of the two Andrews women – was she really called Mercy? – had come up the stairs behind them. She had a smartphone in her hand and it was raised to her ear. She spoke into the phone. 'Yes, they're still here, and with Maggie.'

Bea said smoothly, 'Ah, Mercy, isn't it? Gordon asked us to bring some of Hubert's things over for him but he's not here. Do you know what's happened to him? Maggie says she hasn't a clue. Maggie has not been helpful, but perhaps you know how to contact him?'

Mercy said, 'I really have no idea. Maggie, I thought you didn't have time to do Gordon's place.'

'Nor have I, really. I'll give it a lick and a promise and then I'll be off, and it will be all the quicker if these people didn't come round bothering me.' Maggie had gone back to her washing-up.

Mercy said, 'Well, if there's nothing further, Mrs Abbot? And your partner, is it? Let me show you out. I understand you have some paper or other for me to sign. We can deal with it on our way back through the big house.' She began to descend the stairs. She was wearing trainers, which was why they hadn't heard her before.

171

She was also continuing to talk on her phone. 'Yes, they're on their way out now . . . Yes, I remember. I'll sign the affidavit before they leave and yes, yes . . . Of course I'll read the paper through before I sign it.'

Mercy led the way across the courtyard and back into the house. The kitchen now contained a lanky man with a big nose and a thin boy of indeterminate age. They were wearing kitchen gear and occupied in sorting out a delivery of vegetables. There was no urgency in their movements, and neither man nor boy looked particularly clean.

Bea thought that if they'd come to her for a job she'd have marked them at D minus rather than A plus. No wonder the Tredgolds had asked her to find them replacements.

Mercy nodded to the kitchen staff but didn't speak. Leaving the kitchen behind, she opened the door to the staffroom and ushered Bea and Piers inside. This area had been furnished comfortably enough with easy chairs and a kitchenette area. Dirty mugs and plates stood around in disarray. Mercy said 'Tck!' and looked black.

Bea thought someone was going to get it in the neck for leaving the room like that. The Tredgolds had asked for a cleaner as well, hadn't they?

Mercy cleared a low table and indicated Bea and Piers take a seat. 'The paperwork, if you please?'

Bea handed it over.

Mercy read each page through. She signed the affidavit and handed it back to Bea. 'I didn't sleep here that night. I like to get away after office hours. I'm happy to sign, saying that I was not here.'

Piers said, 'Do you have a theory as to who killed the cats?'

A cool stare, without emotion. 'That was shocking. No, I didn't even see the bodies. I only heard about it later, after the gardener had buried them. And no, I have no idea who'd do such a thing.'

Bea was amused. It wasn't often that women failed to respond to Piers. She said, 'You don't care for cats yourself?'

A shrug. 'I'd like a dog sometime in the future. I prefer dogs.'

'Do you know of anyone in the house who doesn't like cats?'

'The previous chef, I suppose. He was always complaining about the cats finding their way into his kitchen. He fed them titbits, so what did he expect?'

'Anyone else?'

'One of the cleaners said they gave her hay fever.'

'The cleaner who's recently been sacked?'

A stare. 'No, not her. One of the others. There's three cleaners work here full-time at the moment, and we should have four. Each of them is responsible for two floors, or one floor and the coach house.'

'You saw that Mrs Tredgold is putting the house on the market. You understand that the staff will get a bonus when the house is sold. I suppose you'll be looking for another job?'

'I might travel a bit. I've always wanted to do so.'

'And now you can, with the bonus you'll get when the house is sold. How much do you think your bonus will be?'

'I have no idea.' Mercy rose, indicating the interview was finished. 'I'll let you out of the front door, shall I? I suppose you can order a taxi from there.'

As they went through the hall, there was a commotion on the landing above. Mercy looked up with narrowed eyes but made no comment.

Bea hung back, thinking she heard raised voices, but Mercy was anxious to get rid of them. She pressed numbers into an electronic pad by the front door. 'I haven't all day . . .'

Piers and Bea passed out into the sunlit courtyard and the door closed behind them.

Actually the sun was not shining, but the day seemed brighter now they had left the house behind. The gates from the courtyard to the street swung open and they walked through to the pavement. Street noises came as a relief. Signs of life appeared. Cars passed by. A couple of dog walkers chatted together, an elderly woman got into a black taxi, a helmeted moped driver waited at the kerb while his passenger mounted behind him.

Piers had his smartphone out. 'I'll summon an Uber, shall I?'

Bea looked back at the house. 'Your charms didn't work on Mercy Andrews, did they?'

'Mm? No, she must bat for the other side. Where shall we eat?'

'Anywhere, so long as it doesn't take too long.'

The moped revved up and swooped down the road towards them.

The passenger swung an arm out . . .

Bea felt the splash of liquid on her face and throat . . .

The moped roared off into the distance.

Bea screamed and dropped everything she'd been holding . . .

Her eyes! She rubbed at the liquid.

She couldn't open one of her eyes!

She was going to be blind!

Her skin!

She scrubbed at her face.

Sticky!

Piers held her hands away from her face. She fought him off but he persisted. He was saying something but she couldn't hear for the screaming in her head.

Her own voice screaming.

'Call nine-nine-nine.' A man's voice. 'Where's my phone? I'm all fingers and thumbs.'

Piers let Bea go. He was saying something, but she couldn't make sense of it.

She wasn't the only one screaming. A woman was yelling, 'Next time, it'll be acid!'

My face! My eyes!

An excited voice, 'Did you see?'

A woman. 'Did you catch the number plate?'

'Police and ambulance! Yes, an acid attack . . . What's the name of this street?'

A babel of voices, giving the name of the street.

Bea felt her knees give way. She sank to the pavement, leaning against the gates of the Tredgold house. *I'm in shock! I'm going to lose my sight!*

Hard heels on the pavement. 'We need water. Who's got a bottle of water?'

A car drew up. 'Has she been knocked over? Is it a heart attack?'

'The police are coming.'

'And the ambulance. Oh, oh! I feel sick!'

Not half as sick as me. I can't open my right eye. I'm going to pass out.

'Bea, listen to me!' Piers, close to. 'It's not acid!'

'Water? You want water? I've got half a bottle. Here . . .'

Cool liquid on her cheek. A tissue wiping her eyelid.

An intake of breath. 'No, it's not acid, is it? It's a strange colour, isn't it?'

Piers said, 'I think it's some kind of fruit juice. It's not acid. Mango, perhaps?'

A hard finger brushed her face. 'Yes. It's quite thick. Carrot juice, maybe?'

Mango juice? Carrot juice? Then I'm not going to be blind . . . or disfigured?

Her hands were covered with the stuff. Sticky. Nasty. Yes, she could smell it, too, now that she'd calmed down a bit. She could even open her right eye a bit.

Her jacket felt horrible. Sticky. Wet. Ugh.

A siren. A paramedic in a car. 'Let's see what's happened, then. A heart attack, is it?'

Another babel of voices explaining. 'No, no . . . A moped threw . . . It's horrible! Will she lose her sight?'

A man kneeling on the pavement beside her. A quick examination. 'No, no. Did he try to snatch her handbag?'

'Handbag? Where's her handbag?'

'Has someone swiped it? Honestly, nowadays . . .!'

The paramedic was wiping her eyes and face down with some tissues. He was making a good job of it. 'There you are. A bit of swelling, but no damage done.'

Piers said, 'I've got her handbag. She'll be all right, won't she?' He sounded shaken.

'Yes, of course,' said the paramedic, loud and very sure of himself. 'It's just shock, now.'

A police car announced its arrival with its siren. The paramedic stood up and went to speak to the police.

Bea wanted nothing so much as to slide down on the pavement and go to sleep, but there were questions. And more questions. The helpful passers-by faded away one by one. One man, a dog walker, had seen the moped passenger throw something but couldn't give a good description because the driver and his passenger had been wearing black leathers and helmets. He had been so shocked when it happened that he hadn't thought to take the licence number of the moped before it had roared off round the corner.

Piers had been concentrating on getting an Uber and hadn't realized anything was wrong till Bea screamed.

Bea herself had caught a glimpse of the moped coming towards her but couldn't add anything to what the first witness had said.

'You may remember something when you've calmed down,' said the policeman. 'But they didn't get your mobile phone or your handbag, and that's what they're usually after.'

Yes, of course that's it. They wanted my phone or my handbag. Nothing else. They didn't want to . . . to . . . No, of course they were after my handbag.

If I tell the police about the Tredgolds, about having been asked to . . . No, they were after my handbag. I can't cope with any other idea.

She had an overwhelming impulse to laugh. She bent over, gasping.

My handbag, my handbag, my kingdom for a handbag. I'm going mad!

Piers got her sitting with her back to the railings . . . The back of her jacket must be in a dire state and she'd lost a shoe. Where was her shoe?

Where, oh where, has my little shoe gone?

The police were conferring with Piers, taking details of this and that. The paramedic returned to give her a quick once-over. He said, 'You'll be all right now. Take it easy for a bit, eh?'

She nodded. She knew he was right. In principle. She'd been attacked by malice aforethought and there was no great damage done except to her self-esteem.

She, the brave one, the one who sorted out other people's lives for them, had screamed like a hurt baby just because someone had thrown some fruit juice at her.

Police and paramedic were summoned to another incident and rolled away.

The Uber car appeared. Bea was helped to her feet, put into the car and driven away, leaving a couple of used tissues and an empty water bottle on the pavement to mark where the incident had taken place.

Her shoe? She couldn't see it anywhere. Perhaps Piers had picked it up and put it in his pocket? Or something.

Bea stared straight ahead, trying not to think. Not succeeding.

They were out to get you!

'Nonsense!'

They drove straight at you. There was no attempt to snatch your handbag.

'I'm not listening!'

'What did you say?' Piers was concerned about her.

She said, 'Nothing. It's way past our lunchtime. Didn't you say you were hungry?'

He didn't reply but looked surreptitiously at his watch. Was he remembering that Bernice was due that afternoon? Bea couldn't think straight. What time did Bernice usually get back on a Friday afternoon?

They didn't want you dead or they'd have mown you down. They wanted you incapacitated so that you wouldn't delve into their dirty secrets any further.

Bea closed her eyes and tried to close her mind to the voices in her head. She had been attacked in an effort to snatch her handbag. That was all. Nothing else.

She dozed off and jerked upright again only when they reached her house.

She got out, moving stiffly. One foot up and one foot down, diddle diddle dumpling, my son John. Did they teach children those old rhymes nowadays? Once upon a time there'd been a meaning to the rhyme and everyone had known

179

it. Bea wondered what had happened to 'my son John' that he limped.

Piers paid the driver and helped Bea up the stairs and into the house. He even remembered to turn off the alarm and reset it once they were in. Her office manageress, Betty, popped up to report, but on seeing the state Bea was in, shook her head and said there was nothing for anyone to worry about.

Piers said, 'Up the stairs, Bea. Into the shower, and then into bed. I'll bring you up some soup in a minute.'

She looked at the stairs. She couldn't manage them.

Throwing fruit juice at me was meant as a warning. Next time it will be . . .

'Can you manage?' asked Piers.

'Of course. I'm hunky-dory. Though I don't know what that means, exactly.'

He slipped her remaining shoe off and helped her climb the stairs. If his arm hadn't been firmly around her, she'd never have made it. He got her into her bedroom and through that into her en suite. He helped her take off her watch, her earrings and the bracelet. Then she stepped straight into the shower. Fully dressed. She didn't mind that. Her clothes were ruined, anyway.

After a minute or two, she made feeble efforts to undress and throw her clothes out of the shower. He watched her, narrow-eyed, to make sure she could do it. No sex please; we're exhausted. Both of them. He turned on the shower again, and she managed to reach the gel and soap herself all over. When it came to stepping out of the shower, she hesitated. He helped her out, wrapped her in her bath sheet, steered her back into her bedroom and over to the bed.

She said, 'I can manage.'

'No, you can't.' He helped rub her dry, found her nightgown and helped her into it, brushed her wet hair back off her face, pulled the duvet back and got her into bed. He folded the duvet back over her, lowered the blinds at the windows and departed.

She began to shiver. Delayed shock.

That was a warning. Next time . . .

Then tears came, and came, and went on coming until she slept.

Twelve

Friday early evening

Bea woke. The light in her bedroom was all wrong for the early morning. How very odd! She looked at her bedside clock. It wasn't early morning. It was still early evening. Friday was not yet over. How come?

Then she remembered.

She drew in her breath sharply. Blinked, hard.

She had been attacked. Yes, she had been targeted. Quite definitely. Nothing to do with a bag snatcher.

She moaned and pulled the duvet up over her head.

You can't hide for ever.

No, of course she couldn't. She pulled the duvet down and sat up. There was a mug of something on her bedside table. Cold. She took a cautious sip and put it down again. Chicken soup out of a tin, heated in a microwave and left for her to drink when she woke up.

She rolled her head around on her shoulders.

She remembered that Piers had brought her back and made her shower and put her to bed. Presumably it was he who'd left her the soup?

She thought: Drat the man. He's trying to take over. Then she sighed, because it was no good blaming Piers for the mess she'd got herself into.

Someone scrambled up the stairs and shot into the room, landing on her knees on the bed next to Bea. Bernice, Bea's bright teenage ward. Plaits flying. Long-legged, slender body not yet showing signs of puberty. Unbecoming school uniform. Tears in her eyes.

'He said I wasn't to disturb you, but you are awake now, aren't you? Are you all right?'

Bea pulled the girl into her arms. 'I'm fine, just fine. It knocked me out for a bit, but I'm going to be all right.' Her voice was almost normal. 'What time did you get back?'

'That idiot said I wasn't to come in, as if he had the right to tell me what to do! You are all right, aren't you?'

'Someone threw mango juice at me, that's all. Pass me my dressing gown, will you?'

'What was the Tom Cat doing to let it happen?'

Bernice refused to call Piers by his name but

always referred to him as the Tom Cat, since it was his behaviour in the direction of other women which had brought their marriage to an end years ago. Bea knew Piers was now ashamed of what he'd done, and that he was trying to get back into her favour, but the hurt had gone too deep to be healed quickly.

Since Bernice called Piers 'Tom Cat', he responded by referring to her as 'The Brat'.

Bea said, 'It was a couple of muggers. They came out of the blue. We hadn't expected anything like that. No one would. They were after my smartphone or my handbag, of course. But there's no harm done. They didn't get either.'

Bernice put her hands on her non-existent hips. 'Now you're being silly. The Tom Cat might believe that guff but I don't.'

Bea got out of bed, put on her dressing-gown, made her way slowly to the full-length mirror and shuddered. Her hair was all over the place and still slightly sticky. Her eyes looked tired. As well they might.

'I must have another shower.'

Bernice bounced off the bed. 'Promise me you won't have anything more to do with those people? They sound perfectly dreary, anyway, with their cats and their trains and their yachts. Too much money gives people a false idea of themselves.'

Bea tried to smile. 'Bernice, you will have more money than all of them put together when you grow up, but I think you'll remember you're still a human being.'

'Huh! A sense of entitlement, that's what it is.

I see it at school. Some girls think they don't have to learn anything or behave properly because they've got money.'

Bea made her way into the bathroom, slipped off her night gear and stepped into the shower. She hoped Bernice would go away and leave her in peace but feared she wouldn't.

After her second shower, Bea found a clean nightdress to wear and resumed her dressing-gown. The evening might still be young but she was too tired to dress properly.

Bernice hadn't gone away, but was sitting on the side of the bed, frowning and sucking one end of a long plait. 'The thing is, you have to take care of yourself and not take any risks nowadays because you're responsible for me. I mean, who would look after me, if you got yourself killed?'

'They were after my handbag.' Bea seated herself at her dressing table and tried to comb and finger her hair into an approximation of its usual style.

Bernice said, 'The Tom Cat told me all about it. He showed me the drawings he'd made of the people you met. He's quite good at that, isn't he? Though he should have looked after you better. I told him so, and he agreed. He said you'd got signatures from most of the family and all you need now are comments from some members of the staff, but that there's no need for you to do it yourself. Promise me you won't go back there.'

'I promise.' Bea watched her hand tremble as she picked up a lipstick.

'Oh, good,' said Bernice. Squinting at Bea to make sure she was serious.

'I promise not to go near them again,' said Bea. 'You are quite right. I don't need to go back there. I will report to Mrs Tredgold this evening and tell her that—'

'Oh, the Tom Cat has done that already. I stood over him till he did it. He doesn't think you should go back there, either.' She frowned. When Bernice frowned, her eyebrows almost met in the middle. 'You do mean it, don't you? You're not risking it?'

'I mean it,' said Bea. 'I'm grateful to Piers for reporting to Mrs Tredgold. I feel sorry for her – Mrs Tredgold, I mean – because her family are a load of scavengers and spongers.' She considered what she'd just said. 'Can one have a load of scavengers and spongers? Well, I don't see why not.' She hadn't made too bad a job of putting on her lipstick, but she was not going to risk poking mascara into her eyes. One eye still looked red.

'Oh, good,' said Bernice, again. She still didn't look happy. She doubted Bea's promise, didn't she?

Bea didn't. Her innards turned to jelly at the thought of returning to the Tredgold mansion. She couldn't do it. She really could not. Every nerve screamed with fear when she thought about it.

'The thing is,' said Bernice, 'that some people really don't know when to stop. They keep on keeping on when there's no hope of success. They have foolish ideas about sacrificing themselves for some romantic dream. Poetry is full of them. Last Hope Battle. Stupid men running into a fight when they should be running away—'

'You prefer a tactical withdrawal?'

'Yes. That's only sensible, isn't it? I mean, when the odds are overwhelming there is no point in dying in some lone attack on superior odds. Right?'

Bea shivered. Bernice understood that death was stalking the Tredgold house. She also understood that Bea would go the extra mile to see that justice was done. Bernice was afraid that that was exactly what Bea was going to do.

Bea, on the other hand, had no intention of returning to the Danger Zone. She said, 'Agreed.'

'Oh. Well, good.' Bernice still didn't sound convinced.

Bea couldn't think what else she should say to reassure the child.

Bernice swung her plait back over her shoulder. 'I think you should get back into bed. You look tired. I'll bring you up some supper in a minute.'

Telling someone they look tired makes them feel a hundred and one. Bea immediately felt a hundred and two. She said, 'Who's cooking?'

'Tom Cat. You know I can't cook.'

Bea slowly made her way back to bed and sank down on to it. 'Perhaps you should learn. Just in case you're ever stranded with no servants to provide for you.'

Bernice flushed. For a moment Bea thought the child was going to lash out at her.

That was harsh, but the girl has to learn the realities of life or she'll end up like Petra Tredgold with a sense of entitlement which cuts her off from the rest of the world.

'Sorry,' said Bernice, in a tiny voice. She slid off the bed and left the room.

Bea relaxed. For a count of ten.

Then her brain started up. It said, 'Coward.'

I'm not running away. It's a tactical withdrawal. I have every right to get out of this situation. No one can be expected to face an acid attack.

Silence.

She felt tears running down her cheeks and hadn't the strength to brush them away.

Dear Lord, you cannot expect me to go back there. You know it was a warning. You know what's going on in that house. It's evil! Well, I suppose not everyone in that house is evil, but there's a lot of evil there.

Isn't facing evil something that Christians are supposed to do?

Well, yes. Perhaps. If they're wearing the right sort of armour. But I'm only a poor, weak woman who . . .

He laughed. She heard Him laugh, quite distinctly.

She managed a smile, with some reluctance. *All right, I know what you mean, and I'm usually not the fainting, die-away sort, am I? But this is different.*

How different? Remember the Knight's prayer?

She did, vaguely. As a child she'd attended a Sunday school in the local church, and every week they'd recited the Knight's prayer. She'd used it in her morning prayers for many years until one day she'd really thought about what she was saying and had been so frightened that she'd stopped using it. No. It was too much of a commitment to make. Anyway, she was more of a bedtime prayers person nowadays.

He said: Say it.

'My lord, I am ready on the threshold of this new day to go forth, armed with your power, to right wrongs, to overcome evil, to suffer wounds and endure pain if need be . . .'

And there it was. She was not brave enough to suffer wounds and endure pain for someone else. No, definitely not.

Mrs Tredgold cried.

Nothing to do with me!

They drove away all the people who loved her. They shouted at her. They tried to make out she wasn't capable of managing her own affairs.

IT HAS NOTHING TO DO WITH ME!

She came to you for help. She was at her wits' end. And you propose to walk away and leave her to their tender mercies?

She's safe enough where she is.

For how long? How long would it take you, Bea Abbot, to find out where she'd gone? Half an hour? Ten minutes? What's to stop the efficient Ms Andrews from putting her mind to the problem? Items were sent away for repair. Ms Andrews would have arranged that, wouldn't she? Items were not returned to the old address but diverted to the new flat. One phone call to the repairers, enquiring when the goods were to be returned to the house, would give Ms Andrews the new address.

So what are you going to do about it?

Nothing. I can't do anything.

Silence. Then, *Finish the prayer.*

'. . . to suffer wounds and endure pain if need be, but in all things to serve you boldly, faithfully, joyfully, that at the end of the day's labour, kneeling for your blessing, you may find no blot upon my shield.'

Bea said, 'I'm no warrior. I'm no soldier. You can't expect me to expose myself to wounds just because a silly old woman can't control her family.'

A long, reproachful silence.

Bea said, crossly, 'I am NOT a soldier. I didn't sign up for that.'

Didn't you? Something like a sigh.

Bea said all the swear words she could think of. There weren't very many but she gave them some welly, ending, 'So there!'

She thought she heard some more laughter, but she might easily have been mistaken.

There was a kerfuffle at the door and in came Bernice, jostling Piers to get in first, both carrying trays of food. 'We thought we'd eat up here.'

Bea had to smile. 'How decadent. I can't remember when I last ate a proper meal – not just breakfast – in bed. I suppose it was when I was very small and had chickenpox. But I didn't have an appetite then and I do now.'

Piers helped her sit upright and put a tray containing a bowl of stew, vegetables and rice before her, with a spoon to eat it with. 'Marks and Spencer's best. I think it's hot enough. We had a bit of an argument about what power your microwave has but I think it's all right. We'll have ours on our laps as well.' He retreated to the dressing-table stool to eat his.

Bernice seated herself next to Bea on the bed and tackled her dish. 'Why don't you have one of those televisions at the end of your bed that rise up out of nowhere, so that you can watch it late at night?'

'I'm usually too tired to watch anything when I climb into bed at night.' Bea tasted the food and decided that yes, she was indeed hungry.

Bernice frowned at some thought of her own. 'I thought you'd say that a bedroom is meant for other things.'

Bea and Piers suspended operations on their food, trying to grapple with the way this conversation might develop.

Bernice shrugged. 'But what do I know about it, yet?'

Piers said, cautiously, 'Plenty of time for that.'

'This is excellent stew,' said Bea. 'I didn't realize how hungry I was.'

'Chocolate sauce on a banana with cream for afters,' said Bernice. 'I've always wanted to try that. Tom Cat says it's a mishmash and won't be any good but what I say is that if you don't try, you'll never know if you like it or not.'

'True,' murmured Bea. 'Piers, did you indeed ring Mrs Tredgold?'

'I did. She was upset that you'd had such a nasty thing happen to you. She says she doesn't want you taking the matter any further. You're to send her the affidavits you've obtained so far and someone else will get the rest at a later date.'

Bernice licked her spoon clean. 'Your kitchen needs a good clean. You should have an Alexa.' She spoke in a singing voice. 'Alexa, clean the kitchen floor.'

Bea said. 'My cleaner didn't come this week. Toothache.'

Piers joined in the make-believe. 'Alexa, turn the telly on, Channel Four.'

Bea picked up her cue. 'Alexa, draw the curtains.'

Bernice bounced on the bed. 'Alexa, run a bath for me. Oh, wait a minute: Alexa, there's a leak in the tub! Alexa, call the plumber.'

Piers snapped his fingers. 'Alexa, tell the plumber he can't come in with dirty boots on.'

Bernice crowed, 'Alexa, put the plumber in the bath and scrub him clean.'

Bea found herself laughing. 'Alexa, the bathwater has overflowed, and we're all going to be washed away. Call the lifeboat!'

Such nonsense, but it passes the time nicely. They both know that I'm going to go into battle tomorrow but we're not going to talk about it, are we? Alexa, I need full body armour, size sixteen. And a pepper spray, perhaps?

She pushed her empty plate away. 'Thank you, both of you.' She made an attempt to get out of bed. 'I'd better get up and sort the kitchen.'

'No, you don't,' said Piers. 'I'll feed the dishwasher and the Brat will mop the floor.'

'What!' Bernice looked shocked. Then she shrugged and said, 'All right, then. If I have to.'

Bea leaned back on her pillows. 'Thank you, both of you. I'll be all right now.'

Bernice, who was not given to displays of affection, threw her arms around Bea and hugged her. And then sprang away with reddened cheeks. She picked up her tray, crammed dishes and cutlery on it with scant regard for breakages and shot out of the door.

Piers bent over Bea to stroke her cheek. 'I'm sorry I didn't look after you better.'

Bea shook her head. 'Neither of us saw that coming.'

'Bernice has given me a right rollicking and quite right too. I'll clear up downstairs and go home for the night, but I'll be back in the morning. All right?'

'They were after my handbag.'

'If you say so.'

When he'd gone, she stared into the future, repeating to herself, 'They were after my handbag.' That way, she might calm herself enough to get to sleep.

Thirteen

Saturday morning

Bea surprised herself by sleeping a reasonable number of hours and managed to get out of bed only a little after her usual time.

As she dressed and made up her face she heard Bernice run the shower in her rooms at the top of the house, and soon after that she heard Piers turn the key in the lock of the front door and deal with the alarm.

Bea wondered who was on duty that morning in the agency. Was it Betty? In which case, there would be no need to worry about work that day.

Scrutinizing her face in the mirror, Bea thought

no one would really notice that her eyelid was still slightly swollen, but her hair! Oh dear! She would have to work hard to make it lie in its usual style.

Should she wear the bracelet Piers had given her? No, not today.

She went down the stairs to find Piers was about to bring her up a mug of tea. She took it from him with thanks. He'd changed into one of his grey silk shirts and grey trousers. He seemed all right till you looked into his eyes and saw there a mirror of the fear that she was trying to keep at bay. She tried to smile, to reassure him.

He smiled back. A mere twitch of the lips. One coward checking with another.

Bernice was already in the kitchen, dressed in weekend T-shirt and jeans. She was turning over the pages of Piers's sketchbook while slurping down some cornflakes. 'Morning,' she said. 'This woman, here. She looks like the maths teacher in my old school. She thought she was the bee's knees but she was past it, poor dear. Don't know what happened to her. Got the sack, I suppose.'

'Who?' said Piers. 'Oh, that's Charlotte Tredgold. Wannabe poet and journalist.'

'Sounds about right. This man, what's his name? Edgar? I didn't know people still called their children by such stupid names. He's a right idiot, isn't he? Looks like the father of one of my school friends. Lost all his money in some scam or other, serve him right. I was sorry for his daughter, though. She was all right. Brainy. She'll probably make it to uni, no matter what school they have to send her to, now.'

Bea decided that Bernice was too sharp for her own good. She sipped tea, thinking that, with luck, she might live.

Bernice shoved her empty bowl away and turned a page. Silence for a moment, and then, in a sober tone, she said, 'Right little cow, this one.' She held up Piers's drawing of Petra Tredgold. 'We've got a couple like that at school, been sent to us after they'd disgraced themselves elsewhere. The stories they tell! To hear them talk, they've been at it like rabbits since they were twelve. Big shock coming to our boarding school. They can't get away with flouting rules as they used to.'

'How did they get away with it before?'

'No one checked up on what time they were supposed to leave school, and if they said they had a sleepover, their parents believed them. The moment they left school – that is, if they'd bothered to turn up in the first place – they'd change clothes and go out on the town.'

'Surely they couldn't get away with that for long.'

'They said that if they were found out they only had to cry and pretend to be sorry for their parents to forgive them. Their old school took them back each time because their parents threw more and more money into the kitty, until one day they went too far and got themselves expelled.'

Bea pressed her fingers to her temples. She was getting a headache.

Piers handed her a glass of orange juice.

Orange juice? She forced herself to drink some. It was not mango juice. Not. Definitely not.

Bernice waved the sketchbook around,

upsetting Winston the cat, who had thought he might be safe on the table for a while.

Bea picked Winston up, gave him a perfunctory stroke and set him on the floor. Piers got out the sachets of cat food and gave one to Winston. 'There's nothing new about teenage girls misbehaving. The thing is if they look eighteen, they can fool most people into thinking what they do is legal.'

Bernice said, 'I've heard they use their smartphones to find boys, especially boys with transport or access to drugs. Our head wants to take the phones away but the girls say that would infringe their human rights. I don't know who's going to win that one. The thing is, you can't stop people being stupid, can you? They go home at weekends and if you think they've spent time doing their homework and are neatly tucked up in bed by ten then you've got another think coming. Sex and drugs, that's all they think about. They're counting the days till they can leave school.' She sniffed. 'Is that bacon you're cooking? I was thinking of going vegetarian but maybe I won't start just yet.'

Bea poured cereal into a bowl and added milk but no sugar. 'You're not interested in all that, are you?'

'No, but I keep my ears open. I like to know what's going on. The two I'm thinking of won't be around when exam times comes. They'll be on holiday with their parents somewhere in the sun. For "educational purposes". Unless they're down the abortion clinic, of course. Though usually they know how to prevent that.'

Piers cracked eggs into a bowl. 'I think I'm shocked.'

Bernice turned a page or two over. 'This girl, now. What's her name? Carly? Trying to make out she's up for it but she's like one of the hangers-on to the girls I've been telling you about. Thinks she's up for it but isn't. Not yet, anyway. This Carly's not at a private school, is she? Comprehensive, more like.'

She turned back to the page which showed Petra and squinted at it. 'You've pencilled in her eyebrows. Has she had them tattooed? Looks like it. Probably doing Botox for her lips already. Has she got hair extensions? They all want to look the same, don't they? Straight hair, thick eyebrows, boobs out to here. You can't tell one from the other. Mad, innit?'

Piers dished up scrambled eggs and mushrooms on toast for himself and Bea, with a side plate of bacon for Bernice. He offered more tea all round. Bea wasn't sure she could manage any of it. She noticed Piers was picking at his plateful, too. Bernice, of course, attacked her lot with relish. Bernice didn't know what nerves meant.

Unfortunately, Bea did.

Toast and marmalade. Another mug of tea. Somehow Bea got the lot down.

Bernice clattered her knife on to her plate. 'I'm thinking of having my hair cut short. It's such a bore having to put it in plaits. No one else has plaits at school.'

It was Bernice who had insisted on keeping her hair unshorn and putting it into plaits. Now she'd changed her mind. Understandable? Yes, probably. But. Bea said, 'Long, straight hair is fashionable. You don't have to have it in a plait.'

'I like it out of the way when I'm concentrating on something. Besides, what do I need with fashion?'

Mm. She had a point. Some people follow fashion. Bernice could probably be a trendsetter if she put her mind to it. Bea said, 'All right. I'll make an appointment for you at my hairdressers and you can discuss with him what style would suit you best.'

Once her point was gained, Bernice moved on. 'We'll all need dark glasses today. I'm not sure I've got any here. Can you lend me some, Bea? And a scarf, perhaps?'

'What for?' said Piers, stacking dirty plates in the dishwasher. 'You're not coming with me to the Tredgolds.'

Bernice picked up the kitchen scissors and made as if to saw at her plait. 'Of course I'm coming. You couldn't keep me away.'

Bea said, 'No, Bernice. We can't take you.'

'You need me,' said Bernice. 'I'm good at working out what people are like. You can stay at home and I'll go with Piers.'

Bea said, 'Leave your hair alone. I said I'd take you to my hairdresser, if you're sure you want a cut.'

Bernice knew how to bargain. 'When will you take me? This morning?'

'Not this morning,' said Bea. She didn't know when she'd come to the decision to return to the Tredgolds, but there it was, sitting solidly in her stomach. She only hoped she wouldn't sick up her breakfast.

Bernice pretended to saw at her plait. 'What have you got on that you can't go with me this morning? You promised me you wouldn't go back to the Tredgolds, and you are keen on keeping promises, aren't you?'

'I know, but this is something I really have to do. Be a good girl and look after yourself this morning and I'll see if we can get an appointment at the hairdressers this afternoon.'

'You can't leave me alone in this big house. I might get up to all sorts of mischief. I'm coming with you.'

'No,' said Piers and Bea at once.

Bernice shook her head so that her plaits whizzed around. 'You are such children, both of you. We wear dark glasses and carry big bottles of water with us, right?'

'No!' said Bea. 'Look, they were after my handbag, that's all.'

Piers and Bernice looked at one another. Their eyes dropped to Bea's landline.

Piers said, 'Your landline rang last night when we were making supper. It went to voicemail. Someone said, "You've been warned" and rang off. The number had been hidden.'

Bernice said, 'Tom Cat tried reporting it to the police, but they couldn't find the original report and want him to go in and make a complaint. Waste of time. We know who sent it, and we know who was on the moped.'

Bea said, 'We can't *know*!'

'Oh, come on!' said Bernice, slipping off her

stool on to the floor. 'Of course we know. I took one look at the sketches and I knew. So we leave in half an hour?'

As she was going out of the door, Piers called after her. 'Tidy your room and leave your shower clean!'

'Phut!' said Bernice, going down the hall. 'You can't expect me to do the cleaner's work.'

Bea raised her voice. 'My cleaner's got tooth-ache and couldn't come this week. And yes, you will be able to employ someone to do your cleaning for you when you grow up, but you ought to know how to do it properly, so that you can spot any mistakes. This morning, I'll do my shower and you do yours.'

Bernice grumbled all the way up the stairs. Maybe she'd clean the shower and maybe she wouldn't.

Piers said, 'With dark glasses, big bottles of water and some tissues, we'll be safe.'

Bea nodded. The lump in her stomach had travelled up to her throat. She couldn't remember ever having been so frightened before. Oh, perhaps the day she'd got lost in the crowds on Oxford Street? She'd been six years old. A nice man had said he'd look after her and gave her a bar of chocolate, but then it turned out he wasn't so nice and wanted to give her a cuddle. But a woman had rescued her and then the police came and said her parents had been looking everywhere for her and they all went home, rather cross and tearful and she'd never let go of their hands again. Well, not until they died, many years later.

We won't think about dying now. Or about losing your sight.

Piers said to take a taxi. So they did, armed with bottles of water and dark glasses and scarves round their necks.

'Who do you still have to see?' said Bernice, looking up at the imposing frontage of the Tredgold mansion.

'I have to get a signature from Gordon and Hubert, if possible. And then, from any members of staff who happen to be around. Ms Andrews, the housekeeper, for a start. And that's it. In and out in half an hour.' Bea rang the bell and was in the process of announcing herself when the big gates swung open, as if she'd spoken a magic word. They passed through into the courtyard, only to be closely followed by a furniture van with three men up in the cabin. The gates closed behind them.

The front door opened and Ms Andrews stood there, neatly garbed, with a clipboard in her hand. She ignored Bea and her party to concentrate on the van driver. 'You're late. You should have been here an hour ago. All the small stuff, the china and linen has been packed up already, but there's some big pieces you'll have to bring down your-selves. You have a list of them already, I believe?'

She waved them through into the hall.

Ms Andrews then transferred her attention to Bea, to say, 'You again? Oh. Yes, I suppose you need . . .' Then she focused on Bernice. 'The man I know. Who is this?'

'My ward. She is with me for the weekend. We won't trouble you for long.'

'No, you won't. We're busy today. Well, you'd better come on in. I can spare you a minute, but just don't get in the way.'

Piers and Bernice followed Bea into the hall and stopped short. Various cardboard boxes and suitcases stood around in the hall, leaving a passageway through them to the stairs.

The three furniture removal men stood there, looking helpless.

'Use the lift,' said Ms Andrews, indicating the correct door. 'And mind the paintwork.' The men crammed themselves into the lift and the doors closed behind them.

'Who's moving out?' asked Bea.

'No business of yours. Now, I managed to rescue the affidavit you needed me to sign.' Ms Andrews pulled it out from one of the papers on her clipboard and read it through again. She said, 'I did sleep here that night. I do not know who killed the cats. Ahmed committed suicide, and I really don't understand what all the fuss is about.'

She produced a pen and, resting the clipboard against the newel post of the staircase, signed the paper.

Bea and Piers signed as witnesses. Bernice chewed the end of her plait.

Ms Andrews said, 'Now you may go.'

'I still need to get signatures from Gordon and Hubert.'

Ms Andrews consulted her clipboard. 'Oh yes. Gordon said he'd be in this morning. You may go over to the coach house and collect his statement.'

'And Hubert—'

'I'm not sure where he is.' The faintest of frowns. 'He might be over with Gordon, still. You can try there.'

'Also the daily staff, the cleaners and the gardener.'

'They know nothing, but I suppose you have to do your job. They don't normally work on a Saturday morning but we have had an emergency and most of them have come in to help out. They will be having their morning break in a few minutes, and I'll ask them to meet you in the staffroom.'

A hard, young voice rang out from the landing. 'Who's there? Ms Andrews, you said they wouldn't disturb me but a man has just walked into my bedroom, just like that! I gave him what for, I can tell you!'

'A mistake, Petra.' Ms Andrews was almost conciliatory. 'The removal men will be gone in a short while.'

Petra appeared at the top of the stairs to scowl down on Bea and company. 'Oh, it's them again, is it? I thought the old dear from the agency would have got the message by now. Not wanted. She's been warned, hasn't she?'

Bea's fingers curled into claws and she heard a sharp intake of breath from Piers.

Petra leaned on the newel post at the top of the stairs. 'And who's the whippet with them, eh? Another skivvy come to apply for a cleaning job? Well, I can tell you straight off that she's not good enough to deal with my toilet.'

Bernice put her hands on her hips and seemed to grow a couple of inches in height. 'My name is Bernice Holland, and I could buy and sell you and have some change over for Mayfair, if I wished to do so. Yes, I know how to clean a toilet because if you're going to have servants eventually, it's best to know how to do things properly. I go to school because I want to know how to manage the money I'll inherit when I leave university, and I know there's a whole lot more to doing that properly than sitting on my backside and ordering other people around.'

Petra reddened. 'Are you trying to make out that I . . .? Why, you dirty little piece of—'

Bernice interrupted her. 'Want to hear your fortune told? I can tell where you're going to end up and that's on the drugs heap. Or perhaps you'll die having one too many backstreet abortions? Probably you'll still be in your teens when you damage yourself so much you won't be able to claw your way back to health.'

'How dare you! Why, you undersized piece of—'

'I dare because you've threatened me and mine. I may not be able to prove it, but you know and I know what you did yesterday! You may have your family under your thumb and only need to throw a tantrum to get your own way here, but it's a great wide world out there and if you go on this way you'll soon find out money doesn't protect criminals for long. I feel sorry for you, almost, because it's not entirely your fault that you're a waste of space.'

Petra was bug-eyed and incoherent. 'You . . . you . . .!'

Bea and Piers were spellbound, as was Ms Andrews.

Bernice went on, 'I've been lucky. I've got a loving family and people who look after me and care for me enough to tell me off when I go wrong. I've got brains enough to know that that's worth all your doing it with a bit of rough—'

'How did you know that—?'

'Obvious, isn't it? Moped equals rough. You're not old enough to have a licence yet and you're not skilled enough to hit a target fair and square.'

'You can't just—!'

'You're just a common or garden bully,' said Bernice, 'but you don't scare me because I can see what's going to happen to you in the future. So if you don't want to end up in the trash can, you'd better take a good look at yourself.'

Petra shrieked, 'Get her out of here!'

Ms Andrews started to say something to Petra about calming down, but the girl was incandescent with rage. 'I'm going to tear her to—!'

'No fisticuffs, please.' That was Piers, who broke the spell which had bound them by going to the foot of the stairs and looking up at Petra. 'Now, then. You're both out of order. Bernice, you're a guest in this house, so remember your manners. Petra, you started the fight and if you got the worst of it, you've only yourself to blame.'

Petra pointed at Bernice. 'Get her out of here, now!'

Bernice said, 'Humph!' and put her nose in the air. She was not going to leave. Not she!

Petra descended the stairs, thumping on each step in her clumpy, high-wedged shoes. Her hands balled into fists.

The two girls stared at one another with narrowed eyes.

Petra made a sudden rush at Bernice, who side-stepped and let the girl go on past her to stumble into the wall.

Petra screamed and turned back on Bernice. 'I'll get you, see if I don't!'

Bernice didn't even bother to put her hands up. She said, 'Don't even think of attacking me! I've been taking classes in judo and, judging by the spare tyre hanging round your hips, you've done no exercise for months.'

'Get rid of her!' Petra collapsed on to the floor. Tears of temper squeezed out of her eyes and fell down her cheeks.

Ms Andrews drew in her breath but made no move to help the girl.

Bea decided it was time to bring this unseemly incident to a close. She said, 'Did you say we might have a word with some other members of staff today, Ms Andrews? It would save us having to return on Monday.'

'Look where you're going!' A sharp voice from above caused them all to look up. There'd been some bumping and thumping going on while Bernice had been baiting Petra, and now two men descended the stairs, carrying a fragile table between them. It had been encased in bubble wrap but not properly secured. At the same time the lift doors opened and a man struggled out with an odd-shaped and unwieldy object which had been packaged the same way.

Ms Andrews moved swiftly to restore order.

'Petra, that's enough. Mrs Abbot, would you kindly go through to see Gordon, now. As for the portrait painter, he can take the girl to the staffroom and wait there till the rest of the staff have their break.'

Piers raised his eyebrows at Bea, who thought that if they divided up their enquiries they'd be through more quickly and nodded. With narrowed eyes, Bernice watched Petra make her way back up the stairs . . . having to step aside for one of the cleaners, who was pulling a large suitcase down after her.

Bea asked, 'Who's moving out?'

Ms Andrews didn't reply but almost pushed Bea and her party out of the hall and down the corridor to the kitchen quarters.

Bea said, quietly, to Piers, 'That was Maggie bringing down the big suitcase, the cleaner we met at Gordon's place yesterday. Do you think it's Hubert who's leaving?'

Piers shrugged. Equally softly, he said, 'We'll meet up in the kitchen, in about half an hour?' And to Bernice, in an ordinary voice, 'Are you going to stick with me? I'd be interested to hear what you make of things.'

Bernice nodded. 'I suppose.'

'In here.' Ms Andrews opened the door to the staffroom and watched Piers and Bernice go through. Then she shut that door and led the way into the big kitchen at the end.

The tall man in chef's garb was there, as was his spindle-shanked helper. It looked to Bea as if they'd been watching a programme on a small iPad the moment before the door opened but had jumped to attention when they saw Ms Andrews and had started prepping some vegetables. They looked at Ms Andrews with identical wary expressions and ignored Bea altogether.

Ms Andrews opened the door to the covered yard and indicated that Bea go through it, rather like a prison warder making sure the inmate did as they were told. In this case Bea was only too delighted to get out of the house and take some deep breaths of fresh air. The atmosphere inside seemed to be getting worse.

She realized she had forgotten to get Hubert's keys from Piers, but fortunately the door into the coach house was not locked. As she climbed the stairs she listened out for the hum of the model trains chugging but heard the strains of classical music – a guitar solo? – instead. There was no sign of life in the model train room, so she climbed the next set of stairs to Gordon's living quarters.

Emerging into the living room, she found Gordon standing beside an open cardboard box and scratching his head. 'Back again?' he said.

Was he packing for himself, or for Hubert?

Bea said, 'Is Hubert still with you?'

'Thanks for getting me his overnight stuff. No, he's not here. He wandered off. Gone back to his own place, I think. Or visiting a friend? I forget what he said last. He changes his mind every five minutes, poor chap.'

'You'd taken some of his things out of his flat before you sent us there yesterday?'

'Did I? Or did he? He was coming and going. Can't sit still for a minute.'

Was Gordon making this up? He was good at

misdirection, wasn't he? Bea said, 'I understand why Hubert was upset about the cats being killed. I also understand why you might have helped him move out.'

'Me?' Rounded eyes portrayed innocence. Or, rather, his version of innocence.

Bea insisted, 'Just tell me one thing: is Hubert safe wherever it is he's gone?'

A fleeting impression of intelligence crossed his face, and then he went back to presenting himself as the big, bluff, not-too-bright poor relation. 'I really don't understand why you should think he isn't safe.'

Was that a double negative? What exactly did he mean by those words? Hopefully, he meant that wherever Hubert was, he was being well looked after. And if it was his bits and pieces that were in the hall of the big house now, then that tied in with what Gordon appeared to be saying. Hubert was moving himself and favoured bits and pieces of furniture out.

She said, 'He's safe. That's all I need to know. You are packing, too?'

'Me?' He looked around as if puzzled. 'I've got so many books and magazines. Hate to admit it but I'm a bit of a hoarder. Got to prune the collection. There's a meeting next week, I thought I might take some stuff along, see if I can sell it.'

'You're not moving out, too?'

'The trains would take a bit of moving, wouldn't they? It's not feasible. I've thought about it, once or twice but where would I go?'

Bea was pretty sure that if Gordon decided to

move he'd manage it with the minimum of fuss. Would he flee and leave his beloved trains behind? No, he wouldn't. So he probably wasn't thinking of leaving just yet.

'Well,' she said, 'this is just a flying visit to collect the paper Mrs Tredgold wants you to sign.'

'Of course, of course! Did you leave it with me or do you still have it?'

Bea produced her pen and the appropriate piece of paper, Gordon signed and Bea witnessed his signature, hoping that just one witness would do.

She noticed that the open box beside Gordon did indeed contain some books, and there was a gap between those stacked on the top shelf of the bookcase. So Gordon had spoken the truth. She didn't know why she felt he was lying. She was being over-suspicious, that's what.

Now to find Piers and Bernice, collect the signatures from the staff and get out of there. She couldn't wait.

Fourteen

Saturday noon

As Bea stepped out into the covered yard she met Piers and Bernice coming out of the main house.

Bea said, 'That was quick. Did you get them all to sign the papers? Did anyone have anything helpful to say?'

Piers said, 'Yes and no. Is Gordon OK?'

209

'Mm, yes. There was no sign of Hubert or of the clothing we collected for him yesterday. Gordon says Hubert is safe. Gordon himself was packing up some of his books. He claims not to be leaving but to be getting rid of some of his clutter. I'm not sure that I believe him but he wouldn't leave his trains behind, would he?'

Piers stroked his chin. 'That's interesting. It must be catching.'

Bea guessed, 'Hubert's leaving?'

'Nobody mentioned him. It might be Lavinia, which wouldn't be too surprising after what we saw yesterday, but Ms Andrews arranged it so that we couldn't get back into the hall to find out.'

Bernice teetered from one foot to the other. 'I'd like to see the trains. And I'm hungry.'

'In a minute,' said Piers. 'Let's update Bea first. Ms Andrews put us in the staffroom, saying that the cleaners would be down for their break in a minute but warning me to keep it short because they had a lot to do today. She disappeared and three women traipsed in, including Maggie – whom we met yesterday – plus Mercy Andrews. Also, the new chef and his dogsbody who looked as if he were about fifteen but is probably in his late teens.

'While they were making drinks for themselves, I explained what Mrs Tredgold had asked us to do and handed out the relevant letters. Chef and the lad said they couldn't help as they'd only started the job a couple of days ago. They said they needed to get on with what they were paid to do in the kitchen. I said why not, and they departed.

'That left the four women and us. Before we could get on down to it there was a ring on the internal phone. Mercy Andrews took the call and told Maggie that she was needed upstairs straight away. The others went all round-eyed. I could see they wanted to talk about what this meant but couldn't because Mercy was looking daggers at them; daring them to speak out of turn, I suppose.'

'Did Maggie sign her piece of paper before she left?'

'No. She took it with her, saying she'd get it back to me some time. The others settled down but kept on eye on Mercy, if you know what I mean. I could see they weren't going to say anything much in front of her. What they did say were things like, "Well, I slept in my own bed that night," and "More than some did". There was a snigger when one of them said Petra's name, which I don't think Mercy or I were supposed to hear. They were amused and intrigued at being asked to sign the paper, and happy to think they might get a bonus when the house is sold, but they weren't upset or frightened. No one was screaming to be let out of there.'

'You got the impression that Mercy had been told off by her mother – if Ms Andrews is her mother – to make sure the staff didn't talk out of turn?'

'Absolutely. Mercy is all efficiency. And yes, I think she probably is the daughter or niece of the housekeeper, though she isn't anything like that young limb, Carly, who said she was Ms Andrews's niece and was trying to get Hubert into bed. Carly

211

is all boobs and bottoms and nothing much between the ears. Mercy is restrained in manner and dress, better educated and has brains. I asked the women to tell me what each one of them does. Mercy answered for them, saying she acts as office manager and PA to the family. She helps Charlotte with her articles, answers the phone and arranges social events. There's a pecking order in that household. On top is Ms Andrews the elder, then Mercy, followed by Chef. The cleaners are at the bottom of the heap.

'Mercy knows she'll be in for a share in the sale of the house if she *had* slept here, but she hadn't and she wasn't going to pretend that she had. Before any of the others could get down to signing the papers, there was another ring on the phone, which, again, Mercy took. She announced to all and sundry that her mother wanted to see them all in her office straight away. Ms Andrews has them all well-trained, for they upped sticks and departed without a word, leaving me with mouth agape.'

Bea said, 'Ms Andrews wanted to whisk her daughter and the cleaners away to make sure they didn't sign any paperwork or gossip to you about the household . . . Or for another reason?'

Piers shrugged. 'There was a lot of activity in the main body of the house. Even from the staff-room we could hear furniture being moved and men shouting. Mercy acted as if she hadn't heard anything but the other women fidgeted and exchanged looks among themselves. On balance I think Ms Andrews really did need them to deal with whatever was going on in the house. Bernice had found some biscuits which stayed her hunger for a while—'

'Only two,' said Bernice, who was getting restless. 'Can we go now?'

'Let me finish,' said Piers. 'Being left on our own, we wandered out to the kitchen in search of fodder for the Brat, where we found Chef and his dogsbody having a cuppa and a cigarette. They were conspicuously not preparing any food. Having nothing better to do, I asked if I could have a cuppa, and if could they find something for Bernice to eat. They produced biscuits and cups of tea all round. So we sat down with them to enjoy our snack.

'I could see they were curious about what had been going on and sure enough, before I'd even put sugar in my tea, Chef asked me what was going on. I explained what I knew about the cats, Ahmed's supposed suicide and Hubert's disappearance. I enjoyed myself. They froze! I could see them wondering what sort of household they'd wandered into and thinking that they hadn't signed up for this sort of thing. It's odds on they won't turn up for work tomorrow morning, though they might be so afraid of Ms Andrews senior that they'll see today out. I consider it my good deed for the day to have enlightened them about the Tredgolds.'

Bea said, 'So neither Mercy nor any of the cleaners slept in the house on the night Ahmed died?'

'It doesn't look like it. The women – apart from Mercy – might have been persuaded to gossip about the family if I'd had longer with them, but

I would judge them innocent of murdering the cats or the chauffeur.'

Bea said, 'Which takes us back to the family. Gordon kept going on about "the family", too. I just don't get it.'

Bernice jiggled from foot to foot. 'What are we having for lunch? I don't like this place. It's like a prison yard.'

'This way.' Bea tried the door into the kitchens, but it refused to open. Someone had locked or bolted it from the inside? She looked around. They were alone in the covered yard and it did seem very quiet. They were sitting ducks for anyone who wanted to spray them with something from above. No doubt for reasons of security the tall double doors leading out to the courtyard at the front of the house had been padlocked together.

Bea told herself there was no need to panic. 'We should be able to get out through the door that leads into Gordon's place, and from there into the garage and out. You've still got Hubert's keys, haven't you, Piers?'

'Sure.'

Problem. The door that had been opened so easily to Hubert's keys before had also now been bolted on the inside. As Piers tried to open the door, they heard a shutter rolling up inside the coach house.

Piers thumped on the door. 'Gordon, are you there?'

They heard a car start up and be driven out into the courtyard. They heard the engine idle. The shutter was rolled down again. The coach house belonged to Gordon, and if he were planning to

214

go away for a while, of course he'd want to secure it against a break-in. Of course he would.

Bea told herself to breathe slow and deep. They hadn't been locked into the covered yard on purpose. No, of course not. There were plenty of other ways out, weren't there?

Bernice giggled. Nerves. 'Are we trapped?'

'No, of course not,' said Bea. 'There must be a way out to the garden at the back.' Yes, there was. An unobtrusive door had been cut into the tall gates that blocked that exit, too. She tried the small door. That was locked, too.

Gordon had said he had keys to the door, but nothing worked on the bunch Piers had been given. Maybe Hubert had not needed that particular key. There must be a door from the main house into the garden, and he'd have used that, wouldn't he?

Bea told herself she was not going to panic. No. Definitely not.

She returned to the kitchen door and spotted an unobtrusive bell on the wall nearby. 'This is the servants' entrance. They must have deliveries made into the yard here. If we ring this, someone will answer.' She pressed the bell.

No response.

Bernice danced on her toes and chewed the ends of her plait.

Bea wanted to tell her off but restrained herself. They were all feeling the strain, weren't they?

Piers leaned on the bell, hard. They could hear it ring in the distance.

'I'm awfully hungry,' said Bernice, in a small voice.

At long last, the door opened.

Sulky Carly stood there. 'Oh, it's you again. Thought you'd gone. Did you find Hubert for me?' She was wearing another tight top and shorts, neither of which contained her ample equipment.

Bea brushed the girl aside to enter the kitchen. 'Hubert's gone away for some peace and quiet.'

Carly said, 'He'll have to come back soon. Auntie says so. And then . . .' she grinned, 'we'll have some fun, right?'

Piers looked around. On the table were four empty mugs and a couple of cigarette butts in a saucer. No sign of Chef or his assistant. 'Where is everyone?'

Carly shrugged. 'Dunno. I was hungry. I thought there might be some food going in the kitchen but there's no sign. Hubert's fridge is empty but Auntie doesn't mind my helping myself to what's in the family's fridge and freezer.'

Bea picked up a discarded apron from the floor. 'Looks like your new chef's scarpered.'

'I expect there'll be pizzas here, for a start.' Carly opened the door of a huge freezer and poked around inside.

Bernice peered in, too. 'What you got?'

Carly pulled boxes out of the freezer. 'The three cheese one is nice, OK? You still at school?'

'Sure. I've got a few more years to go. How about you?'

'I'm off the moment I turn sixteen. Life's out there, know what I mean?'

'Mm. Wish I could leave, too. But they won't let me. Love your nail polish. What do you call it?'

Carly preened. 'Good, innit? Dunno what the name is. I found it in Boots and well . . . I fancied it, know what I mean?'

Did Carly mean she'd been shoplifting?

Bernice said, 'You're a lot braver than me.'

'Oh, well,' said Carly, accepting Bernice's words as a compliment, which perhaps they were. She held up a large pizza in a box. 'This do you?'

Bernice looked back over her shoulder. 'Bea? What will you have?'

'I don't think we've been invited for lunch.'

'Oh, that's all right.' Carly slapped the pizza on the table and ripped off the packaging. 'Auntie won't mind. I come and go as I please.'

Piers said, 'Carly, do you sleep here sometimes?'

'Uh-huh. I can doss down in Auntie's place in the basement if I get stranded late at night. Mum don't care so long as I'm no trouble.'

Bea said, 'What about Mercy? Does she sleep here, too?'

A shrug. 'Don't think so. Mercy could use Auntie's room if she gets stuck, but I don't think she ever has. Auntie's room's next to the chauffeur's. He's no fun, though. *Was* no fun.' For a moment she remembered Ahmed's death and looked strained. Then she perked up again. Turning to Bernice, she said, 'You go clubbing?' Her tone was only slightly patronizing older sister to younger.

Bernice said, 'We've talked about it. One of my friends does at weekends but she's wrecked on Monday mornings. I'd rather go to a gig, any day.'

Bea turned away to hide a smile. She'd never

known Bernice ask to attend a pop concert and didn't think the girl had ever done so.

Carly set the microwave going. 'You know what? Same here.' Carly was shedding layers of sophistication to reveal a younger and more likeable self.

'Sorry to interrupt,' said Bea. 'Carly, we're looking for someone who's got a moped. Any ideas?'

'I had a boyfriend once that had one. Not my scene. I fell off, the first corner. I'm having driving lessons soon.'

'Nobody who lives in this house has one?'

A shrug. 'We-ell. Not living in. Like, not supposed to be. Unnerstand?'

'Someone's boyfriend, who sneaks in for a cuddle, perhaps?'

'I wouldn't know.' But she did know. Oh, yes, she did.

'Petra has a boyfriend with a moped?'

Carly looked uneasy for the first time. 'Dunno. Might do, I suppose.'

'How many cars are there in the household, and where do they keep them? Not in the coach house, I assume. That's Gordon's territory, isn't it?'

Carly was happier answering this question. 'There's a garage under the garden out back. They dug it all out, built the garage and then covered it over with earth and stuff again. There's a tunnel comes out in the service road at the back. It takes all the family's cars and then some. I've only been down there once.' She shivered. 'A bit spooky, ask me.'

'Room for a moped as well?'

A shrug. 'Masses. How many cars are down

there? I think five or six, maybe seven.' She counted on her fingers. 'The big limo for Mrs T that Ahmed drives, that's one. Auntie has a Volvo, Edgar has a sports car, Lavinia a saloon. Hubert has a hatchback but I don't think he's been using it lately, ditto one for his wife, the one that died. My auntie was saying it ought to be sold, as it's no good sitting there, rusting away. How many's that?'

'Six. What about the gardener, and the chef? What about the cleaners? Can they park their cars there, too?'

Another shrug. 'I suppose. The place is big enough. You could hide an army down there.'

'You don't know anyone who likes to throw acid at people?'

Carly's eyes widened. 'You must be joking! I mean, that's serious bad stuff. No way!'

The microwave pinged and Carly turned her attention to food. She hoicked the pizza out of the microwave, cut it up and pushed half in Bernice's direction. 'Yum, yum.'

Bea motioned to Piers and they made their way out into the corridor and thence to the hall. Bea said, 'Wonders will never cease. How does Bernice do it? She'll have that girl Carly confiding in her before they've finished their pizzas. Do you agree with me that Carly is in the clear re. mopeds and acid throwing?'

'Agreed. It was Petra and boyfriend, wasn't it? It was on my mind to ask where the family kept their cars. I wonder how you get into the basement from inside the house? There must be access from the hall, through one of the doors we haven't tried yet. Do you want to look for a moped down there?'

Bea panicked at the thought. Her heart was racing. Suppose that next time Petra really did throw acid and not mango juice? 'We can't just go barging around searching for a moped. I suppose we could suggest that the police have a look, but we have no proof that my assailant is connected to this house and they wouldn't take our complaint seriously. It was mango juice that was thrown.'

As they opened the door leading into the hall, Piers caught Bea's arm and drew her back into the shadows under the stairs. He murmured, 'Someone's leaving.'

The front door was wide open, and there was a trail of wrapping paper and cardboard leading out into the courtyard. One of the furniture removers was manhandling a heavy crate into the back of the van, which had been drawn up close to the entrance.

A cleaner – not Maggie – was wrapping some china in newspaper and stowing it in a tea chest. Ms Andrews stood over her, her mouth in the thinnest of lines, barely containing impatience.

One of the removal men came down the stairs carrying a piecrust table which had been swathed in plastic. He banged into the newel post at the bottom of the stairs and Mrs Andrews said, in a voice which announced that the speaker was at the end of her tether, 'Careful!' He ducked his head at her and staggered out with his burden to the van.

Another man taped up the last tea chest and hoisted it into his arms. 'That's the lot, missus.' He took his burden outside and lifted it into the van. There was some more shouting, as the furniture was safely secured inside the van.

Bea put her hand on Piers' arm and whispered, 'Those things don't look as if they belong to Hubert. I think this must be Lavinia moving out. Mrs T will want to know where she's going, won't she? Dare we ask or shall we make ourselves scarce?'

'Give it a mo.'

Down the stairs came Lavinia in a brown leather coat lined with sheepskin. An expensive black leather handbag was over her arm and she was carrying a rather beautiful, foot-high gilded clock with a painted dial.

Edgar appeared on the landing in the wake of his wife, bellowing, 'You're not taking that clock.'

'It was my grandfather's,' said Lavinia, keeping her cool. 'I'm only taking the things I can prove are mine.'

Behind Edgar came Maggie the cleaner carrying a leather box and a briefcase.

Edgar was red-faced with fury. 'Lavinia, I order you to—'

Lavinia Tredgold seemed to have aged since the previous day. The bruise on her cheek was now black and yellow. Ignoring her husband, she addressed herself to Ms Andrews. 'Thank you for arranging everything so beautifully. You may tell anyone who asks that I have been called away to assist my brother who's been asked to stand in a by-election. You know the address and can send on any correspondence which may arrive in my absence.'

Edgar pounded down the stairs to catch up

with his wife and tried to wrest the clock from her arms. 'You're not having this!' There was a tussle, and he managed to pull the clock away from Lavinia. He didn't have a firm enough grip on it and it fell to the tiled floor with a crash that echoed around the hall.

There was a tinkle of glass. The back fell open. There was a whirr of displaced springs and one sweet chime.

Then, silence.

Lavinia could not possibly have gone any paler, but she did stagger and put out a hand to the banister to steady herself.

Edgar said, 'You clumsy cow! Now look what you've done!' He turned to Ms Andrews. 'She dropped it. You saw, didn't you! It was she who broke it.'

More silence. Ms Andrews raised her eyebrows, but was prepared neither to agree with him, nor to say he'd lied, either.

Someone else came on to the landing.

Petra. She leaned over the banister, and called out in a loud, sarcastic voice, 'Say "Hello" to Uncle for me, Mother, won't you? But don't expect me to visit you in the sticks.'

Lavinia looked up at her daughter, 'Petra, won't you reconsider—?'

'In your dreams! I'm not leaving London, and that's that!'

'Yes, but the house is going to be sold—'

'Daddy will see I'm all right, which is more than you ever did!'

Lavinia closed her eyes for a second. It was clear that the rejection had hurt her.

A movement by the front door. Mercy Andrews came in from the courtyard to operate a keypad by the door. Was she opening the gates on to the road for the van to leave? Yes. As they listened, it started up and drove off.

Mercy closed the front door and operated on the keypad again . . . lowering the portcullis and bringing up the drawbridge?

Behind her, Bea smelt pizza and felt rather than saw Bernice and Carly arrive to join in the fun. Bea signalled to them to be quiet and they did, rounded eyes taking in the drama.

Lavinia stepped down into the hall. She looked around her. Saying farewell? She said, 'Well, that's it. I did my best.'

Charlotte appeared in the doorway to the big ground-floor reception room. 'Leaving, are you? Well, you won't be missed.'

Lavinia said, 'Charlotte, I know we haven't always seen eye to eye but it is what it is. I have asked . . . No, I have begged Petra to come away with me but she refuses. If at some time in the future she changes her mind, would you be so kind as to—?'

Charlotte repeated Petra's words. 'Hah! In your dreams.'

Lavinia inclined her head. 'Nobody can say I didn't try.' She turned to the cleaners who had been packing up her belongings and pressed money into their hands. 'Thank you for everything. I wish you well in the future.'

The antique clock had been reduced to a heap of metal with cogs, springs and the shattered dial scattered across the floor. Ms Andrews looked at the bits and pieces but made no attempt to pick them up. Instead, she addressed Lavinia. 'I will contact the insurance people about the clock, and I will see that anything you've left behind is sent on to you.'

Lavinia said, 'Thank you,' and looked around her. 'Oh, my jewel case! I thought I gave it to someone to carry down. Where is it? And my laptop?'

Maggie, halfway down the stairs, held them up for Lavinia to see. 'I've got them.'

'Oh, thank you. I couldn't think for a moment what I'd done with them.'

Edgar scuttled up the stairs to where Maggie stood and snatched them from her. Teeth gleaming, he swung them to and fro. 'You saw what happened to your clock, Lavinia. If you want the rest of your precious things, you'll have to go down on your knees and beg for them.'

He waited.

Lavinia made a convulsive movement towards him and then checked herself. Could she bear to grovel to him? No. And yet . . .

Edgar laughed. He threw the box and then the briefcase into the air. They crashed down the stairs. The box slid and bumped down to the hall floor. The laptop fell awkwardly. It was in a heavily padded case, but the sound it made on contact with the tiled floor made Bea wince. Had he broken the screen?

How petty of Edgar! How vindictive!

Ms Andrews never even flinched though both items had landed close to her.

Lavinia managed to keep herself under control,

but her voice went high and low on her. 'Well, Edgar, you are good at breaking things. Let's see how good you are at making your way in life without me. My solicitor will be in touch with you about the divorce. I'm taking my car, because I paid for it. I don't think there's anything more to say, except never ask me for money again.'

She stooped to pick up her jewel box and her briefcase. She didn't check to see what damage he'd done. She didn't even yell an obscenity or two at her husband, for which Bea gave her full marks. Then she walked round the far side of the stairs from where Piers and Bea stood. A door opened and closed. And she was gone.

Presumably that was where the entrance to the underground garage could be found.

Tension eased. Everyone relaxed.

Charlotte said, 'Good riddance. I only wish she'd taken the girl as well.'

Fifteen

Saturday afternoon

Ms Andrews turned her cold eye on the cleaners. 'Pick up all the pieces of the clock before you go back to work, and don't miss any. That's a valuable clock and restoring it will need specialist attention.'

One of the cleaners – not Maggie – muttered

something about their not having had a proper morning break yet.

Bea and Piers looked at one another. If the cleaners went out to the kitchens they would find them lurking in the shadows, which might prove awkward.

Ms Andrews cracked the whip. 'It won't hurt you to take your break a little later than usual. First, pick up all the pieces of the clock and put them in a box. Then I want Mrs Lavinia's bedroom, sitting room and bathroom cleaned. And no pilfering of bits and pieces. If you find anything she's left behind, bring it to me and I will decide what to do with it. Let me know when you've finished and I'll inspect what you've done and then lock those rooms up.'

More muttering, but they did as they were told.

Charlotte had gone red. 'Ms Andrews, you take a lot on yourself.'

'Someone has to see to things.'

Charlotte said, 'You should have asked me first. Lavinia has a three-piece suite which is much more comfortable than mine, and there may be other things of hers which I'd like to have in my rooms, too. I don't want you locking her rooms up before I decide what I want.'

Ms Andrews raised her pale eyebrows. 'That was yesterday. Things have changed.' She lifted her head to address Edgar. 'By the way, Edgar, Mercy tells me you have given her some bills to pay. Unfortunately I am unable to oblige as they have nothing to do with the running of this household.'

Edgar gasped. 'But Mother always used to—'

226

'Your mother isn't here any longer. She left me some signed cheques to pay for the running of the house till the end of the month and after that I shall have to cut off the utilities, which means there will be no water, gas or electricity. You and your sister will probably wish to find yourself alternative accommodation before that time.'

Edgar said, 'That's rubbish! When I see her—'

Charlotte broke in. 'Ms Andrews, stop right there! When we speak to our mother, she will no doubt tell you to—'

Ms Andrews turned her eyes on Charlotte. 'Do you know where she is?'

Charlotte blustered, 'Well, no. Not precisely, but I'm sure that—'

'I suggest you get on with finding yourself somewhere else to live. As each room is cleaned, it will be locked and there will be no further admission except for prospective buyers. And that includes the reception rooms on the ground floor.'

Charlotte said, 'I have my poetry reading here next week! You can't expect—'

'You heard me!'

'But I use the front room one as my office!'

'You have plenty of rooms upstairs.'

'But they are not so . . . so important!'

'No doubt you will manage. And remember, you pay your own bills in future.'

Charlotte gibbered. 'You don't mean that. I mean, there's my usual living expenses, my dues to the Society of Women Writers and Journalists, and my subscriptions to the Royal Academy and the Tate. How, may I ask, am I to maintain my position in society if I cannot pay for them?'

Edgar broke in, 'Mother can't mean to cut us off! Why, the yacht soaks up money and my car—'

'You both inherited enough to see you through to your grave. If you have spent it all, then you will have to cut your coat according to the cloth you have left.'

'Are you mad! You're not suggesting I should sell the yacht? Over my dead body!'

'She can't mean—'

'Yes, she does. Didn't you read the papers that woman made you sign?'

'Mother's off her trolley! When I get hold of her, I'll—' He stamped up and down.

Bea thought that Ms Andrews seemed to be enjoying herself. It was unlikely that Charlotte and Edgar had treated her well in the past and perhaps she was now taking her revenge.

Ms Andrews said, 'I have worked for you for many years, but I don't hear you asking how I shall manage when this house is sold and my job comes to an end. Well, it may interest you to know that I have saved and invested my money wisely, and that I have a decent pension to look forward to. I will continue to look after the house until it is sold and then I will retire.'

Edgar stormed, 'Mother can't do this to us. We'll sue! We'll take her to court! We'll get her committed.'

'She warned you both, time and again, but you wouldn't listen. Now it's time for you two spend-thrifts to get off the gravy train.'

Charlotte looked as if she were going to choke. 'How dare you speak to me like that! When I see my mother—?'

228

'Ah, but when will that be? Please remember that, like you, I slept in this house on the night the cats were killed, and so I will also be getting a share in the sale of the house. We are equal now, Charlotte. I don't have to take orders from you any longer.' A tiny smile. 'It will be amusing to see how you and your brother learn how to make your living in future.'

She took out a bunch of keys, opened a door to the left of the front door and disappeared with her daughter in tow.

Edgar screamed. 'Come back, dammit! How dare you walk out on me!'

Silence.

The hall seemed very empty, as brother and sister looked into the future and found it disturbing.

Bea took Piers's arm and stepped back. She caught Bernice's eye and tipped her head to indicate they should retreat into the kitchen quarters.

Once safely through the door, Carly giggled. 'What a turn up!'

'Let's go to the staffroom for a minute,' said Bea, easing that door open.

'Wow!' said Carly, tagging along with Bernice. 'Didn't she half tear them off a strip! They bloody well deserved it, too. Just wait till I tell my mum!'

The staffroom was empty.

Bea took a seat and patted a chair beside her. 'Carly, come and sit down. You and Mercy are cousins, aren't you? But you don't look alike, or act alike.'

Carly sprawled in the chair. 'We're cousins, all right, but brought up different. Me mum and me aunt were lookers when they were young, but me mum went and fell for no-good men who never stayed longer than to get her pregnant. So there's five of us now, and I'm the second to youngest and the eldest two live round the corner but me mum looks after their kids, too, so's they can work. Tell the truth, we didn't know nothing about me Auntie Anne for years because she'd gone up in the world, like, and we hadn't. Then one day she turned up and said she was sorry to have neglected us and how old was I, and would I like a job with her. And me mum said "No!" at first, because I do help around the house with the kids and that, but it's true I'm not really into school and aren't hardly going to get good exam results, if I bothered to take them at all, that is. So I said I'd think about it, and she gives me a wage and brings me here and it's only then I find out that she wants me to be nice to this old geezer, a real cry baby, who doesn't know how to tie his shoelaces any more.'

'Hubert?'

Carly nodded. 'Auntie explained that his wife had died and he needed cheering up, and it would please the family no end if I could bring him out of the doldrums because no one else had the time to be with him twenty-four hours a day, and that if I could do that, I'd find myself in clover. I said he was a bit old for that, because I'm not stupid, see, and I could see where this was going, and she said that if he wanted to marry me, that would be all right because I wouldn't have to work ever again and could divorce him after a while if I fancied someone younger. And, if it didn't work out but I could just make him feel better about life, then they'd find me a really nice job with a friend in town somewhere that would be easy-going, know what I mean?'

They could imagine that all too well.

It was Bernice who said, 'You mean they'd pass you on to a pimp?'

Carly wriggled, but not very much. 'Well, some-one to look after me. You needn't look so shocked. I mean, it's not as if I haven't been doing it for fun since I was at high school. I'm good at it, and it brings in a bit here and there. This way, I'd get paid a proper wage and have enough to pass some back to me mum. What's not to like?'

Bea said, 'But you could get a job, earn your living . . .' Her voice died away at Carly's look of contempt. Carly preferred an easier option. So Bea said, 'I hardly dare ask. Did you get anywhere with Hubert?'

'Nah. Non-starter. He did try once, but nah. He couldn't do it. He cried. Tell the truth, I feel sorry for him, the poor old thing. He reminded me of me granddad, rest his soul. I do hope he's going to be all right, wherever he is.'

Bernice said, 'Why didn't your aunt use her daughter to make Hubert feel better?'

Carly rolled her eyes. 'Use your head. She's not into men. Period.'

Bernice frowned. 'Well, what about Petra? Oh, no. She's no good. She's his niece.'

Carly grinned. 'That wouldn't have stopped her. But no, Hubert wouldn't have, know what I mean? Besides, Petra's got her own shag.'

231

'Does her boyfriend ever sleep over here?'

'I dunno, do I? There's Auntie's room down the basement next to Ahmed's, the one that I use now and then. She could have used it, I suppose. It's properly furnished with a bed and all. I think it was supposed to be for another live-in maid one time, but that never happened, and Ahmed did say, coupla times, that someone had been sleeping there, off and on. Making noises, like. You know? We all thought it was Petra and her boy, but we knew better than to say anything.'

She sobered up. 'It's all over, innit? Hubert and stuff. I'll have to go back home and get a job.' The prospect did not seem to appeal. Then she brightened up. 'Or go on the game.'

Bea said, 'Your aunt never asked you to get friendly with Kit or Ahmed?'

'What would I want to do that for? I wouldn't, anyway. I mean, we're mates, right? I unnerstand them, I know where they're at, know what I mean? Kit used to slip me extra bacon butties, like. He and Ahmed used to lecture me about taking school seriously and looking for a boy of my own age. They knew what I was trying to do with Hubert, and they didn't approve but they respected me right to live like I want, and I respected them, right?'

'We did wonder whether Petra had ever tried it on with Kit or Ahmed.'

Carly grimaced. 'That she did! Silly cow! Can't think why – she oughta known they wouldn't play ball with her. Yes, she tried it on. They said no and she was dead miffed. She even tried to get Kit sacked, went to her father with some tale about his taking advantage of her here in the staffroom which I don't believe for a minute, but I reckon that Edgar might have been taken in, silly old sod.'

'You think that she complained to her father, and he got Kit the sack by framing him for stealing his watch?'

'Dead right, I do. I said to me aunt, there's no way Kit would steal from Mrs T, and she, me aunt, said she couldn't do anything about it. So he got the sack. I was sorry about that.'

'What did you think about Ahmed dying?'

Carly's eyes shifted to the ceiling, and then to the window. She was going to lie. 'Dunno.'

'You think that was Petra getting her own back on Ahmed for refusing her?'

'She wouldn't want him dead, though. Would she? I did think she might have put something in his thermos, mebbe something to make him drunk, so that when he took the car out to fetch them from the theatre, he'd have a crash and lose his licence.'

'You *know* that she did so? Or guessed?'

Carly licked her lips. 'No, I dunno really. It just came to me, like, that she might have done that, to get her own back. And mebbe somehow it went wrong?'

'She didn't tell you that she'd done that?'

'She don't talk to me. I'm beneath her notice, like. Silly cow.' She turned sullen. 'Can I go now, please?'

'One more thing,' said Bea. 'Your aunt seems very much in charge today. Do you think she's acting off her own bat or has she perhaps had a letter or a phone call from Mrs Tredgold giving her instructions as to what to do about the house? Shutting off the water, for instance, makes the place uninhabitable.'

Carly got up, pulling her tiny skirt down, and checking that her boobs were more or less tucked in. 'You ask her. I don't know nothing about anything, right?' She pranced out, jiggling her rump at them.

Piers said, 'Now does she really know something, or was she making that up?'

Bernice said, 'I liked her, before. I don't, now.'

Piers corrected her. 'You still like her, but you're sorry she's chosen a certain way of life.'

Bernice narrowed her eyes at him. 'Don't tell me: you fancy her!'

Piers shook his head, laughing. 'Not my style.'

'What is your style, then?' Becoming aggressive.

Piers flicked a glance at Bea and fiddled with his pencil.

Bea, pretty sure she'd gone pink, said, 'Let's get on, shall we? We really must try to get those last few papers signed by the cleaners, and then we can call it a day.'

The door opened and Maggie the cleaner came in. 'Don't mind me. I've been having one of my hot flushes, and I said to madam, "If I don't have a cuppa now, I'll be passing out on you," so she said I could take ten minutes, which is what I'm going to do.'

'It's good to see you, Maggie,' said Bea. 'Do you know where Gordon has gone to? Or Hubert, for that matter?'

Maggie turned her back on Bea to switch the kettle on and talked to the air in front of her. '"Now, don't you go gossiping," madam said. As if I would. Would I tell family secrets to complete strangers? Of course I wouldn't. I have a bad habit of talking to myself, though, and if you're listening then I can't stop you, can I?'

'We're listening,' said Bea.

Maggie put a teabag and some sugar in a big mug and filled up with boiling water from the kettle. 'June's a friend of mine, used to clean for Mrs Tredgold till they trumped up some charge that she'd stolen a diamond ring. As if she would!' Maggie snorted. 'Anyway, June and I, we've been worried sick about Hubert, but we reckoned as he's best off with Gordon who, to give him his due, has looked after him well. Gordon's all right, you know. This morning, early, he rang me to say he wouldn't be needing me for a bit as he was taking Hubert away and I was to let some people into the coach house who are coming to pack up his train sets on Monday. So he's moving out too. All the nice people are moving out, and what's left . . . well . . .!'

Bea and Piers exchanged glances. Was this good news?

Bernice set her jaw. 'I'd like to see the trains.'

Bea said, 'I don't think we can, today.'

Maggie put some milk in her tea and blew on the surface. Then she reached into a pocket and withdrew a wodge of papers, which she tossed on to the table in front of Bea. 'I seem to have picked up some papers. Can't think why. I might as well drop them into the wastepaper basket,

235

except that that's full and who's going to empty it? That's what I want to know. It's all very well doing overtime, but I should be taking my youngest niece out this afternoon, and she can play up something chronic if she don't get her own way. Takes after my sister, the one that's having twins at the end of the month.'

Bea cautiously picked up the papers and unfolded them. 'Wow!'

Maggie stood by the window, looking out with her back to them. '"Papers," madam says. "I don't want to hear of any of you signing no papers, right?" Who does she think she is, telling us what to say? We'll all be out of a job when she's got the house ready for sale, anyway. Mrs T used to treat us right, and if she ever wants a cleaner she can trust, then she'll know where to find me and June, too. Unnerstood?'

Bea was a happy bunny. She was holding papers from a number of people, not only Maggie and June but someone else as well. 'I'll make sure to tell her. I see you've got round to talking to some of the others. That was clever of you.'

'I'm not talking to you. I'm just thinking aloud. I thought there was no point in asking that new cleaner. She don't know nothing, and if she can more than write her name, I'd be surprised. But us oldies had a fine old time in the pub last night. There was me old mate June, and the gardener and me mate that's upstairs now, kowtowing to her Highness like we have to do if we want to keep our jobs. So we talked it over and we decided that what Mrs T really wanted to know is who killed Ahmed. And the cats. I said we could make a guess, like, couldn't we? I said we could fold the paper over so nobody else could see what we'd written down and I wouldn't read what anyone else had written, and they wouldn't read what I wrote, neither.'

'Understood,' said Bea. 'And, thank you. I'll give the papers to Mrs T tonight.'

Maggie fished her teabag out, dropped it in a nearby saucer and took a gulp of very hot tea. 'Ah, that's better. The cup that cheers, they say, and they're right about that.'

She looked around. There were half-empty mugs, odd plates, plus the paper napkins Carly and Bernice had used when eating their pizzas. 'Dunno who's going to clean up in here today. There's only so much a person can do. Well, I'm back to the job, now. And I haven't gossiped to a soul while I've been down here, right?'

Maggie took a step towards the door and it opened to reveal Ms Andrews, in a fine, cold temper.

'Maggie? What are you doing here? I thought I asked you to finish cleaning Mrs Lavinia's rooms so that I can lock them up.'

'Didn't I have to go to the loo and get myself a cuppa? What you should be saying is what are these people doing in our staffroom, making themselves free of our teabags and milk, no doubt. And before you ask, I wouldn't demean myself by gossiping with them, right?'

'That's correct,' said Bea. She made a show of looking at her watch as she put the wad of papers into her handbag. 'She said you'd told her not to gossip. Ms Andrews, you know I was asked

237

to get signatures of all the staff here? I have to check, but I believe I'm still short of—'

'I'm afraid you're out of luck. My staff have all gone home now except for Maggie, and I don't think she's able to help you now, is she?'

'Wouldn't dream of it,' said Maggie. 'I'm on my way, but I'm giving you fair warning, Ms Andrews. I won't work a minute after two. I've got my family to consider, overtime or no overtime.' And off she went.

Ms Andrews kept the door open, waiting for Bea to leave. 'Don't let me keep you any longer, Mrs Abbot. I will see if I can arrange for you to meet with the rest of the staff on Monday. That is, if they wish to be involved any further in what has been a most distasteful affair.'

'Understood,' said Bea, pretending to accept this offer while thinking it unlikely it would ever happen. She frowned at Bernice, who had taken out her phone and was fiddling with it. Couldn't the girl leave it alone for ten minutes?

Bea brought herself back to the present. 'Ms Andrews, there's just one thing. I would like you to accompany us out of the house and see that we get safely into a taxi.'

Ms Andrews narrowed her eyes. 'Why on earth should I act as nanny for you?'

'Yesterday when we were waiting for a taxi in the street, a moped drove past us and the passenger threw an orange-coloured fruit juice at me. It was an alarming experience. If it had been an acid attack, then I'd be in hospital facing months of painful treatment and the criminal and his or her accomplice would be looking at a lengthy jail sentence.'

Ms Andrews let the door close softly behind her. Was it the first she'd heard of the incident? Mm, yes. She was horrified, and not trying to conceal it. She started to speak and then checked herself. Had she got the message that Bea thought someone connected to the household had been involved? Yes, she had. And she was now thinking who that might be, and what this might mean for the family. In the end all she said was, 'I don't see what that has to do with me. Obviously, it was just a prank.'

Bea said, 'Someone phoned to say it was a warning.'

The woman put a hand to her throat. 'The police are involved?'

'We called an ambulance and the police. The paramedics attended but when they realized it was not an acid attack, they left us to go home under our own steam.'

Ms Andrews's eyes flickered and then narrowed. 'Can you identify the perpetrators? Did you get the number plate?'

Piers said, 'They were two youngsters, judging by their shape and size. A boy at the front and a girl at the back, wearing helmets. As for the number plate, I think if I saw it again I'd recognize it.'

'You mean that you can't be sure? You didn't give the police the number?'

Bea dodged that one. 'I believe you allow someone, not a member of the household, to keep his moped in the garage here?'

Ms Andrews was relieved. A cold anger displaced her earlier concern. 'You didn't see the number plate. You have no proof, have you?' She made a rapid recovery. 'How very dreadful! This is such a quiet neighbourhood, too. I suppose they were bag snatchers, looking for a tourist to rob.'

'I don't think so,' said Piers. 'Would you give us permission to go down into the garage to see if there is a moped there? It might jog my memory about the licence plate.'

'What! No. Ridiculous! No. If there were such a vehicle on the premises – which I doubt – then you could take a note of any moped's number and swear that it was the one you saw yesterday, which would be a miscarriage of justice. I can't allow that. You have no proof that anyone in this household is connected to the matter.'

'That's true,' said Bea, 'and there was no great harm done yesterday. But what about today?'

Sixteen

Saturday afternoon, continued

'Well, what about today?' Ms Andrews had recovered her aplomb now she understood there was no proof which might incriminate the family.

Bea said, 'Suppose someone repeats the incident, using acid this time?'

'Unlikely. What you saw yesterday was a

neighbourhood bad boy, out to frighten people without doing any real harm. Nothing like that could ever be connected with this house.'

Bea said, 'How can you guarantee that?'

'Well . . .' improvising rapidly, 'I know you are imagining things, but I will make sure everyone hears about the terrible thing that happened to one of our guests. I shall say that if it happens again the police will be looking for the moped involved.'

'That's fine as far as it goes,' said Bea, 'and might well do the trick – for tomorrow. In the meantime, you can ensure our safety by accompanying us out on to the street and waiting with us till we get into a taxi.'

'Ridiculous! I have other things to do with my time.'

'Very well. I do understand that you are a busy woman. So why don't you ask your daughter to accompany us, to stand waiting on the pavement until a taxi arrives?'

The woman blenched. She could read that scenario as well as Bea could. Like Bea, she could picture Mercy standing at the kerbside as a moped started up and drove towards her, and the moped's passenger swung a bottle containing acid at the girl . . .

Ms Andrews's hands contracted to claws.

'Would you risk her face?' said Bea. 'Or the loss of an eye?'

The woman's voice cracked. 'What a remarkable imagination you have!'

Piers said, 'So, will you let us see if there is a moped in the basement?'

'No! No, I . . . There's nothing like that here, I'm sure of it. I mean, that if any of the young people's friends might, occasionally . . . but they'd be at work at this time of day, wouldn't they?'

'On a Saturday afternoon?'

'No. Well, perhaps. But if you are going to spread rumours that someone in this house might encourage that sort of behaviour, then it will be Mr Tredgold's solicitor who will be in touch with you, asking for damages for libel.' She had recovered herself. The moment when she might have cracked had passed.

'What libel?' said Bea. 'We have been careful only to speak the truth.'

'Well . . .' Again Ms Andrews improvised. 'You might be speaking the truth as you perceive it, but you yourselves are not so innocent, are you? From what my niece, Carly, tells me, your man here is not averse to touching her inappropriately. What do you say to that?'

Bea exploded. 'What nonsense!'

Piers began to laugh. 'Now that is slander! I've never touched the girl!'

Ms Andrews thought she was on to a winner. 'Are you saying my niece is a liar? That's not what she'll say in court!'

Bernice piped up. 'Sorry, Ms Andrews. I've been with him all morning. Stuck to him like glue till he went off with Mrs Abbot for a while. He was never alone with Carly. I was, but you're not going to make out that I tried to seduce her, are you? Carly and I have spent a lot of time together today. We've talked about all sorts, especially the odd things that have been happening in this household.'

Ms Andrews drew back. 'I . . . well . . . she must have been mistaken.'

'No, *you* were mistaken,' said Bea. 'I believe an apology is in order.'

'I . . . I was mistaken.'

Bernice held out her phone.

An eerie voice was heard, like an echo. Ms Andrews. '. . . I was mistaken.'

Had Bernice been taping the conversation on her smartphone?

Everyone in the room thought about what words Bernice might have recorded.

Ms Andrews lunged for the phone.

Bernice was quicker. She hugged it to her and darted behind Piers.

Bea said, 'Ms Andrews, I do understand your wish to be loyal to the family and to protect them as far as possible. We are outsiders and have a different slant on things. We have heard testimony that various strange things have been happening here recently but that none of them have been brought to the attention of the police. Oh, except for Ahmed's demise, which was dismissed as suicide.'

'That is what it was. He committed suicide.'

'Perhaps he did, though it seems unlikely. So far, either through your efforts at damage control or by sheer luck, the family have not fallen under suspicion of committing any crime but if we, your guests, are attacked on leaving your house today, you may count on it that we will not be toeing the party line. We will

243

be screaming blue murder and I can guarantee the police will listen.'

Ms Andrews folded her arms. 'Now you are being ridiculous.'

'Will you or your daughter accompany us as we leave and wait with us in the street till we are safely in a taxi?'

'No. We have far better things to do with our time.'

Piers said, 'There's a way out of this. Ms Andrews, *you* phone for a taxi, and ask it to come to fetch us from inside the courtyard. Don't get an Uber. Get a black cab because they're distinctive and can't be mistaken for a private car. Then *you* open the gates to let the taxi into the courtyard and close them after we leave. You have video cameras covering the courtyard for security purposes, so no one else could come inside the gates, could they? If another vehicle did come into the courtyard, the cameras would register its presence and, if anything untoward were to happen, the police would be able to look at your video footage.'

Slowly, the woman nodded. 'Very well. I'll take you to the hall, phone for a black cab and ask them to collect you from the courtyard. There's no need to involve Mercy.'

She got out her phone and spoke softly into it. She held the door open, and this time Bea, Piers and Bernice took the hint and followed her out of the staffroom, down the corridor and through the door into the hall.

Their footsteps echoed on the hall floor.

Bea lifted her head, listening. Was that the

whine of a hoover upstairs, where Maggie was finishing her work? There was no other sound to be heard. Apart from that hot spot of noise upstairs, the house felt as if the life had been drained out of it.

Ms Andrews killed one call and dialled again. This time she spoke out loud, asking for a taxi to fetch guests from inside the courtyard of the house. She keyed in the code to open the front door. For a long moment she stood in the open doorway, looking out. Listening.

For a moped? Cars flashed by on the road outside. Not many, but a few.

No moped.

Ms Andrews lifted her phone as it pinged. She had received a message. She said, 'The taxi is here.' She keyed open the big gates to let the cab into the courtyard.

The cab drew up at the front door and the three of them got in. Piers told the driver to take them to the nearest Tube station. The gates to the court-yard began to close as they drove out.

Piers screwed round in his seat. 'What's that behind us?'

Was that a moped, idling by the kerb some way down the road?

Bernice reached out to grasp Bea's arm. 'Oh!' Her eyes were wide with a mixture of excitement and terror.

'It's all right,' said Bea, and tried to relax. 'They can't know it's us in this cab. It may not be them, anyway. It might be some local lad having a laugh.'

Piers had his phone out. 'Bernice, get your phone ready. If they pass us, take a photo, will you?'

'They're coming!' Bernice bounced around in her seat.

'Keep the windows up!' Bea, seated in the middle, was struggling to see, too.

A moped with two people, both helmeted, mounted the pavement and roared along towards them, scattering the odd pedestrian.

A young woman pushing a baby in a buggy crashed into a garden wall.

An older woman, walking with a stick, staggered into a gateway and clutched at the wall to save herself from falling.

Still riding on the pavement, the moped drew abreast of the taxi.

Piers lifted his phone to take a picture.

'Hey!' The taxi driver slowed. 'What's up with them, eh?'

'Bag snatchers!' yelled Bea. 'They tried to get us yesterday.'

The moped kept pace with them. Did it look like the one they'd seen yesterday? Yes, it did.

Bernice yelled, 'I can't see their faces!'

The passenger was holding something . . . a bottle?

Though helmeted and clad in black leather, by her shape it seemed to be a girl. She rapped on the window and yelled, 'Open up!'

The taxi driver, cursing, swung the cab into the middle of the road.

The moped followed them on to the road.

The passenger thumped the glass again.

Mouthing obscenities, the taxi driver swung his cab sharply to the left, causing the moped to swerve back on to the pavement which luckily was empty this time.

'Bloody . . .!' The taxi driver was incandescent.

The bottle shot out of the passenger's gloved hand, fell on the pavement and rolled away.

She was going to fall off.

No, at the last minute she righted herself, clinging to the driver's jacket.

'Get that!' The taxi driver stood on his brakes.

Someone screamed. Bea, or Bernice?

A man walking two dogs on the opposite pavement had got out his phone. Was he ringing the police?

The moped roared off down the pavement, back on to the road, and away.

'Gotcha!' said Piers. 'Number plate was muddied, but I think I got it.'

Bea was trembling, but in control of herself. Just about. 'We've got to get that bottle.'

The taxi driver said, 'If those something somethings have marked my cab . . .!' He drew to a halt, and parked.

He got out of his cab. Shaking.

So was Bernice. Her eyes were huge. Tears welled. 'I couldn't get a good enough shot!'

Piers reached across Bea to hold Bernice's hands. 'You did good, Brat.'

Bernice wailed, 'I thought I'd be fine! I thought it was going to be a great adventure but it isn't like that!'

Bea pulled the child into her arms and held her tight.

The taxi driver was lighting a cigarette with hands that still shook. 'What was that about, then?'

Piers opened the car door and, moving with care, got out on to the pavement.

The young woman pushing the buggy sat on the pavement, having a little weep. The older woman was being helped back on to her feet by a young man, who'd been driving past in his van. He'd parked askew and left the van door open. Traffic built up behind him.

The man with the two dogs wound his way through the traffic to reach their side of the road. 'I've called the police.'

The taxi driver was swearing under his breath. And smoking. Alternately.

Bea stroked Bernice's smooth head.

They were both crying.

Piers said to the taxi driver, 'You saved our lives.'

'Look what they've done to my bloody cab!'

The cap had come off the bottle, and its contents lay in a viscous puddle on the pavement. The liquid had splashed up on to the door of the cab, where it had already started to eat into the paintwork.

Bernice howled and hid her face in Bea's shoulder.

Bea tried to comfort her, while needing comfort herself.

That first phone call which Ms Andrews made before we left the staffroom . . . She was letting someone know that we were about to leave. We'd been at the house for hours. Petra and her boyfriend might have been waiting for us to leave earlier, perhaps . . . but they would have had a long wait. No, at some point the word went round that we were in the staffroom, trying to get the cleaners to talk. They could have learned that from Mercy Andrews, who chivvied the staff out earlier . . . or from her mother, who came in to make sure that Maggie wasn't going to talk.

A police siren heralded the arrival of the cavalry.

The police are going to treat it like an isolated road rage incident. They will say, 'Boys will be boys!' But the cab driver won't let them get away with that. He's hopping mad, and rightly so. I hope he has insurance. Surely all black cab drivers have insurance? But this incident means he'll lose time and money . . .

Bea's head reeled with trying to think through all the various possibilities.

Piers dealt with the police while Bea sat in the cab, cuddling Bernice. Piers was being calm and sensible. He wasn't ranting and raving like the cab driver. He showed the police the pictures he'd taken of the moped, and after some discussion, managed to send them by email to the police officer in charge.

The police lifted the bottle from the pavement with great care. 'Bad stuff,' they said. 'Limescale remover. Acid. Could have done a lot of damage.'

The taxi driver exploded. 'It did do a lot of damage. Look at my ruddy cab! If I get my hands on them . . .!'

Piers said, 'The girl wore leather gauntlets, as you can see from my photos. But she may have handled the bottle earlier, when she bought it at a shop or lifted it from her home. You might get some fingerprints off it, with luck.'

They nodded. 'Could you identify . . .?'

No, of course Piers couldn't. Nor could Bea or Bernice. 'They wore helmets. You couldn't see anything of their faces.'

Could the police decipher the moped's number plate? It wasn't easy to read – perhaps it had been deliberately muddied?

If the police fail to work out what that number is, and if the Tredgolds get rid of that moped tonight, there'll be nothing to connect them with the crime.

Bernice began to shiver.

Bea said to the police, 'My ward is in shock. I think I am, too. Perhaps I could take her home and we could give you a statement tomorrow? Here's my card.'

The policeman said, 'You couldn't identify them?'

Bea shook her head.

'I wish I could have seen them,' said Bernice. 'I wish their helmets had come off and I'd seen them. But they didn't, and I didn't.' She was on the verge of tears again. 'I hope they rot in hell!'

Everyone took everyone else's details and the police called another cab to whisk Bea, Bernice and Piers home.

They didn't talk on the journey, but tried to relax and not think too much . . .

Too many problems.

Too many people with motives.

As they turned into their road, Bernice sat upright. 'I'm hungry!'

Piers said, 'I suppose I am too. No lunch. I'll get out here and shop for some ready meals. All right by you, Bea? Have you enough money for the fare?'

'I can pay by card if necessary.'

He got out at the traffic lights, and Bea tried to remember which pocket she'd put her keys in. And found them as they drew to a halt, double parking outside her house.

Once inside, with the alarm turned off, Bernice turned to Bea and hugged her. 'If you were to die, I couldn't bear it.'

Bea held the girl fast. 'Same here. I shouldn't have taken you there.'

Bernice lifted her head. 'You didn't take me. I decided to go. You couldn't have stopped me. I thought I would be good at the detecting lark, but all I did was upset that horrible girl Petra, and then she . . .' She peered up at Bea. 'It was her, wasn't it? On the bike?'

'I don't know. Probably.'

'Was it my fault that they came after us?'

'No. I'd upset her before that.' Bea tried to smile. 'Mind you, I did enjoy your taking her apart. She got the truth and the whole truth, possibly for the first time in her life.'

Bernice wasn't sure what to make of that. 'So I'm only partly to blame?'

'Don't give in to false guilt. Right is right, and wrong is wrong, and innocent people don't go round armed with bottles of acid to chuck at anyone who looks at them in a funny way.'

'I didn't just look at her, though.'

'You demolished her sense of entitlement. You

251

cut her down to size. But don't forget, she was after me anyway, because she knows I'm not going to endorse her claim to have stayed the night when the cats were killed.'

Bernice drew back. 'I forgot that's what it's all about. No, it isn't really about the cats, is it? It's about Ahmed dying, and the others losing their jobs.'

Bea said, 'The two things might not be connected.'

'Of course they are. That girl did the lot!'

'I'm not so sure about that, Bernice. I haven't got it all worked out yet. I'm hungry and thirsty and tired and worried to death. Give me a chance to get myself sorted out and we'll talk about this again.'

Piers rang the bell. Didn't he have his key?

Ah, but he had his arms full of shopping. He marched straight through to the kitchen and spread out his purchases. 'Fish and chips, hot. Apple pies, ditto. Cream from the corner shop. Fresh orange juice to drink, and . . .' with a flourish, '. . . an orchid each for the two most wonderful ladies I have ever had the privilege to know.'

The orchid for Bea was white and pink, with multiple buds on each of its six stems. The one for Bernice was purple and pink and just as luxurious. And expensive.

Bea blinked a tear away. She shook her head at him. 'You shouldn't.' And then she smiled.

Bernice's mouth fell open. 'For me? I've never been given flowers before.'

'The first of many,' said Piers, unwrapping the

252

food. 'You deserve it, both of you. Now, sit. Eat. Don't talk.'

Bernice said, 'Bea thinks—'

'That's enough, Brat. You did well today, but you've had something to eat earlier and we haven't. We're famished. Give us a chance to catch up.'

'Tom Cat!' replied Bernice, but without an edge to her voice for once.

They ate. Every last chip. Every last flake of pastry.

Piers ran his finger round the cream pot and closed his eyes.

'Don't fall asleep yet,' said Bea. 'I'm not dragging your dead weight into the sitting room. The way I'm feeling, I couldn't lift you on to the settee without falling over myself.'

Bernice had also run out of energy. 'Isn't your cleaner ever coming?'

'On a Saturday afternoon?' Bea started to clear the table but was suddenly overcome with fatigue. 'I'll see to it later. I'm not sure I can even climb the stairs.'

'You poor old things,' said Bernice. 'Let's put you into a couple of easy chairs and cover you over with rugs and you can have a nice little nap like the geriatrics you are.'

'Geriatric yourself,' said Piers, dragging himself along to the sitting room. 'You wait, my girl. Tangling with murderers takes it out of you.' He collapsed on to the settee, eased off his shoes and put his feet up.

Bea sank into her big chair by the fireplace. 'Forty winks. That's what my father used to call it. He said he'd have forty winks and be as right as rain.'

Bernice put her hands on her hips. 'If you think I don't know what you're up to, then you're mistaken. I am not going to be left behind when Bea goes to see Mrs Tredgold.'

Piers murmured, 'Is that what you think she's going to do? Do you really think she'd leave you in my charge?'

'Of course not,' said Bernice. 'You'll go with her. And I'm coming, too. Do you want me to look up his will while you're having your forty winks?'

'Whose will?' said Piers, closing his eyes and relaxing his length with a contented sigh.

'Yes, please,' said Bea. 'Do you know how?'

'Do I know how to ask Alexa? Haven't I the latest in phones? What sort of question is that?'

'Silly me,' said Bea, closing her eyes.

A gentle zzzing sound came from Piers.

Bernice said, happily, 'I knew, I just knew he'd snore!'

Seventeen

Saturday late afternoon

The sun shimmered on water in the dock. Bea wished they were going to take a dip in a swimming bath somewhere. Or perhaps dive into the sea off a sandy beach? She wished they were about to have a cream tea in a cafe in Cornwall, or that they were setting out for a walk in some leafy wood with nothing to be heard but the voice of a bird.

Instead, they'd taken a taxi and arrived in the rejuvenated Docklands on a day when most of its anthill of workers was absent. Bea wished she were able to take time off, too.

Oh, well. Onward and upward, and the good Lord be with us.

The doorman at Mrs Tredgold's building said he couldn't let them in without checking that they'd be welcome upstairs. Good. At least the first line of protection was in place.

Bea rather hoped Mrs Tredgold would say she was unavailable. But of course she didn't.

Bernice, who had changed into a slightly more formal long-sleeved T-shirt and black jeans and brushed out her long hair to hang free down her back, seemed unimpressed with their surroundings. In fact, she stuck her nose in the air and said, 'If I had enough money to live here, I'd fly my guests in by helicopter and land them on the roof so they wouldn't have to deal with London traffic.'

Piers rolled his eyes. 'Or tell them to take the Tube.'

Bea didn't comment. They were all nervous, weren't they?

They travelled up in the lift to the penthouse suite. Bernice's eyes widened when she stepped out into the hall and caught a glimpse of the astonishing scenery outside. 'Is that a garden? Up here in the clouds?'

There were indeed young trees in pots outside, and was that fake or real grass as well? The garden – as Mrs Tredgold had promised – had arrived.

'Mrs Abbot.' The new housekeeper stepped forward with a smile. 'Thank you so much for recommending me. I am going to be very happy here and yes, my cat loves it, too. Mrs Tredgold is expecting you. There's a breeze outside, so she's in the sitting room this afternoon.' She turned to Piers. 'And you are Mr Piers, who's going to paint her portrait? And this is Mrs Abbot's ward, Bernice?'

Someone had been doing their homework, hadn't they? Bea was pleased. This house-keeper's appointment was going to work out to the benefit of all concerned.

They trooped into the huge sitting room with windows overlooking the brand-new garden and the panoramic view of London. A door halfway along the back wall was ajar, no doubt to get a through draught.

Bea's eyes went to the card table at the far end, around which clustered four upright chairs. No one was sitting there now, but the chairs were at odd angles and there were playing cards, notepads and pencils still laid out on the baize surface. Someone had been playing bridge recently? Bea could guess who.

Mrs Tredgold said, 'Come in, Mrs Abbot. I expected you before this.' She was sitting in a modern recliner, with her stick at her side and a black-and-white cat on her lap. 'Forgive me for not rising but I'm providing a comfortable seat for my latest guest. He took to me at once, I am happy to say.' She twisted her head round to welcome Piers and Bernice. 'Good to see you again, Piers. Are you ready to start work, now? And I see you've brought Mrs Abbot's ward with you. One of the Holland dynasty, I understand. An interesting child. Do make yourselves comfortable.'

Piers and Bernice went towards the window, where they found seats. Piers undid his satchel to get out the tools of his trade.

Mrs T patted the arm of a chair next to her. 'Mrs Abbot, you must sit beside me, where I can see you more clearly. You'll join me in a cup of tea?'

'Thank you,' said Bea, drawing an occasional table close to her chair, and laying out her paperwork. 'A cup of tea would be most acceptable.'

Mrs Tredgold said, 'You have some news for me? I am all ears.'

Bea said, 'I have some information for you, but I am not at all sure you want to hear it. Would you like me to put everything back into my folder and dump it in the wastepaper bin?'

'What a strange idea.' Yet the older woman's voice cracked. Was that fear flickering at the back of her eyes? Probably. But she mastered it to say, 'Carry on.'

Bea said, 'You asked me to discover who killed your two cats. I have been at some pains to talk to the members of your household, some of whom were helpful and some not. I think we can rule certain people out but I cannot give you the proof you wanted.'

Mrs Tredgold said, 'That is truly disappointing.' Did a trace of satisfaction hang in the air? 'Do tell me what you've discovered.'

Bea took a deep breath. 'You weren't really interested in the death of the cats, were you?'

Mrs Tredgold shifted in her chair. 'Don't bandy words with me, young woman.'

Bea shook her head. 'You haven't been open with me from the beginning. You've known all along who did it. You couldn't prove it but you knew, all right. Only the knowledge was distressing and you didn't know what to do about it. You were not prepared to take the matter to the police as you considered, correctly, that they would do very little if anything to protect you or—'

'Protect me? What on earth do you mean?' Mrs Tredgold made a sharp movement and the cat leaped off her lap and disappeared. She said, 'Mrs Abbot, you are being absurd. My life is not in danger.'

Bea was silent, because she rather thought it was.

Mrs Tredgold closed her eyes and slumped in her chair. In a small voice she said, 'You won't help me, then?'

'I can't, unless you are prepared to be honest with me.'

'I don't want the police involved.'

'I understand that, but you know as well as I do that these things can escalate to a point at which your life might well be under threat.'

'Ridiculous!' Mrs Tredgold made a restless movement, looking anywhere but at Bea. 'Where is that tea, eh? I could do with a cup.' Then she turned back to Bea. 'So, you failed me, eh? I had thought better of you. What is your excuse?'

'You didn't give me enough information.' Bea extracted some sheets of paper from the pile in front of her and held them up. 'Shall I throw these away, or would you like me to go on?'

Mrs Tredgold sighed. 'Continue, since you've already got so far.'

'Wills are in the public domain after probate has been granted. My ward copied this one out for me. Your husband, Marcus Tredgold, left a considerable fortune to each of his children, and you were the residuary legatee. But he also mentioned two other people, didn't he? There's a clause stating that his faithful secretary, Anne Andrews, and her daughter, Mercy Andrews, had already been provided for. I haven't had time to get a copy of Mercy's birth certificate, but I suspect it will name your husband Marcus as her father. Am I right?'

There was a long silence.

The afternoon had clouded over. Rain spat at the windows.

Bea said, 'I can leave now if you wish, but I think it might ease you to talk about it.'

Mrs Tredgold said, 'It's the elephant in the room, isn't it? It is the big problem that nobody dares to mention but that is always there, and which affects everything that happens. Anne was a typist in my husband's office in the good old days before computers. She was his mistress for many, many years. All through his first marriage. You knew he'd been married before he met me? Well, he

259

had. She died. Anne thought Marcus would marry her when his first wife died, but he didn't. He married me instead. Why? Because I came from the same moneyed background? Because I was not the flighty sort and knew how to keep my mouth shut? Because I was good looking enough and had the right sort of county background?

'He made it clear that as his wife I would run his household, bear his children and be seen in public when it mattered, but that Anne's position was never to be questioned. He bought an annuity for her and a house in Kensington. In addition, he paid her a generous allowance over and above her office wages. He visited her twice a week. They never appeared together in public but I knew all about it. I could smell her on him, every time he came back from her. I thought that when I had the children he'd forget about her, but it didn't work that way.

'Why did I put up with it? For selfish reasons. I was fond of him, I enjoyed our lifestyle, we had the children together and I understood that some men need more than one woman at a time. I hated her. Fortunately we hardly ever met. Then I made a big mistake. I made a scene when he visited her instead of taking me out on my birthday. He was furious. He said I had broken the terms of our agreement, though heaven knows I never signed anything, and the terms seemed to vary according to how he felt about the matter. He devised a nice punishment for me, though.'

'He got Anne with child, and that child was Mercy.'

'Yes. At every step he kept me informed about

the child's welfare and upbringing. The very best schools, of course. A better car for Anne. I thought of divorce, often. Our own children were growing up and then away at boarding school. They'd been delightful when they were small, but their nanny and their boarding school had taught them a sense of entitlement which made me uneasy. I'm old fashioned, you see. I'd been brought up to regard myself as a steward of inherited wealth, and to be responsible for anyone who worked for me. Marcus considered the fact that he'd made so much money meant he was cleverer than anyone else and didn't have to care about what happened to other people. He passed that opinion on to his children without ensuring they knew how to earn money or look after it themselves.'

'Hubert didn't go down that road?'

'No. Dear Hubert was bookish and plunged into the obscure world of genealogy. He was the only one who understood the work ethic. His job was never going to bring in any money, but I was proud of him. Hubert married a fellow worker at the Institute of Genealogists. They rarely took a holiday and lived thriftily. I'd hoped they'd have children, but it never happened.'

'Edgar married, too.'

'I thought he'd made a good choice with Lavinia, who came from much the same background as I did. He was attracted to her cool good looks, and through her charity work she was in contact with minor and sometimes not so minor royalty, a section of society he couldn't reach by himself. I hoped she would persuade

him to take to that life and he did, for a while
. . . until he realized what hard work it could be.
At that point she lost her attraction for him.'

'When did your children learn about Anne?'

'I don't think they knew for years, but soon
after he was diagnosed with cancer Marcus
moved her into the house as our housekeeper and
gave her a suite of rooms. She brought Mercy
with her as her assistant. The children came to
understand it pretty quickly then. As for Marcus,
the specialists tried everything, but well . . . it
was no good. He could have had the most expensive nurses in the world but he liked to have one
or other of us beside him all the time – especially
at night. I saw how much it meant to him so I
didn't make a fuss. I am something of a coward,
you see. She did love him, you know.'

'He didn't make any further provision for her
in his will?'

'Not beyond what he'd already settled on them.
Besides that, he trusted me to see that they'd never
want for anything. He said they'd be at a loose
end when he'd gone and asked me to keep them
on in the house as long as I could. Nothing was
written down. I could have repudiated the deal, I
suppose, but I sympathized with Anne because
she'd spent her whole life waiting for Marcus to
acknowledge her. We never speak of the past but
have moved smoothly into a different relationship.
I have never given her an order but always made
requests or suggestions. In turn she has never
criticized me or thwarted any of my wishes.'

'When Marcus died, the children were given a
lump sum of money each?'

'Hubert invested his inheritance wisely and should be all right, whatever happens to me. The only capital expenditure he made was to buy a small magazine, which will never make any money but brings him some kudos. He can well afford its outgoings. The other two played ducks and drakes with their inheritance. I tried to give them good advice but it fell on deaf ears. Charlotte despises me because I have "no soul for poetry" as she puts it. She fell under the influence of one smoothie after the other. They could produce ancestors back to the Conqueror but had no intention of ever earning their living or of marrying her. They encouraged her to invest in the wildest of schemes – she even bought a racehorse at one point, if you please – and lost the lot. Edgar fell in with a group who are only happy when they're spending money, preferably on bigger and bigger yachts. They don't do any real sailing; just motor from port to party.

'After Marcus died, I grew tired of the children's squabbles and of a life lived in the public eye. I moved out of the big rooms on the ground floor up to the penthouse where I could be nice and quiet. I missed Marcus, but I was content with my lot. I was well served by the people who looked after me and I didn't have to take any notice of what went on in the rest of the house.'

'You discovered bridge and betting on the horses. You reconnected with Gordon. Until . . .'

'Yes, dear.' A quick smile. 'It was a good life until Edgar and Charlotte got through their capital and started to badger me to pay their debts. I could see that unless they altered their way of life, helping them would serve no purpose but to send good money after bad. I calculated that at their present rate they could get through everything I had left, including the house, within five years. So I struck. I refused to help them unless they helped themselves, and that they would not do.'

'Not Hubert.'

'No, not Hubert; he told the others to leave me alone but they wouldn't. Perhaps they couldn't. Their debts, their sense of entitlement . . . Some days I locked the door to my suite and took the phone off the hook and refused to let anyone in.'

'Did you know that Lavinia has left Edgar?'

'Has she?' Yet there was knowledge in her eyes. 'How strange.'

Bea said, 'I suspect she rang you last night to say she had had enough and was planning to leave today. I did wonder at first whether you'd give her sanctuary here. You liked and trusted her, didn't you? She was one of the three you played bridge with. The others were Hubert and Gordon. When one of them couldn't come, you invited Kit to join you instead.'

'I knew Lavinia was unhappy with Edgar. She is a proud woman and she felt she should stick to her marriage vows, but over the years and particularly of late, she's come to realize that Edgar is going to continue to abuse her, and her daughter doesn't listen to anything she says. She has money of her own, though less than it was since she's paid Edgar's debts time and again. So yes, I knew she was thinking of returning to her roots. Her brother is in politics. She thinks she can be of use to him. She was wise to go.'

There was a tap on the door and the house-keeper wheeled in a hostess trolley laden with tea, a plate of tiny sandwiches and some slices of cake.

'Splendid,' said Mrs Tredgold, leaning forward in her chair to indicate where the housekeeper should leave the trolley. 'Will you pour, dear? Oh, and I gave your little cat a fright and he jumped down. I don't know where he's gone, do you?'

Bernice spoke up from a chair by the window. 'He came to me first, and then he disappeared somewhere. He likes me. What's his name?'

'He's called Pippin,' said the housekeeper, pouring tea for one and all. Bea and Piers refused anything to eat, but Bernice took something of everything in sight. Mrs Tredgold took a tiny bite out of a sandwich and left the rest on her plate.

Bea thought of what Mrs Tredgold had said and what she'd skated over. It seemed to Bea that Marcia Tredgold was a perfect example of a woman who had had a sheltered life and always looked for the best in people. She was, Bea thought, slightly naive.

Bea waited till Mrs Tredgold had finished her cup of tea to say, 'Someone opened a window in your flat and dropped one of your cats out on to the roof of Hubert's conservatory. Was that because he stood up for you?'

'What nonsense. There was nothing sinister in it, although of course it had terrible repercus-sions. I've always thought that June, one of my cleaners, must have done it, perhaps irritated by Mitzi getting in her way. A momentary loss of control. She probably assumed the cat would scramble down into Hubert's balcony and that would be that. You couldn't expect her to own up, could you?'

Bea shook her head. 'You know perfectly well she was got rid of by a different pretext on another occasion. I can think of only one reason why you kept the knowledge of the culprit to yourself, and that was that it would have been more painful to Hubert to hear it than if you kept quiet about it.'

Mrs Tredgold's eyes sparkled with tears. 'I'd had quite a few callers that morning. Family. Friends. It was the most terrible accident. I can still see Lavinia's face, as she came rushing in to my sitting room, crying out that Hubert had fallen through the glass roof. . . Though it wasn't Hubert who'd fallen, as it happened, but his wife. We rushed to the window, and there . . . All that blood. Hubert howled like a wolf. It was awful! Awful!' There were beads of sweat on her forehead. She wiped them away. 'No one was to blame.'

'Hubert blamed himself, didn't he? Was it he who'd opened the window in your flat for you that day? Old windows tend to stick if they haven't been opened for a while. Did you ask him to open it? I'm not saying he threw the cat out, because if he had done so, he'd have blurted it out straight away. But he is still blaming himself for something. What is it? Was it just because he let his wife go up the ladder and didn't go himself? Or was it because he thought you'd done it yourself?'

Mrs T paled. Her fingers scrabbled on her lap. Eventually she said, 'He's the over-conscientious sort. I've tried to get him to talk to therapists and he refuses. His distress is terrible. I don't know how to help him.'

'Try telling him the truth. Tell him who put the cat out of the window, and he will be able to put the matter into perspective.'

Mrs Tredgold said, 'You have the weirdest imagination. Hubert's feeling guilty because he didn't go up the ladder to rescue Mitzi. He's not as bad at heights as Charlotte but he let Stefanie go up the ladder while he held it steady at the bottom.'

'You are protecting someone. Who is it? Did Stefanie herself put the cat out? Did she then run down the stairs in a panic and try to rescue the situation by going up the ladder herself?'

'Now you're being ridiculous.'

'Well, it wasn't Hubert. I agree he'd have confessed if he'd done it. And it wasn't your cleaner, June, either. So it must be either Anne Andrews or her daughter, or some other member of your family.'

Mrs Tredgold knocked her teacup over. Fortunately it was empty. She stared at Bea, her mouth working.

A shadowy figure shot into the room from the far door . . . the door that had been conveniently left ajar . . . the door that had concealed a listener. Or even two listeners?

Hubert was shaking. 'Mother? Was it Petra? I know she didn't like the cats but . . . She wouldn't have done that, would she? Why didn't you tell me?'

Mrs Tredgold said, in a voice that quavered, 'Teenagers lie when they're in trouble, don't they? She was so worried we would stop loving her if the truth came out. She didn't think it through. She was shattered, afterwards.'

I know that Petra is capable of considerable nastiness and this fits . . . and yet? It just feels so convenient.

Mrs Tredgold seized her son's hand. 'Try to understand. I couldn't give her away. She didn't mean anyone to get hurt. She dropped the cat out of the window, thinking it would scramble down. When you went to the rescue, Petra thought you'd put everything right. But when Stefanie died, poor Petra was so sorry. She cried so hard. I promised her I'd never tell anyone that I'd seen her . . . Forgive me, Hubert. I didn't know what to do for the best.'

'No-o-o!' He crumpled into an awkward heap at his mother's feet. 'Why didn't you say? I thought it was you! I saw you at the window! I couldn't understand why you didn't say! Then I thought I must have imagined it! That my mind was going. I thought I was going mad!'

A second shadowy figure came out of hiding. Gordon. Of course. Marcia would never have abandoned either of them. Bea wondered exactly how many bedrooms there were in this flat and how many Mrs T was going to take in. Well, Gordon had a place of his own. Perhaps he wasn't sleeping here.

Gordon patted Hubert's shoulder and helped him to his feet. 'There now, my boy. Cry it all out. You'll feel better now you know what really happened.'

Hubert sobbed. 'How could she! Does she think

268

she'll never have to answer for anything she does?'

Yes, probably. And judging by the way Mrs Tredgold has handled this revelation, Petra will indeed get away with it.

Gordon helped Hubert to sit on a chair beside his mother, who pressed his knee. Both were in tears.

Gordon said, 'There, there.'

'Oh, Hubert! I'm so sorry!'

'It's been eating away at me, thinking I'd seen you at the window and knowing it couldn't have been you, because you'd have said, wouldn't you? I thought my mind was playing tricks on me and—'

'Oh, Hubert! Wouldn't I have said if it had been me?'

'I don't know! The therapist said I was substituting my feelings for my mother or some such and I thought that was nonsense, and he went on about—'

'I'll kill that man,' said Gordon, meaning it.

'Oh, my dear boy.' Mrs Tredgold tried to pull him into her arms, clumsily. He was too tall and ungainly and she was in an awkward position, reaching forward to him at an angle. She cried out, 'Oh, my back!' And subsided into the recliner, holding up her hand and closing her eyes.

'Mother!'

Mrs Tredgold was clearly in pain. She whispered, 'It's all right. Give me a minute. It will pass.'

Bernice spoke up from the window. 'Sorry to interrupt, but I don't think we should eat any more of this cake. It's disgusting!'

269

Eighteen

All eyes were on Mrs Tredgold.

Gordon lowered the back of the recliner and, once Mrs Tredgold was in a horizontal position, the look of pain on her face gradually eased.

Hubert hovered. 'Shall I get you a glass of water?'

Gordon had taken charge. 'No, no. She'll be all right in a minute.'

And indeed, she was soon able to smile, and indicated that she wished to be returned to an upright position. 'A blip. Thank you, Gordon. I'm all right now, Hubert. No need to look so worried. I'll be glad to get Andy, my physio, back to look after me.'

Hubert seated himself beside her, holding one of her hands. 'You gave me such a fright!'

'I'm fine, really.' She gave Hubert's hand a little squeeze and held out her other one to Gordon. 'Dear Gordon. If only I'd stuck with you all along.'

Gordon held her hand in both of his. 'We were too young. We didn't understand commitment.'

She nodded. 'I know. Thank you, both of you. I am so fortunate to have you in my life. And now we know who dropped the cat on to the conservatory, we can all be comfortable about it. Right, Hubert?'

'Yes, yes. I suppose so. It's such a relief to know it wasn't all in my head. If only you'd told me!'

'I couldn't, dear. Not after I'd promised her I wouldn't.'

A long sigh. 'I suppose I can understand how it happened and why you covered up for her. It's tragic that my poor dear wife had to suffer but nobody could have foreseen that the glass would break, or that she would be injured.'

Gordon said, 'It's best to have these things out in the open, Hubert. Remember, I've been telling you—'

'That my dear wife wouldn't want me to follow her into the grave while I can still be of use in the world. Yes, I remember, and I will try to put the whole affair behind me now.'

'Good boy!' said Mrs Tredgold, reviving. 'Now, would someone be so kind as to pour me a fresh cup of tea? And I think I might fancy a sandwich now. How about you, Gordon? And Hubert? I don't have a bell to ring for help yet, but if you could just pop into the kitchen, I'm sure our new housekeeper will be happy to oblige with a fresh pot for us.'

It was Gordon who went. Of course. Hubert continued to hold his mother's hand, and she to smile on him.

Let's all play Happy Families, shall we?

For the time being.

Bea wondered if Mrs Tredgold would want to hear the rest of her report. But perhaps she'd had enough excitement for one day. Bea also wondered if Hubert would ever recover and if he would marry again. She was surprised how

271

easily Mrs Tredgold had forgiven young Petra for bringing about the death of her aunt. The death had not been intentional, but still . . .

Of course, Mrs Tredgold didn't know about the acid attack, did she?

Or who had killed her cats?

Or did she? It was difficult to know exactly how much Mrs Tredgold knew about anything. When Bea had first met the older woman, Mrs Tredgold had given the impression of being the puppet master, moving the pieces of her family around at will. Then Bea had learned that Mrs Tredgold had wept when her staff had been driven away and that she'd been unable to stop the family's bullying. Perhaps the truth lay somewhere in between strength and weakness, as indeed it did for most people.

Mrs Tredgold had compromised about Anne Andrews, had covered up Petra's role in the death of Hubert's wife and in due course would probably have arranged matters so that she could move out of the family home without causing everyone to go to panic stations. Only the cats had been killed, which had panicked Mrs T into calling Bea in for help.

Did Mrs Tredgold now feel that she didn't need Bea's help any longer?

Mm. Yes. Quite possibly.

How far had Mrs Tredgold really wanted Bea to go in her search for the truth? Perhaps just enough to give her leverage against the bullying of her family, but not enough to have anyone handed over to the police?

Gordon returned, saying a fresh pot of tea was

coming up. He seated himself on the other side of Mrs Tredgold, who smiled on him, too.

Bea gave a little cough. 'Would you like me to continue, Mrs Tredgold? I really think we should. You are still in a vulnerable position.'

'On no, dear. No one knows I'm here except for these two lovely men, and they'll look after me beautifully, I know.'

'I beg to differ. Back at the big house, there's one mailbox on the gates. I suppose Mercy collects the mail daily and takes it back into the house to be sorted out for various members of the family. There must have been a lot of extra mail dealing with your buying this place and arranging for telephone and internet to be connected. There would be instructions to decorators and the restorers who took your favourite pieces away only to have them returned to your new address.'

'Yes, dear, but I was very clever. All that went through Gordon.'

'Letters for Gordon would have been collected and distributed along with the others. You don't think Mercy would notice he was getting mail from estate agents and solicitors and computer people? From decorators and restorers? Perhaps she thought at first that it was Gordon who was moving out, but when she noticed the restorers were taking pictures and other small pieces of furniture from your rooms, never to be returned, then she must have drawn the correct conclusion. And told her mother.

'Moreover, either Mercy or her mother answers the phone when a call is made to the house and not to individual persons. Gordon was in and out.

273

When he was out, didn't Mercy take messages for him? Appointments with decorators or service people could be changed if the date or time became inconvenient. People mislay details of precisely which day or which flat they should deliver to. So they'd ring Gordon, and if he were out, then Anne or Mercy would take the call. Those two women knew early on what you were doing, but for reasons of their own they kept their mouths shut.'

Mrs Tredgold looked alarmed for a moment but then she relaxed. 'Well, I don't think that's a real problem.'

'In other words, you don't think either of them killed your cats. Which means you have a good idea who did.'

Rightly or wrongly, Mrs T has adopted the idea that her young granddaughter – who was to be forgiven everything because of her youth – had dropped Mitzi out of the window and caused the death of Hubert's wife. Mrs Tredgold has taken the view that it was an accident, and we can't really blame the child for an accident, can we?

If you followed that idea along to its logical conclusion, then Mrs Tredgold will also say that Petra killed the cats. It would be so convenient if everyone accepted that. And if anyone were so impertinent as to ask for a motive, then she'd say that Petra must have developed a phobia about cats after she'd inadvertently caused her aunt's death. And then, because it would be ridiculous to assume two killers in one household, Mrs T is going to say that for some reason Petra had fed Ahmed a dose of something which had done for him, too. Purely by accident, of course, and not meaning to kill him. And then Mrs Tredgold will claim that her grandchild had panicked, as of course, dear, she must have done, being so young, and that Petra had covered up her 'mistake' by leaving a suicide note on his phone.

It all hung together so nicely.

So conveniently.

The police had accepted that Ahmed had committed suicide, so there was no need to look into anyone else's actions, was there?

If Bea was right, then any minute now Mrs Tredgold would dismiss Bea from the case.

Which is exactly what she did.

'Now, dear, I am very grateful to you for helping me sort out the misunderstanding over the death of poor Hubert's wife, and perhaps we should draw a line under your investigation. I'll pay you well for what you've done and we'll leave it at that.'

Bea set her teeth. She was not prepared to leave it at that. In the first place, she'd put herself out to do some work for Mrs T only to be attacked in the street. And, in the second place, Bea believed that Mrs T was still at risk.

So she said, 'Wouldn't you like to know who claims to have stayed in the house the night the cats were killed? And who everyone thinks did the deed?'

'Well, yes. I suppose that would be amusing.'

She's playing it down.

Why is she not anxious to have the truth come out? Who is she covering up for, and why?

Bea riffled through the papers in front of her and selected one, which she held up for Mrs Tredgold to see. 'I have signatures from most, if not all, of the people concerned. First, Gordon signed to say he slept in the coach house the night the cats were killed. He said that he'd seen Hubert in the garden and taken him back to the coach house to sleep. If you accept that . . .?'

'I do. Dear Gordon. Dear Hubert. I knew neither of them would ever hurt Mitzi and Poppy.'

'Fine.' Bea selected three more. 'I saw Lavinia. She signed to say she'd slept there that night. She said that their daughter had a sleepover somewhere else and didn't come back to their quarters that night. She was prepared to give me the contact details for the sleepover. She added that Edgar had come into her room about midnight to report that Petra was out and she'd reminded him of the arrangement.'

'No, no!' said Mrs Tredgold, becoming agitated. 'I'm sure that's wrong. Lavinia must have the dates wrong.'

Bea said, 'Edgar agrees with you. He says Petra was there. Petra also signed to say she was there. It's up to you to decide.'

Edgar wanted Petra to receive a share of the sale of the house and therefore he'd maintain up hill and down dale that she slept there the night the cats were killed. He hadn't realized yet that his mother was going to say that it was Petra who'd done the dirty deed.

For reasons of her own, Mrs Tredgold wanted to put the blame for the slaughter of the cats on Petra. So she needed the girl to claim to have slept in the house that night. If it was decided that the girl had killed the cats, she'd automatically lose her share of the sale of the house. But, if she wasn't at the house that night, she couldn't claim a share of the loot. Either way, Petra lost out.

Unless, of course, the girl had used the conveniently vacant bedroom in the basement . . . with her boyfriend . . . who might or might not confirm their presence in the house . . .

Bea wasn't particularly concerned about the girl losing her share of the money, and in some ways Bea thought it would be only natural justice if that did happen, but it must be for the right reason.

Mrs Tredgold was almost smiling. She said, 'Poor Petra. So young and so difficult. I know Lavinia has had a terrible time with her. The girl has got in with the wrong crowd, of course. She's been led astray. I'm grieved to think she has behaved so badly, but she's young and I'm sure she'll pull herself together when she realizes what she's done. Young people nowadays, they might as well be living on a different planet. They never know what month it is, never mind what year.'

Bea thought that Petra could probably identify not only the month and year, but also the date and the hour. However. She held up the next paper. 'Charlotte signed to say she was there. Kit Crossley confirms that he saw Edgar and Charlotte late that evening and both were preparing for bed. Next: Ms Andrews signed to say she slept there. Her daughter, Mercy, didn't. However, it is just possible that young Carly, Ms Andrews's niece, may have slept in the house that night, either up in Hubert's flat while he was over with Gordon or making use of the extra bedroom in the basement . . . That is, if Petra wasn't already there. Some of these people signed without really

277

considering what might happen if they'd made a false declaration.'

'Really?' Mrs Tredgold was thinking hard. Was she deciding whether or not she should try to lay the blame on one of the other young women, rather than on Petra? Which would she choose? Mercy . . . or Carly? In Bea's estimation, neither would be a good bet for a fall guy. It would be far more realistic to stick to blaming Petra.

'Well, well,' said Mrs Tredgold. 'That's all very interesting, but it doesn't alter the facts: Edgar, Lavinia and Petra, Charlotte, Hubert and Gordon all slept there, as did Anne Andrews, but not her daughter or Carly. Eight people. I'm including Ahmed, of course.'

Bea felt her temper rise. 'Blood money.' How dare Mrs Tredgold dump all the blame on Petra! 'It's called blood money when the family of the killer pays off the victim's family to avoid prosecution.'

Gordon said, 'Now, come on! That's no way to talk!'

'Isn't it?' said Bea. 'I was asked to get these signatures and I have done so. I have failed to find evidence which will stand up in court as to who killed the cats and arranged for Ahmed to die, but I have come to certain conclusions. Mrs Tredgold originally suggested that it was up to me to decide who killed the cats and now—'

'Yes, dear, and you've done a good job. But the final decision must rest with me.'

Bea said, between her teeth, 'That is your right. But before you make that decision you might like to take into consideration one or two things I learned from those who have served you loyally for years and who know the family well. You asked me to tell your staff members that they would be getting a bonus when the house is sold. Those who had worked with you longest had very definite ideas about who was responsible for the deaths of the cats. They decided that each of them should write down the name of the person they believed to be responsible. They folded the papers over and did not show what they had written to anyone before passing them on to me.'

Mrs Tredgold looked troubled. She held out her hand for the papers. 'Give those to me. I'll read them later. Gossiping women can't be trusted. It will only muddy the waters for me to read out what they've said.'

'Don't you want to know who they thought it was? It's interesting that they all gave the same name.'

'They talked about it among themselves and that's why they all said the same.' Mrs Tredgold flicked the papers open and read the name each one of them had given. Her expression of mild interest did not change. 'As I thought, they were influenced, wrongly, of course, by talking to one another. These papers are irrelevant.'

Bea stared at Mrs Tredgold. How could she not believe what her faithful servants had said? Bea decided to make one last try. 'There is one other thing which you might wish to take into consideration. Piers rang you last night to tell you that on leaving your house some sticky yellow liquid had been thrown at me by the passenger on a moped. When it was realized that the liquid was some sort of fruit juice, the matter was dismissed as a prank. Perhaps, it was thought, someone after my handbag?'

Mrs Tredgold's attention sharpened. 'Yes, Piers told me about that. But you were not hurt. He also said that you couldn't identify your attackers.' She shifted uncomfortably in her chair and avoided Bea's eye. Bea considered that Mrs Tredgold probably had a very good idea who the people on the moped might have been.

Bea confirmed, 'No, I wasn't hurt, but I was badly frightened. All I saw was two young people on a moped, wearing helmets and black leather clothing.'

'How do you know they were young?'

'Body language. Both were slim and lissom. The driver was taller with broad shoulders. The passenger was not as tall and she had a womanly figure. It's true that I didn't see their faces or the licence number of the moped. What you don't know is that later that day I received a message on my phone, saying that that attack had been a warning.'

Gordon frowned. 'Really?'

Hubert was open-mouthed. 'But that's terrible!'

They were shocked. Neither of them had known about the attack.

Mrs Tredgold hadn't passed the news of this 'incident' on to them. Surely she should have done so if she hadn't feared to raise the subject and start the two men wondering if there were any connection to her family?

'You received a warning?' Suddenly Mrs

Tredgold looked every day of her age. Had she guessed what was coming?

'Yes, I did,' said Bea, watching Mrs Tredgold. 'I was tempted to give up and not return to your house to collect the rest of the information you'd asked for. Piers didn't want me to return. But I did. The attack was repeated, but this time we managed to get into a taxi before the moped reached us. This time acid was used. We were not hurt but the taxi was scarred and the driver wants the police to prosecute. And yes, the police are taking the matter seriously this time.'

'Could you identify the people concerned?' Mrs Tredgold was hoping for the best and fearing the worst.

'We managed to take photos on our phones as we were attacked and as the moped drove off afterwards. We got the licence plate. It was dirty but the police think they can work out what it was. Yes, the police have that information now. Also, they retrieved the bottle which had contained the acid and are testing it for fingerprints.'

Mrs Tredgold put her hand to her throat. 'No doubt the pranksters were wearing gloves.'

'Yes. But one or other, or perhaps both of them, would have handled the bottle beforehand and may well have left prints. I'm sure the police will be very thorough in investigating the matter. We did ask Ms Andrews if we might check for the presence of a moped in the underground garage at the house, but she refused to let us do so. No doubt when the police return, armed with a search warrant—'

281

'Enough!' Mrs Tredgold had become agitated. 'You have gone too far. You must go now! I have things to do! I am not well!'

Gordon drew back. 'Marcia, you don't mean that you knew—'

'No, of course I didn't!' said Mrs Tredgold. 'It might have crossed my mind when Piers said . . . But I never thought, didn't think the little fool would be so . . . But she's so headstrong, won't listen to anyone who . . . Oh, what am I going to do?'

Bea said, 'You were prepared to let Petra take the blame for causing the death of Hubert's wife. You were prepared to let her take the blame for killing your cats. Possibly you were also prepared to let her take the blame for Ahmed's death, even though you rather hoped that little matter had been solved by the police accepting the suicide note? But you didn't think she'd be up to an acid attack? Is that one crime too many?'

'I . . . I don't feel well.'

Gordon stood up. 'That's quite enough, Mrs Abbot. I think you'd better leave.'

Hubert was all concern. 'Mother, do you want to lie down?'

Mrs Tredgold closed her eyes and made little movements with her hands as if to push people away from her.

Bea got to her feet, but she wasn't finished yet. 'I believe that your granddaughter and her friend are guilty of the two attacks, yes. And yes, they ought to answer for it. Was Petra also guilty of killing the cats? I don't think so, and neither do the people who have loved and served you for

282

years. Was Petra guilty of killing Ahmed? I doubt it. I really don't understand what happened there. What I do know is that you think it's easier to blame Petra for everything than to look into what really happened. Please, Mrs Tredgold! For your own sake, it is not wise to leave the investigation where it is.'

Gordon turned on Bea. 'What on earth do you mean?'

Bea said, 'She knows. There's more than one person living in that house who wishes her ill. I don't know why, but I believe Mrs Tredgold is protecting the real killer by throwing the blame on Petra. This is understandable but not sensible. Think about it. Someone who is capable of bringing about the death of another person is capable of trying again, especially if they think they've got away with it first time round.'

Mrs Tredgold turned her face from Bea and clutched Gordon's arm. 'Tell her to go. Tell her I'll pay her bill, but that's enough. I don't want to see her again.'

'Yes, but Marcia—'

'I'm tired. Get rid of her.'

Bea picked up her handbag. 'When this is all over, your old chef, Kit Crossley, your physio Andy, and your faithful cleaners June and Maggie would be delighted to work for you again. But not until justice has been done.'

Gordon loomed over Bea. 'Didn't you hear her? She has asked you to go.'

Looking into his concerned face, Bea suddenly realized why Mrs Tredgold was so anxious to divert attention from the real villain in the case.

Bea felt faint. She took a step back. 'Oh, I see it all! How dreadful! But, Mrs Tredgold, you can't give in to blackmail!'

'Can't do what?' Mrs Tredgold attempted to smile. 'You are ridiculous! Please, go!'

Bea felt as if she'd been poleaxed. She couldn't think straight. The sudden flash of knowledge that she'd had evaporated. Surely she'd been mistaken! She said, 'Yes, I'll go. I can't do any good by staying.'

She looked around for Piers and Bernice, who had been quiet all afternoon.

Piers looked up from his sketchbook, nodded and began to put it away in his satchel. 'Ready?'

Bernice was not ready to go. She was standing by the doors which led on to the balcony, struggling to get one open.

Bea said, 'Bernice?'

'Sorry. Sorry,' said Bernice. 'I'm feeling a bit sick and I can't open the window. The cat's been sick, too. I think the cake was poisoned!'

Nineteen

Saturday late afternoon, continued

Bernice's colour was indeed poor.

Piers was the nearest to her. He sprang up to wrestle with the catch on the door and managed to force it open.

Bernice stumbled out into the open air, taking deep breaths, holding on to her head. Unsteady on her feet.

The cake? Bea looked at the trolley which the housekeeper had brought in, laden with plates of sandwiches and cake. The sandwiches looked homemade. The cake was a lemon drizzle bought affair, cut in slices. Only the end piece was missing. The one Bernice had taken?

Bea shot out to join Bernice, who was weeping and moaning. Her forehead was cool. She wasn't running a temperature . . . or was she?

Bernice put a finger down her throat and retched. Nothing came up.

Piers shot some words at Bea and disappeared. What had he said? She hadn't caught it. Never mind that!

Bea held the child's long hair back, as she retched again . . . and again.

Bernice said, 'I feel awful! Oh! I only ate a bit! It was horrible.'

'You think it was the cake? No one but you ate the cake.'

'Ooooh!' Bernice doubled over, retching. Nothing came up.

Piers appeared, holding a glass of dull-looking water. 'Drink this! Mustard solution. It will bring everything up.' He held it to her mouth.

'Ugh! Nasty!' Bernice tried to fend him off, but he persisted.

'Best to get it all up.'

Bea whispered, 'You think she's been poisoned?'

'Dunno. Best not take any chances.'

Bernice drank. Tried to hold it down. Vomited.

285

Copiously. Into a big flowerpot. A sickly sweet odour arose.

'Finish it!' Piers held the glass to Bernice's mouth again. She tried to push him away, but he persisted.

She drained the glass and vomited again. Not so much came up this time. She bent over the flowerpot, limp. Head down.

Bea held her shoulders.

The girl was trembling. At last she lifted her head. 'I'm feeling better. It was the cake, I think. It tasted horrible. I only took a couple of bites. The cat took a bite, too. I think he was sick behind the chair I was on.'

Piers disappeared again.

Bea steered Bernice away from the flowerpot and its odour. The child wept, quietly. She was shivering. Shock.

Bea found a tissue in her pocket and wiped the girl's face.

Bernice continued to shake. Bea enclosed her in her arms and held her fast.

I should never have brought her. What sort of guardian am I to put my ward in danger? I shall never forgive myself if she's been poisoned. Should we get her to hospital to be pumped out? Well, she has been sick. She's probably all right. Dare I take the risk? No.

I must get a sample of her vomit so that the police can trace the poison.

There was a commotion indoors. Gordon shouted something.

Piers replied quietly, but in a forceful manner.

Mrs Tredgold cried out, 'No, no!'

Hubert said, 'Don't distress yourself, Mother.'

Another voice – the housekeeper? – raised in a scream. Grief! 'No, no! Not my cat!'

Piers said something else, quietly.

Bernice stirred in Bea's arms. 'Is the cat all right?'

'I don't know.' Bea continued to hold on to the girl.

Bernice stopped shaking. Her body was warm against Bea's.

A phone rang inside the apartment, and someone – Gordon? – answered.

Bernice said, 'The cake tasted funny. Was it poisoned? I'm not going to die, am I? It tasted horrible. The cat thought so, too. But he was curious. He nibbled a bit and then he was sick.' A deep breath. 'I tried to tell you the cake was funny, didn't I? But you were all shouting at one another and didn't hear me. I should have made you listen.'

'You didn't poison the cake. You tried to warn us. You have nothing to blame yourself with.'

'Should I apologize to the housekeeper for not looking after her cat?'

'You can say how sorry you are but you have no need to apologize. After all, it was she who brought the cake in for us to eat. And no, before you ask, I don't think she'd have done so if she'd known it was poisoned. She wouldn't risk the life of her cat.'

Deep breathing while Bernice thought about that. Then she said, 'Piers knew what to do. He's all right, really, isn't he?'

It was the first time ever that she'd called him by his proper name. Bea said, 'Yes, he is.'

Bernice disengaged herself from Bea's arms. 'I must look a mess. Ugh, I've got sick on my hair. I'm just so bored with having long hair. It gets in the way.'

'Let's go and wash it off. Clean ourselves up.'

'And go home straight away?'

'Someone has got to look into the business of the cake, but not us. We'll leave that to the police. Find a bathroom, have a good wash and we'll get out of here. I don't know where the bathrooms are. Somewhere off the hall, I suppose. Do you want me to come with you?'

'I'm not a child!' Bernice stepped back into the sitting room and went across it into the hall beyond.

Bea followed her, trying to work out what had happened in their absence.

The housekeeper was crouched on the floor, watching as Piers busied himself over the tiny black-and-white bundle on the floor. The cat had been sick, yes. But it was moving. It wasn't dead.

Piers handed the cat to its owner, who was crying and crooning, 'Come on, my lovely, tell me you're not dead.'

Mrs Tredgold was distressed. 'The cat's going to be all right, isn't she?'

Piers helped the housekeeper to her feet. She was still crying and still talking to the cat, who was stirring feebly in her arms. Piers helped the woman back through the room and into the hall and closed the door behind them.

Bea watched them go and thought about what was going to happen if the cat died.

Gordon came into the room from the hall,

ushering in someone they hadn't expected. He said, 'It's Ms Andrews, Marcia. When the doorman rang through to tell me she was here I told her to go away, but she said it was vitally important that she sees you.'

Mrs Tredgold sat upright and reached for her stick. 'What! How did you know where to find me?'

Anne Andrews was wearing an outdoor jacket and towing a tote bag on wheels. She was, perhaps, looking a trifle paler than usual, but still composed. She said, 'I brought you some of your night things, all that I had time to pack in a hurry. My daughter and I've known for ages that you were planning to move. Did you really think you could send all your favourite pictures for cleaning without my noticing that they never came back? Of course I contacted the restorers to find out what had happened to them. And there were phone calls asking for confirmation of times to deliver this and that. We've had this address for ages. But if you didn't want to tell us, then I wasn't going to say anything.'

'Then why have you come?'

'Your son and daughter have just found out where you are.'

'No! How? We've been so careful.'

'Not careful enough. Normally my daughter fetches the post from the box in the courtyard but today she neglected her usual tasks to help Lavinia pack. By ill fortune Charlotte, who was expecting some letter or other, went out to fetch the mail instead. She spotted an envelope addressed to Gordon with the logo of the picture restorer on it and opened it. As she said, why would he have a picture restorer writing to him when he doesn't have any pictures? Inside was a bill for the cleaning of some of Mrs Tredgold's favourite pictures which Charlotte knew had recently vanished from her mother's rooms, together with the new address to which they had been delivered.'

Gordon said, 'So that's how they found out! What bad luck!'

Ms Andrews twitched a smile. 'Believe me, it's not the only bit of correspondence which has been misdirected in recent months. Mercy has always spotted them in the past and set them aside for you to deal with but it's been a difficult day, what with Mrs Abbot and her friends disrupting our routine. Not that there was that much routine, given Lavinia's decision to leave. It wasn't surprising that Mercy forgot the post.

'When she found the restorer's bill, Charlotte took it to Edgar and they stormed down to confront me in my office. I told them I knew you'd been planning to go and they lost it. They screamed at me that I was a traitor and worse. They began to push at me, first on one side and then on the other. I found their lack of control disturbing. I backed up against the wall and got my mobile out. I said that if either of them laid a hand on me again, I'd call the police and have the pair of them arrested for assault. They saw that I meant it, so they backed off. Charlotte countered by giving me the sack.'

Gordon was the first to speak. 'Ms Andrews, they can't sack you, can they?'

Mrs Tredgold had her hand to her mouth. 'I can't believe that they laid hands on you! No, they can't sack you. They don't pay your wages.'

Hubert was puzzled. 'Ms Andrews, I don't understand. How would Charlotte and Edgar cope without you to run the house for them?'

Ms Andrews softened into a smile for Hubert. 'I know that, and you know that, but they are beyond reason, and I don't see how I can stay on now.'

Mrs Tredgold put her hand over her eyes. 'It's all going wrong. I never meant it to be like this.'

Bernice, huge-eyed and pale but clean and tidy, slipped back into the room. She nodded to Bea, and mouthed, 'Can we go now?'

Bea shook her head and mouthed back, 'In a minute.'

Ms Andrews hadn't noticed Bernice's return. She said, 'They gave me twenty-four hours to pack and get out. Mrs Tredgold, I need longer than that. There's a lot needs sorting out. I need to get the accounts up to date, there's a carpenter booked tomorrow to replace a rotten floorboard at the top and the boiler service is due. If I have to go, then I want to leave everything in good order. I told Edgar and Charlotte that we'd have to see what you said about my leaving so soon. Charlotte went all quiet and said we would see, indeed we would. She left, I suppose to ring you to confirm that I'd been sacked.'

Mrs T said, 'Well, she may have tried but I'd switched my phone off to have a little nap. It's been a difficult day.'

'For me, too. I was left with Edgar, who said

he wanted me out of the house there and then. He stormed off, shouting for Petra, and I . . . I didn't know what to do. I tried ringing you but couldn't get through. I pride myself on thinking clearly but for once I was at a loss. Mercy had heard the shouting and came to join me. I told her what had happened. We agreed she'd start packing up my things while I got some of Mrs Tredgold's belongings together.' She indicated the tote bag. 'I managed to get a few of your things together: nightdress, underwear and so on. It's a start. You'll have to send someone for the rest.

'Charlotte came back after a while but went straight up to see Edgar and then there was a lot more shouting and banging of doors. It was on my mind that they'd be over to see you soon and that I must warn you. I tried your number again and again, but you didn't pick up. Is there a landline here yet? Perhaps if you'd give me the number . . .? That is, if you trust me with it.'

'Of course I trust you,' said Mrs Tredgold. 'You do have somewhere to go, don't you? Marcus told me he'd made provision for both of you. Mercy lives in the house in Kensington, doesn't she?'

'Yes. She's a good girl. Now this job is finished I think she'll probably be off to the States. She's always talked about going one day and now is the time for her to get away and make a fresh start. I told her I couldn't rest until I'd warned you what had happened. She said she'd carry on with the packing while I came to see if you were all right. I know we've never been close, Marcia . . .' and perhaps it was the first time Ms Andrews had ever called her employer by her Christian name, '. . . but we've known one another a long time. I'm glad to see you are in good health and well looked after.'

Mrs Tredgold lay back in her chair. 'Oh, Anne, you don't know the half of it.' She pointed to the trolley. 'The cake. Bernice was sick, and the poor dear little cat. I'm jinxed.'

'No, no,' said Gordon, distressed for her.

Mrs Tredgold would not be comforted. 'It was meant for me. I was meant to eat it and die!'

Hubert said, 'No, no!' But he was showing the whites of his eyes in shock. The stress was beginning to take its toll on him. Was he going to go to pieces again?

Piers came back in, shutting the door behind him. 'The cake. The housekeeper says it was handed in downstairs this afternoon by someone who said it had been left out of a delivery from the supermarket by mistake. The doorman sent it up when he had a minute. The housekeeper thought nothing of it and served it up in all innocence.'

'Man or woman?' That was Gordon, who was catching on fast.

'The housekeeper doesn't know. I've checked and the doorman who was on duty earlier this afternoon has now gone off for the weekend. His replacement doesn't know anything.'

Gordon said, 'We should tell the police.'

Mrs Tredgold shook her head. 'No, no. We can't. It's . . . The thing is, it's family. I'm sure it was just a prank. Young people can be so thoughtless.'

Hubert couldn't take that. 'Mother, that was no

293

prank! If you think Petra could have been responsible for . . . Well, I admit she hasn't much sense, but to poison a cake? No! I don't believe it.'

'Neither do I,' said Bea, drawing all eyes to her. 'Mrs Tredgold, this has to stop. I know you've tried to keep a lid on things but you can't ignore an attempt to poison you. If you won't call the police then I will.'

Mrs Tredgold clutched at her chest. 'You can't! You don't know what you're saying!'

'Oh yes, I do,' said Bea.

Gordon was anxious. 'My dear, I think Mrs Abbot is right.'

'No, you mustn't! You don't understand!'

Bea said, 'I do understand, Mrs Tredgold. It's now clear to me who you are protecting and why. I don't blame you for trying to hush things up. You've been sitting on a land mine for some time, but your running away has actually set off the explosion you've been dreading.'

Mrs Tredgold gasped, 'You don't know anything!'

'One by one your faithful staff and the sympathetic members of your family have been hounded out of the household. Kit Crossley and your cleaner June, framed for theft. Andy, the physio, accused of vandalism. Hubert, driven to a breakdown by a prank that went wrong. You must agree that all that is true.'

Mrs Tredgold nodded, her eyes huge.

Bea said, knowing this was the crucial question, 'Then why wasn't Gordon targeted?'

Silence. Everyone's eyes switched to Gordon, who blinked. And looked stunned.

Hubert drew back. 'Are you trying to say that it was Gordon who's been driving us all mad? That it was he who got rid of Mother's staff? No, I don't believe it. He's been good to me. Like a father. Better than my own father.'

Gordon nodded. 'Mrs Abbot, I must admit you have a point. I have wondered, several times, why nobody has tried to get me out. I wouldn't hurt Marcia for the world. I've tried to be her friend, to be a friend to the whole family, and Heaven knows I don't understand what's been going on. I tell myself that I'm not a threat to anyone, but neither were the other people who've been got rid of. Yes, I've been on tenterhooks wondering when an attempt is going to be made to get me out, but it hasn't happened.'

Bea said, 'The attempt was made some time ago, Gordon. It worked, but you never knew about it.'

Mrs Tredgold said, 'Please! Please, Mrs Abbot. Go no further! You're right, of course, but I'll pay you double, whatever you ask! Just don't say any more.'

The housekeeper put her head round the door. 'Some more members of the family have rung through to say they are on their way up to see you, Mrs Tredgold. I don't know who they are, and I don't care. I'm not staying here. You'll have to find someone else to look after you in future.' She retreated, shutting the door behind her.

Gordon said, 'Marcia, I don't understand.'

Bea said, 'She was protecting you, Gordon. She's known all along who was responsible for what was happening to her family and to her loyal staff.'

'But what have I done?' He genuinely didn't know.

Bea said, 'It's not what you've done, but what someone wanted you to do.'

The door to the hall was flung open and young Petra was pushed, head first, into the room. She had lost her usual air of superiority, and one of her bra straps had broken and was hanging free. She had a long red scratch down her arm, and her hair was all over the place. She was weeping.

She looked a mess. And frightened. She fell to the floor and stayed there.

Charlotte loomed in the doorway behind the girl. Four square. Solid. A female warrior lacking only a winged helmet and a shield.

Edgar hovered behind his sister, bleating, 'Oh, come on, now!'

Charlotte put her hands on her hips to survey the room. 'Having tea, are we? Did we enjoy the cake I sent up for you?'

Mrs Tredgold said, in a faint voice, 'Charlotte, not now. I'll talk to you in a minute, when these other people have gone home.'

'No. It's good to have witnesses. I want this settled once and for all.' She stirred Petra's prone body with her hefty shoe. 'She's come to confess what she's done. To make sure everyone knows exactly what she's been up to. When that's out of the way, we can settle what's to be done about the house and the future and we can all go back to being happy again.'

296

Gordon said, 'I don't understand.'

Charlotte threw him a glance of disdain. 'Of course you don't. Men like you should be castrated at birth. You're the scum of the earth, the—'

'Steady on,' said Gordon.

Petra had regressed to her real age. Snot ran from her nose. One side of her face was red and blotchy. She sobbed, 'I didn't do it! At least, not all of it. I swear I didn't.'

Charlotte pulled a chair up beside her mother and sat in it, knees well apart. 'Stop that, my girl! You know what we agreed. You'll confess to what you've done and be sent off to boarding school or I turn you over to the police, who will deal with you like any other juvenile delinquent. You don't want a taste of prison, do you?'

'No, but I—'

'Enough! Stand up straight when I'm talking to you, you little shit. Did you really think you could cheat me out of what is my due?'

The girl tried to stand and didn't make it. 'No, I—'

'So come on. Tell the nice ladies and gentlemen what we agreed. First, you were cross with Mitzi because she clawed your leg and you dropped her out of Granny's window, right? You were so frightened by what happened to Stefanie that you didn't say anything about it. Correct?'

'I—' A glance up at Charlotte from under her brows. Then, 'Yes, I suppose so.'

'Stop snivelling! The next thing you did was to make mischief with the staff. It amused you to hide things like your father's watch and see everyone else running around, looking for them. Right?'

Petra held out her hands to her father. 'Daddy, I didn't—'

'Yes, you did,' said Charlotte. 'Who else in the house would do such things?'

'Daddy!'

Bea thought it was time to intervene. 'Yes, Edgar. Come clean. It was you who framed Kit for stealing your watch, wasn't it?'

Edgar went pink. 'I . . . er . . . I might have mislaid it, and mistakenly thought . . . Well, you know how it is.'

'You framed Kit. Right. You can at least clear your daughter of that matter.'

Edgar swallowed. 'Yes, but Petra did other things, didn't she? I mean, Charlotte says there were some acid attacks! I can't believe it of you! What would your mother say? Charlotte's right, Petra, you have got to make a clean breast of it and then we can start again.'

The girl sank to her knees and curled her arms around her. Her hair fell over her face. There was a livid bruise forming on her left arm.

Charlotte smacked her lips. She was enjoying this, wasn't she? 'So she should. Now, Petra, let's get down to the nitty-gritty. You might not have planted the watch, but you were very happy to see the chef go because he'd never treated you as you felt you deserved. So on the night he'd been given the sack, you lured the cats down to the main kitchen and cut their throats. You thought everyone would jump to the conclusion that Chef had done it in response to being sacked. Unfortunately for you, he left early, and I heard you come in much later.'

Petra sobbed. 'You didn't see us. No one saw us.'

'I saw you. You woke me, falling into the hall and letting the door bang shut when you came up from the garage. Too much to drink, eh? It makes you clumsy. I came out on the landing to see what all the fuss was about and I saw you telling the lad with you how to put on the alarm which covers the garage and the back door. I would have come down and given you a piece of my mind but I was in my nightwear and then you bolted off downstairs and I thought it could wait. You'd snuck back into the house to have sex with him, hadn't you? Dirty little trollop that you are.'

The girl shook her head but didn't speak.

'Then,' said Charlotte, 'you realized there was a problem. You were supposed to have had a sleepover at a friend's house that night. If you got that confirmed, then you had an alibi for killing the cats, but that meant you wouldn't get any money from the sale of the house. On the other hand, if you said you'd returned and had slept downstairs, then you might be accused of killing the cats, which meant you'd lose the money anyway. Either way, you lose out! You are not due any of the money from the sale of the house. Understood?'

The girl shuddered and tried to make herself even smaller.

Edgar groaned but didn't speak.

Actually, if she did sleep in the house that night, and she didn't kill the cats – and I'm pretty sure she didn't – then she is in line for a payout from the sale of the house.

Charlotte continued, 'Then there was the nasty affair of the chauffeur. You hated him because he'd rejected your advances, right? So you took some of your mother's sleeping tablets, ground them up and put them in Ahmed's thermos flask while he was taking Edgar and Lavinia to the theatre. I hope you only intended to make him too drowsy to drive, which would have caused him to lose his job. Unfortunately you miscalculated and he went into a coma. You went down with your father when he came back from the theatre to confront Ahmed. It must have been quite a shock to find you'd actually done so much damage. But it was easy to stage a suicide. You used his mobile to send a message to Mother, just saying sorry, and spread some bank notes around. Nobody was going to query that he'd stolen some money and was sorry for it, were they?'

Except that Petra wouldn't have had access to so much money . . . or would she? What about all that money which was in the handbag which Charlotte so conveniently left behind her on her first visit? Where did that come from, and where did it end up? Could Petra have laid her hands on it? No, probably not.

'Finally,' said Charlotte, 'you overreached yourself completely by fooling around on the moped with your boyfriend, attacking Mrs Abbot. Why? Because she'd seen right through you as soon as you met and was going to tell your granny who'd been such a bad girl. Right? Incompetent as usual, you failed to frighten her with your first attempt, and then you aimed so badly you hit a taxi and not your target! This time Mrs Abbot and her friend were ready for you and took photographs. Do you honestly think you can get away with this? I can tell you this for nothing. Your boyfriend will talk when he realizes what sort of mess you've got him into. What can I say but that you deserve everything that's coming to you!'

Charlotte swung round on Mrs Tredgold. 'If you need her to write out and sign a confession, I'll make sure she does so. And you'll not make excuses for her this time, Edgar!'

Edgar dithered, on the balls of his feet, fingers to mouth. 'I can't believe it! My own daughter!'

Charlotte clapped her hands together. 'Sorted. Now, all that remains is the mopping up. Mummy won't want all this to come out in public, will you? So what I suggest is that Petra is shipped off to a single-sex boarding school somewhere far from town with no weekend leave, where she can't get into any more trouble. You'll pay for that, won't you, Mummy? As for the house, you can make that over to me and Edgar, so that we can continue to live there as we should. All household bills to you as before.'

Mrs Tredgold shut her eyes and leaned back in her chair. Her attitude said she was accepting defeat.

Bea, however, had not. She said, 'That's a reasonable account of what's been happening, Charlotte, with a couple of omissions. Haven't you forgotten something?'

Twenty

Charlotte lowered her head. A dangerous bull ready to charge? 'What?'

'The doctored cake for one thing. Who prepared that? And where did the money come from that was found at Ahmed's bedside?'

'Hah!' Charlotte dismissed this as unimportant. 'The money? He'd stolen it, of course. As for the cake, that was a message I left for my mother, to let her know I knew where she was.'

'Surely you didn't intend to poison your mother, did you?'

A stare. 'No, of course not. I smeared the top with mustard. It would look all right but taste nasty.'

'It made my ward sick, and the housekeeper's cat.'

'What business did they have of eating cake intended for my mother? Ridiculous!'

Bea said, 'I'm delighted it wasn't poisonous. That saves us from having to take my ward to hospital, with all the investigations that would have followed. And I'm glad you've owned up to interfering with the cake and given us so much detail about the other things that have happened. So much so, that I can't believe you didn't know all about them from the beginning. It's almost as

302

if you were in Petra's shoes while all this was going on.'

Charlotte grinned. A death's head grin. 'I kept an eye on her, yes.'

'And beat her up today? Or was that Edgar, exercising his authority as her father?'

Edgar wrung his hands. 'I smacked her once, that's true. She lied to me and . . . Well, what is a father to do? She was seeing that scumbag, when I'd told her . . .! And her mother had warned her, too. But I didn't know, honest I didn't, I didn't realize till Charlotte set about Petra herself and I told her to stop, and that's when she, Charlotte, told me what had been going on. If I'd known, I'd never have allowed it, believe me!'

'Oh, I believe you didn't think Petra was at the bottom of everything,' said Bea. 'Neither do I. She might have dropped the cat out of her granny's window, though I'm not at all sure about that. Did you do that, Petra?'

Petra lifted her head a fraction.

Charlotte lashed out with her foot, catching the girl on her shoulder.

'Stop that!' Bernice swooped in to stand over Petra. Hands on hips, Bernice confronted Charlotte. 'That is no way to behave. I agree she's a piece of shit, but you can't set about her like that!'

Charlotte's face darkened. 'Why, you . . .!'

Gordon stepped between them. 'Charlotte, that really is enough.'

Bernice helped Petra to a chair. 'I don't know much about the justice system, but if a girl is accused of a crime, doesn't she need a solicitor or something?'

Charlotte showed her teeth. 'You think she needs an acceptable adult to look after her interests? I agree. Her father and I are in charge here. And you, my girl, are well out of order.' Charlotte turned on her mother. 'Call your lapdog off, right?'

Mrs Tredgold's face was ashen. 'Charlotte, this is not right, indeed it is not.'

Charlotte smirked. 'You want I should tell all these lovely people your dreadful secret? Won't they just love to hear about it, eh?'

'No, that's . . . Charlotte, I beg of you!'

Gordon said, 'Marcia, what's going on?'

Charlotte laughed. 'As if you didn't know!'

Gordon said, 'But I don't know. Marcia, if you want me to go away, you only have to say the word, but I can't stand by and listen—'

'Hypocrite!' Charlotte spat the word out. 'Liar! Rapist!'

Gordon took a step back. 'What!'

Charlotte leaned over to grasp her mother's arm. In a low voice she said, 'You don't really want it all to come out, do you?'

Bea took charge. 'That's enough, Charlotte. And more than enough. Gordon, she thinks she's got some dirt on you and she's held that over her mother all this time. That's why Mrs Tredgold has let this horrible affair go on for so long. She couldn't bear the thought of your being exposed to the world.'

'But what have I ever done that . . .' His eyes narrowed. 'No, I don't believe it. She couldn't have thought . . . No, no! I don't believe it. She must be mad!'

304

Bea said, 'Can you bear to tell us what actually happened?'

Gordon blinked. 'What? But . . . It was nothing. I mean, I didn't take any notice. No, you can't be serious. Marcia, has she implied that I—?'

'Raped me. Yes.' Charlotte looked triumphant. 'I had to go away and have a termination, didn't I? I have the papers to prove it!'

Bea said, '*Someone* had a termination, yes. But not you, Charlotte. It was Petra, wasn't it?'

Petra shrank in her chair. She licked her lips. 'Daddy, I didn't know what I was doing. I was so young and my boyfriend at the time didn't know what to do, either. Then he heard of someone who could help us, but they said I had to cough up in advance . . . I'd got into trouble using your card before and you'd switched numbers so that I couldn't use it again. Aunt Charlotte caught me trying to use her card and made me confess. She said she'd pay for me to get an abortion. She said it would be best if I didn't use my own name but hers, and when it was all over she kept the paperwork. She's held that over me all this time.'

Bea said, 'It all begins to make sense, doesn't it? Mrs Tredgold, you should listen to the gossip in your household more often. Your staff had a very good idea of what was happening. They knew Petra had been in trouble and hinted as much to me. They knew that Charlotte had made advances to your chef and your chauffeur, both of whom rejected her as politely as they could. She even tried it on with Piers, here . . .'

Piers nodded. 'Incredible, but true.'

Bea went on, 'Charlotte's not had any luck getting a man of her own and so she tries to flirt with anyone who comes into her orbit. I fear she spins herself fantasies about men. She can't allow herself to believe that she's not attractive to the opposite sex so if they reject her it must be their fault, and not hers. Gordon was obviously going to be a target from the beginning, not only because he was living in close proximity to her but he had the audacity to prefer you, her mother, to her. Gordon, she did try it on with you, didn't she?'

Gordon reddened, as people sometimes do when admitting to a shameful act, or when innocent of the accusation. 'Yes, she did. It was embarrassing. I could hardly believe it. I told her she must have had too much to drink. I said I'd forget it ever happened, and I did. I mean . . . ridiculous! She's Marcia's daughter, for heaven's sake. I put it out of my mind.'

Bea said, 'Charlotte didn't forget, though. When she found out that her mother was going to tighten the purse strings, she used the paperwork from Petra's abortion to blackmail Mrs Tredgold, and from that moment on she was off and away, hands free. Whatever she did, Mrs Tredgold and Petra would have to cover for her. Now, Petra might or might not have dropped the cat on to Hubert's conservatory. Did you do that, Petra?'

Bernice, standing behind Petra, pressed her shoulder. 'Tell her the truth, Petra.'

Petra shook her head. A tiny movement, but a telling one.

Bea said, 'No. It was Charlotte who did that, wasn't it? Mrs Tredgold caught her daughter in the act but kept silent because Charlotte threatened to expose Gordon as a rapist if she said anything.'

Gordon said, 'Marcia, you should have known me better!'

'I did,' said Mrs Tredgold, in a thread of a voice, 'but what could I do when she showed me the paperwork of her abortion? She threatened to publish it, and no matter how innocent I thought you were, the scandal would have ruined you.'

Bea said, 'Yes, Mrs Tredgold, I do see that you were in a cleft stick. You couldn't think how to stop Charlotte as she got rid of one after the other of the people around you. You tried inconspicuously to make arrangements to move. I don't really think that would ever have got Charlotte off your back, and with one part of your mind you realized that, but you didn't know what else to do. Then Charlotte wanted to switch domestic staff agencies, and you snatched at the opportunity to bring someone else in from the outside, to observe what was happening. That's why you invented that elaborate rigmarole of the statements you wanted me to get signed. You were lashing out in all directions, trying to find someone, anyone, to help you. Ahmed's death provided the trigger for you to leave and this has brought about the present position.'

Bea continued, 'Petra is a very silly girl and has behaved badly. She is not entirely to blame because she has been encouraged to think she's something special. She suffers from the same problem as Charlotte and Edgar, who think money makes you invulnerable. When I started to ask questions, I was attacked by Petra and her boyfriend. Petra, did you think that up of your own accord or did your aunt suggest it to you?'

Petra wept. 'You were so horrid, and I thought no one could possibly know who . . . and Auntie said . . . and it was only fruit juice, for heaven's sake. You should have taken the hint, you really should!'

Bea sighed. 'So Petra and her boyfriend were responsible for both attacks on me. The police have photographs of the moped and they also have the bottle which contained the acid which damaged the taxi. The taxi driver will make sure they take the matter seriously unless—'

'Unless I pay them off?' said Mrs Tredgold.

'Do you really think you should? Did you throw the acid? No. Petra did. Is it right for someone else to be punished instead of her?'

Charlotte said, 'Well, Edgar won't be able to pay him off. He hasn't a penny to fly with.'

Bea said, 'He has assets. Let him sell his yacht and find something useful to do. If Mrs Tredgold is kind, she'll let him have a share of the sale of the house, though Lavinia will stick him for alimony. Like you, Charlotte, Edgar has been a little too free with his fists, attacking first his wife and then his daughter.'

Charlotte folded her arms and looked smug. 'I don't care what happens to Edgar. He's made his bed and he'll have to lie on it. You can't touch me. Remember, I have the paperwork for an abortion in my name. My mother has to support me, because I only have to lift the phone and tell the police and they'll arrest Gordon for raping me, and she doesn't want that, does she?'

Mrs Tredgold lifted her hands in a gesture of despair.

Gordon put his hand on her shoulder. 'That's enough, Marcia. Let her do her worst. You can't go through the rest of your life worrying about what Charlotte might say or do.'

Bea applauded. 'Quite right. Remember that Charlotte loses her hold on her mother if she does make her complaint public. What's more, Gordon, there are now a number of people who have heard Petra tell the truth about her abortion. She can testify against her aunt, and if that's not enough, all of us here can bear witness to what Charlotte has admitted to doing. So that deals with Charlotte's blackmail attempt.'

Petra pushed back her hair from her face. 'Oh, what's to become of me?'

Edgar was no help. 'How should I know? You little fool! Don't you see what a terrible position you've put me in? I'm in debt already. Even if I sell the yacht tomorrow . . . There's Lavinia wanting her pound of flesh and if she takes half of what's left . . . How am I going to live? And if Mother turns me out . . . Where am I to go?'

Mrs Tredgold said, 'Everyone who slept in the house on the night the cats were killed – except for the one who did it – gets a share of the sale price. That, it now transpires, excludes Charlotte, because she killed the cats. Am I right, Gordon?'

'I believe you are.'

'Yes,' said Bea. 'Charlotte described everything as if Petra had been responsible, whereas in fact it was all down to her. She killed the cats, thinking to put the blame on the chef because he'd refused her advances. The same goes for Ahmed, though I don't think she intended to kill him, merely to get him the sack by putting him to sleep for a while so that he'd upset Edgar by not fetching him from the theatre.'

Charlotte spat. 'Try telling that to the police. Who's going to believe that story? And I can assure you, my mother won't even try.'

Bea took a chance. 'You think your family will close ranks to keep you out of jail? What about the staff? They knew what was going on. Did you know that they laughed at you behind your back?'

That got to Charlotte. She propelled herself out of her chair, reaching for Bea with thick, powerful arms. 'They didn't! Those men wanted me! They watched me all the time! They lusted after me!'

'Steady!' Piers stepped in front of Bea.

Charlotte swung round to find herself enclosed in a circle of wary faces.

Petra, overexcited, made the mistake of laughing hysterically and pointing at Charlotte's face.

Charlotte grabbed the girl and tossed her to and fro as if she were a dog playing with a toy.

Petra screamed.

Gordon and Piers tried pull Petra away, but Charlotte had a firm hold on her. She shouted, 'Back! Back! Or I'll . . .' She looked around and made for the open door on to the balcony. 'You back off, or I'll throw her over the wall!'

Charlotte pulled Petra outside. The girl screamed, thinly.

Piers and Gordon shouted, 'No!'

Ms Andrews launched herself after Charlotte, throwing herself at Charlotte's thick legs. They tumbled to the ground in a writhing heap of arms and legs. Ms Andrews picked herself up and brushed herself down. 'I can't think what made me do that. It would have been so much neater all round if both of the bitches went overboard.'

Charlotte lay there, breathing hard, jaws snapping, eyes wild.

Gordon retrieved Petra and handed her back to Edgar, who didn't seem to know what to do with her.

Charlotte scrambled to her knees. She hissed at Ms Andrews, 'Whore!'

'True,' said Ms Andrews. 'But a successful whore, you must admit. Now, Marcia, that's quite enough. Call the police!'

Charlotte pushed herself awkwardly to her feet. 'No! You can't!'

'Call them.' Ms Andrews was stony-faced. 'Or I will.'

Charlotte's heavy head swung back and forth. 'You wouldn't dare! I'll tell them . . . I'll tell them you threatened to throw me over the side of the building!' She made a lumbering run and hoisted herself up on to the parapet. 'See . . .!'

She tottered on the ledge, vertigo overtaking her.

This time nobody tried to stop her.

With a throaty scream, she dropped out of sight.

'Oh, my God!' Petra clutched her father, who was open-mouthed.

Gordon snapped open his phone. 'Ambulance!'

Piers leaned over the balustrade. 'She didn't kill anyone on the way down. There's people down there, looking up. Not tending her. She's dead.'

Mrs Tredgold said, in a faint voice, 'She was upset. She's no good at heights. She didn't mean to kill herself. It was an accident. Surely we can we deal with it in the family?'

'No,' said Bea. 'We need the police.'

Piers said, 'You can't hush this up. Questions will be asked. Where did she fall from and why?'

Mrs Tredgold said, 'Mrs Abbot, please! I'm willing to pay you a bonus for what you've done.'

'That won't work, said Bea. 'For several reasons. Kit, Andy and June were falsely accused and lost their jobs. Aren't they owed something for that? Worse, Ahmed has been branded a thief and a suicide, and I'm not having that. Even if you could hush those things up with cash, the police have evidence that a taxi-driver's cab was sprayed with acid . . . and who did it. If you won't call the police and have everything out in the open, then I will.'

'Agreed,' said Ms Andrews.

'Agreed,' said Gordon. 'I'll call the police.'

Petra wailed, 'What's to become of me? Am I going to prison?'

Gordon said, 'You'll take your chances in the system, like everyone else.'

Mrs T said, 'I'll get you a solicitor.'

Gordon rang the police.

* * *

The police came.

Mrs Tredgold, clearly distressed, put the best possible slant on the event.

Taking statements took time.

Bernice was exempted because of her age, but the others took it in turns to say what they'd seen . . . keeping it nice and short. Bea reckoned it was going to be hard for the Crown Prosecution Service to work out who ought and who ought not to be prosecuted. It was possible that even Petra might end up with just a slap on her wrist.

Mrs T said she'd go to see Ahmed's family herself and ensure that they received his share of the sale of the house. She also said she'd recompense June for being wrongfully accused of theft, Andy of vandalism and the taxi driver for the damage to his vehicle.

Ms Andrews sank into the background, not volunteering any information which could incriminate Petra or Charlotte further.

Gordon and Hubert acted as bookends to Mrs T, who gave the performance of her life as a misguided but loving grandmother . . . which was near enough the truth to satisfy most people, if not all. And the rest were going to keep their mouths shut, weren't they?

It was a subdued trio of Bea, Piers and Bernice who eventually reached home. Exhausted.

'I'll cook,' said Piers, dragging himself out of the taxi and finding a front door key.

'Order a takeaway,' said Bea, her arm around Bernice as they toiled up the steps and into the house.

Piers killed the alarm, led the way to the kitchen and reached for the takeaway menus. 'What do you fancy?'

Bea said, 'Bernice, I'm sorry. I should never have taken you to the Tredgolds.'

'You couldn't stop me, just as the Tredgolds couldn't stop Petra.'

'I should have tried harder.'

Piers put his arm around Bernice. 'I expect we'll all have flashbacks about it. And it's true, normally teenagers don't get exposed to such stuff. But you're a little soldier, aren't you, Bernice? You've seen more in your short life than most people have seen by the time they're eighty.'

'I'm not that tough.' In a small voice.

'None of us are,' said Bea, 'but we have resources. We know when and where to ask for healing.'

For a long moment all three were silent. Bea gave thanks for their deliverance and asked for wisdom in the future. Perhaps the others did, too.

Bernice perked up. 'Are the shops still open? Can I get my hair cut now?'

Bea and Piers looked at their watches. Unbelievably, it was only six o'clock.

'Too late,' said Piers. He ran his hand round the back of his neck. His hair had grown a trifle shaggy. 'I could do with a trim, too.'

Bea said, 'I'll see when my hairdresser can fit you in, Bernice. If you're going to cut your hair it should be done by someone good. Next weekend, perhaps.'

Bernice nudged Piers. 'You forced me to drink that mustard stuff. You made me vomit when it

314

wasn't necessary.' She was half accusatory, and half joking.

'Wouldn't you have done the same?'

Bernice frowned. And then nodded. She nudged him again and this time it was definitely a gesture of affection. She looked at Bea. 'What do you think will happen to Petra and the rest of them?'

Bea said, 'Mrs Tredgold will probably settle Edgar in a smaller place somewhere. I'm sure she won't let him starve. I expect Ms Andrews and her daughter will look after the house till it's sold and then she'll retire and Mercy will go on her travels. Petra? She may get some kind of rap on her hand for her misdeeds but I'm sure Mrs T won't abandon her. I hope she can make a fresh start, perhaps going to stay with her mother or at a boarding school?'

Bernice sighed, worldly-wise. 'I don't suppose they'll ever be satisfied, whatever she gives them. I suppose she could buy them an annuity each and say that's it!'

'Good idea,' said Bea, impressed by Bernice's thinking.

Bernice said, 'Mrs T's new housekeeper said she'd stay on now her cat's going to be all right. Do you think Gordon will marry Mrs T? I mean, they seem comfortable together.'

Bea refrained from looking at Piers. Did Bernice understand that Marcia and Gordon were not the only couple who were comfortable together? Perhaps she did.

Bea said, 'He's very capable. I expect he's got some place all ready to put his trains in. Or maybe he'll decide to stay where he is in the coach house.'

Piers rubbed his eyes. 'I've done half a dozen sketches of Mrs T and none of them please me. Perhaps because she's such a complex character? I don't feel I've done her justice but I don't think I'll try again. Except . . .' He reached for his satchel. 'Perhaps . . . one more try?'

Bea and Bernice exchanged glances. Bea said, 'We won't wait for him to surface. I'll order some food in. Or . . . I've just remembered that there's a fish pie in the fridge which Kit made earlier. We can have that with some frozen veg, and fresh fruit for afters.'

And it was good.

When they'd finished eating, Bernice said, 'I feel better. I expect you two oldies will want an early night. That's all right by me. I can always watch something on Netflix.'

Piers's phone pinged. He picked it up and frowned. 'You know I said a French businessman had cancelled his sittings for next week? Well, he's come back to me, asking if I can fit him in soonest. I could take the first Eurostar out on Monday morning.'

Bernice said, 'But you'll come back, won't you?'

Piers looked at Bea.

What should she say? Did she want him to return? Yes, she did. She nodded.

It need not mean anything much.

One step at a time, right?

She might even wear his bracelet again tomorrow.

Lightning Source UK Ltd.
Milton Keynes UK
UKHW041918031120
372744UK00001B/40

9 780727 892515